Blood Habits Die Hard

JEREMY HANDEL

CHAMPAGNE BOOK GROUP

This is a work of fiction. The characters, incidents and dialogues in this book are of the author's imagination and are not to be construed as real. Any resemblance to actual events or persons, living or dead, is completely coincidental.

Published by Champagne Book Group
2373 NE Evergreen Avenue, Albany OR 97321 U.S.A.

~~~

First Edition 2021

pISBN: 978-1-77155-448-0

Cover Art by Sevannah Storm

www.champagnebooks.com

Version_1

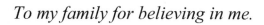

To my family for believing in me.

Chapter One

I am alone.

The only one of my kind in the world, perhaps to have ever existed. I've some idea of how I came to be, but no memory of any life before being here.

It's difficult to guarantee I'm alive right now. I have a short pulse, small heartbeat, and feel little in terms of emotion. "I think, therefore I am," is the best description of myself.

Living in the trees, I stay in the shadows at all times. Among the badgers, bats, and bandicoots, I hunt under cover of total darkness.

According to stories I've read over the years, I think I'm some kind of vampire. I don't know this for a fact, however, blood—human blood—is the one thing I can ingest for sustenance.

I'm crepuscular by nature because sunlight makes me ill. It may not kill me, but the vomiting and ocular discharge are enough to turn me off the whole experience.

While unable to fly, elevating myself enough to jump to almost any surface is a simple task.

Though lacking in super strength, I *do* move faster than anything else on the planet, especially when I've got a full stomach.

With no family or friends of which to speak, I have the freedom to be whatever I please. However, I have no option other than to be anything other than what my biology dictates. There are stories told of others like me in the world, but my investigations concluded nothing other than old wives tales of fanatics, sycophants, and agoraphobics.

No one else can be made into a vampire, try as I might. I am not the pandemic virus popular culture would portray.

There's no possibility of me being anything other than alone.

I've walked everywhere on the planet's surface, and some parts of the ocean humans don't yet have the technology to visit. My physiology doesn't require oxygen in the way it's typically conceived of and my bones can stand up to immense pressure, so I spent the latter half of the 20th century with aquatic life—emerging to feed once a day.

There is no desire within me to help advance humanity. They've performed every imaginable act of horror, and they are not worthy of my vastly superior knowledge of healing, nutrition, and energy consumption. The wars, greed, famine, and the total disregard for life laid the groundwork for their destruction, and there is nothing I can do about it. If there was, I wouldn't go out of my way to stop it. It makes no difference to me. Humans would either fear me or worship me if I ever exposed myself to the world, and neither sounded like a position I wanted. I could have ruled the world if I wished to, and someday I may still. There's plenty of time.

I remain unknown to the people of the world—a gatekeeper of secrets.

At the turn of the century, humans waged the War to End All Wars. After the turmoil in the Middle East came to a head, the world split itself into two factions divided by class: the Noors who controlled a vast majority of the wealth, and the Sooth who had the bulk of the population on their side, but far less in the way of resources.

Whether man, woman, child, or elderly, every human on the planet played some role in the war. Children were set to work in the factories, making clothing and munitions. The elderly, most of which were too fragile to fight or perform physical labor, were implanted with brain chips that let them command the military's drone air force from the comfort of their homes.

The war touched every country on the planet, and anyone who lived to tell the tale had a battle scar.

After the dust settled, the Creatures took to hunting in the open. For years I'd been aware of their existence and their whereabouts beneath the Adirondack Mountains. They created an intricate system of tunnels much like a colony of ants might make.

They were surprisingly smart for such savage beasts. They were unpredictable when they were on the prowl. For decades they operated by themselves, but they were learning how to do so in packs faster than expected. Sometimes you would find one alone; I surmised those were wolves breaking away from a pack to form their own.

In my time, I'd done my best to stay out of people's affairs, so when I discovered the beasts, I kept it to myself.

The devils were monstrously hideous. Their torsos were largely human-like, with similar pectoral and abdominal musculature. Their blank, expressionless faces had two slits with which to smell and a gaping hole filled with razor-sharp needles they used to devour their prey. Their glassy, oval-shaped heads looked like giant eyeballs sitting atop lanky, slender bodies. They had bumpy, translucent, brown skin that stretched over their long, thin spider legs, to the talons at the end of their feet. Their claws were perfect for eating, and rarely did they walk upright.

I'd studied them and discovered they tracked movement by scent and sound and were aware of only what smelled of blood. On more than one occasion, I'd seen them crack skulls and eat the contents like a peanut.

When the war concluded, the Creatures made their existence known to the planet. Like me, they consumed human blood, and they stalked their prey at night. Whether they needed to because the sun made them sick, I didn't know. However, I *did* know whatever coaxed them from hiding gave them a ticket to the buffet.

Every night they hunted—creeping their way into rooms, hiding under beds and in the shadows. People were no longer safe anywhere and, based on where they chose to live, it appeared they were taking it more seriously. They took residence in low quality buildings made of a specialized substance called Polymer-Xeta.

The material was initially designed to increase a stealth ship's ability to avoid detection. It was repurposed as cheap building material when tests proved the substance harmful if inhaled. Using the substance for buildings was the moral equivalent of force-feeding asbestos to the communities' inhabitants—an act the ruling class felt was population control. Aside from causing cancer in lab rats and incurable cysts inside of people, it *did* serve one purpose: the Creatures were unable to smell through it. The few neighborhoods with Polymer-Xeta buildings were packed ass to ankles with Sooths.

At first, I was content to let the monsters feed to their heart's desire. They had their business, I had mine, and in general, there was no issue staying out of their way. My studies showed they were interested in tracking only people, and they never wanted to bother me during meals. There were times I thought they may have been staring at me, but always shrugged it off as a coincidence.

I'd figured the people of earth would eventually determine a way to force the beasts back underground. People were losing the battle every day. The population was wearing thin, and they weren't reproducing fast enough to keep their numbers high. For the first time in my existence, my food supply was in danger. The monsters didn't leave anything behind when they fed, so there was never anything left for me to harvest, were I desperate enough to even want to attempt it. No matter what happened with the Creatures, I needed blood to feed on, and if they ate too many people, there wouldn't be enough for me.

Initially, I took residence in one of the places most touched by destruction—downtown Chicago. Despite being the drop zone for dozens of missiles during the war, downtown Chicago still had enough of an infrastructure for me to hide in. There were not many places for one to take refuge, but I created nests on several rooftops and throughout the abandoned subway system. There were similar hideouts in the ruins of every major city in the world—and most of the minor ones. I was always within a close radius of a stash house and made sure to keep them stocked with blood bags for me to consume if needed.

Right outside of the city proper, I stayed hidden in a forest preserve that remained relatively untouched by the chaos of the war.

I liked being in the trees—free of eyes, free of the Creatures…or so, I thought.

~ * ~

The night's hunt started like any other. At nightfall, I arose from my slumber, stretched my limbs, and made my way to the border of the southernmost part of the Chicago Sector: Sooth City. Formerly Chicago's south side, Sooth City had the most concentrated population in the country. Thanks to hundred-foot electrified fences with manned outposts, AI drones flying in patterns around the city, sensors buried deep underground, and a host of additional security measures, the area inside the wall was largely safe from attacks.

The town's headmaster, Juan Carlos DeSantos came from a long line of so-called "wartime heroes" who fought battle after battle with impeccable success. He'd been a general in the war, and the Sooth were lucky to have such a competent leader, otherwise the Noor may have been able to use their mech suits and bomber ships to destroy the Sooth entirely. After the war, the city's council of elders elected him to be the protector of Sooth City by unanimous vote.

Humans were the least safe in Sooth City, so I hunted the area less often than others as I wanted it to stay that way. Jumping over the hundred-foot fence was a bit tricky and enough of an inconvenience for me to notice. Despite the large number of them for me to hunt, most people were under strict surveillance when they weren't directly in their homes, so getting around the city was more difficult than simply picking off a straggler making a run between townships.

I hopped onto the top of a tree a few miles outside the city limits to survey the area. There were a lot of people outside, even in the outskirts of Sooth City. Most were performing security tasks—the walls were manned at the towers.

There was a lone security officer in the distance standing watch over the northeast tower of the encampment. The short, stocky man was at one of the smaller towers along the city's perimeter. Like a falcon stalking a kill, I surveyed for the better part of an hour, waiting to see that there were no other predators in the vicinity. As far as I could tell there were no Creatures around to give me any problems.

I made my move.

Darting through the shadows, I used my speed to ensure nothing could focus on me. Each step, a calculated effort toward my prey.

Stopping at the edge of the tree line, I took one more look to be sure there were no additional humans around, that there was nothing other than me and my food.

The guard sat on the chair in his outpost, completely unaware of my existence, completely unaware his life force was going to be drained for the sake of mine.

I salivated as I got closer, anticipating the rich metallic flavor of my next meal. I moved in, closed my eyes, and bit into the air, expecting the salty taste of skin between my teeth.

Opening my eyes, I saw one of the Creatures hovering over a fresh kill, scooping mounds of stomach flesh into its gaping mouth with its claws, blood dripping down its jowls. In between each mouthful, the monster let out a hideous clicking sound which echoed throughout the trees, I assumed to let the rest of the pack know the kill was claimed.

I decided to try and steal some food from the blood-soaked beast. I had shared meals with Creatures in the past, so it seemed like a good idea at the time. I inched closer to the body—steady with my steps to make sure it didn't detect me, despite being positive it couldn't. When I was three feet away from the Creature, it stopped, looked up, and made eye contact.

As I headed in for a drop of blood, the behemoth swiped at me. I ducked and missed the claw by a centimeter. It took furious swipes at the air and, after several more attempts to take my head off, I took it personally.

Air whooshed by me as I stepped back to avoid taking another claw to the face. I worked my way around the Creature, jumping as it took swings in my direction with arms the length of vaulting poles. It was no use. The Creature moved at breakneck speed, and I couldn't get in close enough to get a bite.

Instead of trying to out-maneuver the thing, I decided to leave the area. I took several leaps backward and ran as fast as I could. I glanced behind me to make sure it wasn't following me and was satisfied I was out of range. Slowing, then stopping completely, I let the silence of the night engulf me.

My closest lair was inside of Lake Forest, IL, an hour away from Sooth City. I wasn't as fast as normal thanks to a lack of sustenance, so it took more time getting there than it would have been if my meal had not been interrupted.

Once there, I went to grab a container where I kept spare bags of blood. I was disappointed to find my lair was destroyed. The place had been ransacked. There were no animals around, and I came to the conclusion that one or more Creatures were attracted to the food that'd been stashed inside.

I wasn't exactly sure what to do. I didn't have the time to find another victim, and my next stash house was much too far away to beat the sun.

Damn it. What if another hunt was interrupted? Would my other stash houses be as empty? I might need to find a new backup plan.

As the sun rose, my stomach rumbled. I knew hunger wouldn't kill me, which offered some solace, however it did cause a sharp, perpetual pain that made sleep difficult.

The Creatures were getting too close for comfort. Previously, I was content to let them feed as they would, but if they were able to see me, it posed a real problem.

Replaying the encounter, I was convinced the beast must have been aware of me. It looked at me. I was sure of it. It didn't make sense. I walked among the monsters more than once without any fear of repercussions.

This time was different.

In the centuries I'd been alive, I never questioned my findings or theories. I was unmistakably correct regarding every discovery I'd made. In this instance, I was wrong. If the Creatures had always been able to see, they'd hidden it well. If *not*, they'd found a new way of sensing their surroundings. Either way, I was threatened beyond any force I'd encountered in my travels.

If I wanted to continue feeding normally, I needed humans to be more effective at killing.

As much as I wanted to remain in the shadows, the time had come for me to take action against a foe I never thought I'd have to actually face.

My era of apathy ended. The time to fight had come.

~ * ~

I went to sleep hungry for the first time I could remember. I'd been hungry before, but I never had to go more than one night without eating.

There was plenty of weaponry hidden throughout the world. However, my best bet was to find a way to earn the humans' trust, give them whatever information I could gather, and use them to help me destroy the Creatures. To survive, I was going to abandon my life as I knew it. I'd never had any worries regarding my survival before, and never assumed I would.

As I contemplated such an extreme change, there was an immense pressure emanating from the barely-beating heart inside my chest...I was afraid.

In any given circumstance, my attitude was of a teenager, unafraid of any consequences. I assumed I would live forever no matter what I did, and I grew anxious at the idea of confronting my mortality. All I wanted to do was hide away from the world, but the world was slapping me in the face with the message that the time to come out of the shadows and expose myself to those who would fear and misunderstand me was at hand.

I needed to conceal my identity and live with the humans for as long as I could, and the best place to accomplish my goal was Sooth City.

A stranger appearing at Sooth City was sure to raise questions among the inhabitants, most specifically DeSantos, so I gave myself the best backstory possible. The last thing I wanted to do was let anyone know I was invisible to the Creatures. Back in the old days, before the war, I'd seen all the movies, and I knew what happened when humans discovered a species unlike themselves. I preferred not to be strapped to an operating table and dissected alive.

I chose the alias Trevor Mason—a former research scientist who'd studied Abnormal Evolutionary Science at Northwestern University. During the war, Mason was a private in the Sooth Marine Corps and retired after receiving a Purple Heart for valor in combat.

At the end of the war, he traveled the country in silence, moving at night and sleeping during the day, gathering information on the Creatures without getting too close.

Humans always loved a war hero, and they would naturally assume my Marine training helped me acquire the skills needed to elude danger for as many years as I had.

In my travels, I'd collected enough materials to recreate any documents I might require to prove my identity. Mason had a birth certificate, social security number, and academic credentials. I even owned a thesis paper on the effects of nuclear fallout and the resulting evolution of local flora and fauna.

With my alias ready to go, the next part of the plan was to make my way to one of my supply locations. There, I would find everything I needed to blend in with the humans and defend myself if absolutely necessary.

I fell asleep in my favorite place for the last time.

Chapter Two

The next night, I gathered my things. I kept most of my tree houses to the bare essentials, so there wasn't much packing. The real purpose was to make sure no humans stumbled upon any of my homes. Something intelligent living in the woods by itself would not be tolerated and it was sure to cause alarm if the Sooth found my belongings.

Hunger pains were still growing in the pit of my stomach, but I ignored them as best as I could and continued.

My first stop was to a cache twenty miles outside of Sooth City. Buried underneath the abandoned railway system was my largest North American hideout. It housed an emergency supply of food I'd stolen from blood drives, a change of clothes, and several other things I would need in order to make sure I survived.

I got to the cache entrance an hour after the sun went down completely—an early start for me. I approached the metal grate where I'd hidden the secret door. Brushing the leaves and dirt aside, I stuck my fingers in one of the openings then pulled.

By design, the door would have been arduous and elaborate for a human to lift without assistance, so I was confident I'd find everything untouched. I casually strolled in, unlocked the second security door, and pulled the handle.

A shuffling noise came from the back corner where I kept the safe with my blood stash.

Immediately, I knew what it was.

One of the Creatures found another entrance into my lair.

When making a nest, I always explored the surrounding area for potential entrances and escape routes, so I couldn't figure out how the

Creature got there. Everything appeared to be fine until I saw the tunnel next to the Creature.

Standing in the doorway, I watched it devour my only food supply for miles. I'd be too weak to make it to Sooth City with the supplies I had, and I couldn't leave without a bit of sustenance and the documents I'd need.

I continued forward.

Inside, I carefully studied the Creature for any change in behavior. One step into the room, and it seemed happy to continue eating its meal, so I kept going. To get to the locker where I kept the weapons and spare clothes, I passed within three feet of the Creature's range. Taking slow, deliberate steps, I made my way around the feasting Creature and made it to the locker. I breathed a sigh of relief, put my hand around the handle of the locker, and rotated it. The door creaked at the hinges, so I briefly stopped to make sure I hadn't been heard. The monster was content to sit there, slurping blood.

In the bunker there was a trunk that had several handguns in belt holsters, boxes of ammo, extra magazines, and a duffel bag. At the top of the locker, there was a bar holding several articles of clothing. I took what I could—a handgun, a few magazines, a pair of cargo pants, a T-shirt, tactical vest, and boots, all black, and put them in the bag.

With everything packed and more-or-less ready to go, my hunger alerted me to one of the blood bags the Creature had thrown to the side. I had one chance to eat something prior to my arrival at Sooth City. Once I got there, blood was going to be a challenge to come by, especially without killing anyone.

I put the duffel bag strap across my shoulder, bent my knees slightly, and crept toward the stray bag of blood lying next to the Creature's feet. I did my best not to alter the air in the room any more than I already had.

When I was within two feet, I bent further and extended my arm. The exact second my flesh made contact with the bag, the monster halted, lifted its head, and sniffed the air around it. I tightened my grip around the bag and tried to pick it up off the ground.

Out of nowhere, the beast bellowed a metallic squeal that echoed throughout the tunnel system. I fell back, let go of the bag of blood, and watched it spill onto the floor. It took wild, furious swipes in my general direction. It knew I was there but couldn't locate my position enough to land a blow.

I rolled to my stomach, got to my feet then leaped toward the exit, over the Creature. I landed and an enormous pressure swept my legs out from under me. My face slammed against the door as I fell.

When I opened my eyes, the Creature was staring directly at me from the other side of the room.

Slowly at first, it crept toward me, exposing its red, dripping teeth. I unzipped the duffel bag, took a handgun then flipped the safety off. As if it sensed it were in danger, the Creature charged. When it got close enough, I got out of the way. The Creature rammed headfirst into the concrete wall, leaving a significant dent and a cloud of dust.

It tried to stand up but couldn't, so I squeezed my finger on the trigger until the chambers were empty.

The noise stopped, and the Creature lay there. Every few seconds, its chest cavity inflated and deflated. I knelt above the semi-slain beast. Though it was, for all intents and purposes, without a face, there was a sense of longing in the Creatures giant glassy head.

It didn't have to communicate; I knew what it wanted. I put one more magazine in my handgun, pointed the gun at the monster's face, closed my eyes, then pulled the trigger. A loud bang echoed in the room and dissipated into the darkness.

I went to look for any blood bags that may have been left behind but found nothing.

Something about shooting the Creature was unnatural to me. It was the first non-human life I'd taken and, ironically, the most uniquely human interaction I had with one of the Creatures so far. The blank expression on the dead monster's face burned into my brain like a soldering iron, and I couldn't shake it.

There was an intelligence to the Creature. It was aware of my existence in a way I assumed they were utterly incapable.

Had it smelled me?

None of the others I'd come in contact with had noticed me—this one did.

Could it see me?

The notion was unlikely—they were largely unable to see.

How had it found my hideout? Had it smelled the blood bags through the ground, through the safe, and through the plastic bag? I'd never seen any evidence they were able to smell blood outside of a human body.

Nothing in my research showed me they were anything other than bloodthirsty animals. However, life in peril always found a way to adapt, and it was time to readjust what I thought I knew.

I took a knife from my pocket and decided to cut into the Creature's face to see what I could find. I noticed new muscles and ocular layers that hadn't been there previously.

The Creatures were evolving to match their surroundings faster than any species in history. They were above ground for a relatively short amount of time, and already they were developing defense mechanisms to help them adapt. If I didn't act, they were going to annihilate my blood supply for good.

Back above ground, where the entrance to my hideout was hidden, I took a seat and rested a moment.

I stayed behind for the duration of the night to clean what I could and take inventory of what was left. There was nothing for me to eat, but I did find the documents I needed, a flask, some rubber tubing, and several hypodermic needles.

Since I hadn't planned for a Creature attack, by the time I got outside, the sun would be rising in a few hours.

Not wanting to sleep in the same room as a dead Creature, I decided to bury myself and my duffel bag in the dirt outside like a vampire from a movie. It wasn't my favorite way to sleep, but it was safe and comfortable enough for one day.

I used the energy I had left to burrow a hole in the ground deep enough for me and the duffel bag to lay in. I scooped mounds of dirt from the ground—careful to make neat piles to camouflage myself. When I finished, I brushed the foliage onto myself.

I rarely slept underground. I forgot how cold it was.

Another night without eating.

I ignored it as best I could, but the pain grew with each passing second. I closed my eyes, and as the warmth from the sun seeped its way through the soil, I dozed off.

~ * ~

Now awake and under the midnight sky, I desperately needed to eat something. It would take me in the opposite direction, but I decided to hunt in Noor Village, a township fifty miles away from Sooth City. The suburb-like town was far, but not so far I would have to beat the sun. I was in danger of a Creature attack, but this time would be different.

I also had a hideout near there. I assumed the place was ransacked by a Creature, but it was enough for me to seek shelter if I needed. I guessed there wouldn't be any blood there. However, there was a bed for me to sleep in.

There was more risk traveling to places owned by the Noor. Though no more than a few soldiers manned most of their outposts, they possessed the means to afford the kinds of over-the-top security measures the Sooth simply could not. The Sooth gained their power from sheer numbers, and the Noor used their immense wealth to build robotic countermeasures and security systems which required almost no human interaction. The Noor and Sooth were equally matched, and the feud had been at a standstill for years.

There was a military encampment on the outskirts of Noor Village. Miles away from any location of importance, they didn't guard it as thoroughly as the rest of the country.

I'd hunted there several times in the past. It wasn't always easy. The Noor were armed to the teeth and trained in every possible method of combat, new and old. The best chance I had was to wait and pick one off when, and if, they left the group.

~ * ~

I arrived at the outpost after midnight. Three men guarded the camp, and they were sitting around a fire. Each guard kept a rifle close. I could feel their heartbeats from my position in the trees. While the men warmed their hands next to the fire, I chose the one to be my meal for the evening.

Tall, muscular, and dark-haired, a soldier with the name "Willis" written on his name tag was my target. Blood pulsed behind his jugular, calling me to come and take a bite.

Leaves shuffled behind me. I turned and saw one of the Creatures lessening the space between it and the soldiers.

Unwilling to let another meal get away from me, I yelled out, "it's coming from the north!"

The guards jumped to attention, rifles at the ready. Each soldier pointed their weapon in a different direction: one facing north, one west, and one east. The Creature closed in on them, running so fast it almost hovered above the ground.

The men waited calmly. I had assumed they were goofing off, warming their hands at the fire while talking shit, but they were focused, in charge of the situation, and seemingly unafraid of the danger looming in the forest.

I leaped from the tree a hundred feet in front of the Creature and ran. Behind me, the Creature was gaining ground.

"Help me, you assholes!" I shouted as I made it to the tree line.

The soldiers all shifted in my direction.

A split second after I exited the forest, the sound of laser fire engulfed me. The soldiers fired blindly into the night, their gazes locked ahead of them.

I dove behind the line of men shooting at the Creature. After a moment, it collapsed like a sack of laundry and remained motionless.

The guards turned simultaneously and saw me lying on the ground.

One of the men stepped toward me, and the next thing in my vision was the butt of a rifle a centimeter from my face.

~ * ~

I woke up groggy and sweating. I wanted to move my hands but they were tied behind a chair. My limbs and joints were tight, and I had difficulty holding my head up after not eating in two nights. The rope binding my chest, hands, and feet was an inch thick and even though I struggled, I was stuck.

The three men from outside surrounded me, keeping their rifles trained directly on my face. I wanted to laugh at the idea of something as banal as a gun being able to kill me, but I didn't want to tip my hand. I did, after all, plan on eating one of them if not all three. Under normal circumstances I would have been able to break through the ropes, but every one of my muscles were tired and I lacked the strength to escape.

"What the fuck are you doing out here at night?" Willis asked me.

I didn't answer.

Willis drew back his fist and, after what seemed like an eternity, punched me in the cheek.

"Don't make me ask again," he growled.

"I was trying to make my way to Noor Village." I let my voice quiver and hoped my pretend fear would prevent more punches.

"What for?" one of the others asked, this one with "Harrison" written on his name tag.

"I have important research I have to show to Raymond Harrington," I lied.

Harrington was the head of Noor Village and had access to the vast resources and networks available to Noor leaders.

"Bullshit," Harrison said. "What kind of research?"

"The kind that will send the Sooth running for their teddy bears," I said quietly. I had to say something to appeal to their anti-Sooth sensibilities.

They waited a moment longer, staring at one another to determine whether what I was saying was worth lowering their guard. My ploy did the trick. All three men visibly relaxed their shoulders and lowered their weapons.

"What's your name?" the third man, Johnson, asked.

"Dr. Trevor Mason," I said, adding a slight tremble to my voice. "I used to research abnormal evolution prior to the Creatures. Now I study them."

Johnson walked behind me and drew his knife. He bent over and cut my hands free.

When I was free of the rope, I massaged my wrists.

"So, what's this information you have for Mr. Harrington?"

Willis asked.

Willis tried to turn around and make eye contact with me, but I leaped into the air, landing directly behind him and sinking my teeth into his shoulder. He howled while blood poured from his neck and stained his uniform a deep, dark red. The warm blood filled my mouth, slid down my throat, and dispersed into my bloodstream, replenishing me.

Johnson and Harrison removed their handguns and shot at me. While I drained Willis, several bullets entered my chest cavity and escaped through the other side.

Once I was finished with him, I turned my attention to the other two guards. I was satisfied with my meal, so I didn't feel the need to drink from either of the remaining men. I swiftly ran behind Johnson, put my hands on either side of his head and twisted until I heard a snap. Before Harrison was able to react, I was behind him snapping his head around as far as it could go.

I dropped the body, and it slumped onto the ground in front of me.

The three men lay there in the center of the room in complete silence.

Taking a rubber tube from my bag, I stuck one of my hypodermic needles inside, then grabbed a flask and attached the tube at the opposite end. I crammed the needle into Johnson's jugular vein, then sat back and waited for the flask to fill. When it was full, I put the container in my back pocket in case I needed instant access.

Finally, a good night.

Sooth City was too far away from Noor Village to get there before the sun rose, so I decided to spend another night in the dirt. I didn't want to, but there was sure to be a shift change at sunrise, and I needed to get away from there without anyone discovering the bodies. Luckily, Johnson, Willis, and Harrison hadn't alerted anyone to my arrival, so there was time for me to clean up and rest for a bit.

I left the bunker satisfied that there were no Creatures in the vicinity. Apparently, the massacre had gone unnoticed. I knew it wouldn't last though. Creatures had an impeccable sense of smell, and it was only a matter of time until one of them stumbled onto the scene or dug their way into the bunker.

~ * ~

By the following night, my arms and legs were no longer weakened. I attributed it to the food I'd eaten the previous night.

I was ready to make the trip to Sooth City. The journey was not a particularly far one for me, but I needed to appear human the entire time, so I couldn't travel as fast as I would under normal circumstances.

There were enough supplies to last me the trip, barring any unforeseen Creature attacks. After two surprise attacks and some new theories regarding their evolution, I knew it best to keep an extra careful eye on any of the Creatures I happened to come in contact with.

There was one stash house along the way for me to use as a way-point, so I traveled with nothing other than the essentials. The only thing I needed was a flask with enough volume to keep me sated while I went to the city limits.

My clothes were covered in bloodstains. I disrobed and took the black clothing I'd stashed in my bag. After all, I couldn't arrive at Sooth City in bloody clothing. They would be expecting a much more solid explanation of how I was able to survive. Unfortunately, my persona wasn't particularly adept at looking like a badass. I put on the extra clothing and threw my bloody rags into the corner of the room.

After taking an inventory, I zipped my bag and placed it on the table.

I left Noor Village the following evening and headed south in the direction of Sooth City. There were forests along the way for me to hide in so I wouldn't have to pass through any of the guarded neighborhoods.

In the past, I was able to blend without issue. This time, something in my gut told me it was going to be different. I wasn't sure if the Creatures noticing me was a hindrance or not. On the one hand, it made it more likely the Sooth would accept me, and, on the other, it would make the trip far more dangerous.

It didn't *exactly* matter. Both were inconsequential as long as I made it to the city in one piece.

I needed to make sure I arrived at my destination. The rest would fall into place, regardless. Juan Carlos DeSantos was notoriously unreasonable, and I had to make a plan to ensure he would hear my story without blinking.

There was a cold urge in my stomach telling me I should run and keep hiding like I'd done for so many years. However, my instinct to survive outweighed my desire to make myself less anxious about my life.

~ * ~

I made it to the southern Noor border several hours later without incident. No alarms went off which meant no one noticed me coming through the forest.

Outside of the fence, I stopped once again to check for Creatures. I was being overly cautious even though I hadn't seen any signs in several hours.

The forest's night sky was unmarred by city lights, and there was a faint glow of fading stars between the lines of darkness.

My nerves stood on end, and my focus was clear and concise. Each movement was deliberate and full of intent as I inched my way closer and closer to the fence posts.

I was expecting a Creature attack at any moment. I could almost feel them pacing behind me—smelling the blood in the flask I carried.

At that moment, I decided to drink the contents. Should I get caught I didn't want the guards to discover it, and I was growing more and more aware that a Creature could find me at any moment. I unzipped my bag, took the bottle out then gulped the contents.

I no longer trusted the flask to contain the smell of the blood left on the inside, so I threw it into the forest. There was shuffling heading toward the direction I tossed the blood bottle—the sound of tree branches breaking underneath something's weight.

I was right. I *could* feel the Creatures. I caught a lucky break when they didn't attack me for drinking. For the sake of my hypothesis, I estimated they were close enough to get to me when I finished consuming the blood.

Factoring in their excessive speed, I calculated their smell range to be somewhere around three miles. It was a disconcerting thought. If I wanted to eat, I had a short window of time to do so until my meal was interrupted.

I continued as if nothing happened and made it to my next stash house without additional run-ins.

This particular hideout was buried underground in a suburban fallout shelter built in the 20th century. To my knowledge, no one had visited or even stumbled upon the bunker in close to twenty-five years. I lifted the patch of plastic grass covering the entrance hole and tossed it to the side. I took the circular handle and twisted it until the latch came loose. I climbed inside, closing the door as I entered.

Inside, broken bottles and bags of blood lined the floor. The blood stains had oxidized into brown circles. The hole in the middle of the floor told me everything I needed to know. I could no longer count on my underground bunkers to have any supplies left, now that the Creatures knew how to get in. They were becoming more adept at targeting specific locations and creating entrances to the places they wanted to get to.

I sighed, took a deep breath, and did an inventory of what remained.

All the ammunition, clothing, and equipment I'd stored there was intact. I looked for the fridge I kept the blood in. It wasn't there. I stopped at the hole in the ground and knelt. The hole was the right shape and size.

They'd taken it and ran.

Just below the surface, right where the Creature made the first turn, there was a single container of blood resting on the ground. The bag wasn't within reach, so I hopped in. Moving carefully, I picked up the rectangular container and retreated out of the hole. Through the echoes in the tunnel, dirt was shifting and the sound of something scraping against the walls filled my ears. More Creatures were coming.

I backed away from the hole, careful not to make any noise, gulping the contents of the blood bag to save time. I finished my meal as I got to the hatch and tossed the pack behind me as far as I could. I saw the Creature's shadow in the distance and expected them to stop at the bag to investigate the contents. They continued barreling toward me. I twisted the circular handle. When it opened, I jumped into the night sky, slamming the lid behind me.

A loud thud hit the bottom of the door. The Creature stopped after that.

I climbed to the top of the tallest tree I could find and stared intently at the bunker. The loud pounding continued as the Creatures attempted to force their way out. The hatch broke open. Two Creatures exited the hole and took in their surroundings.

I stayed in the trees.

After ten seconds of thinking I was safe, one of the Creatures turned its big, glossy head toward me and started clicking, exposing a mass of jagged fangs.

It leaped toward me. I went to a neighboring tree fifty feet away, a split second before it approached my position. The beast broke the tree branch clean off and tumbled to the ground—taking several more branches with it on the way. The Creature struggled to gain its bearings but eventually did so.

The second one continued the pursuit ahead of the other. I dodged both of them, hopping from treetop to treetop as they failed to get their footing enough to land on a tree branch without breaking it. For the better part of an hour, they chased me, putting me further out of the way of Sooth City. The Creatures must have gotten bored of falling because they finally stopped.

There was no longer any doubt in my mind. At some point, the Creatures had developed the ability to see.

I was in as much trouble as the humans.

Getting to Sooth City was imperative. Otherwise, there would be nothing left for me to save.

The chase had taken far more time than I would have liked, and the sun was starting to make its way above the tree line. For the third time in as many days, I had to bury myself. In my time alive, I resorted to burying myself only in the most desperate of times. However, times of desperation were closing in on me. I was experiencing new feelings there'd been no previous reason to comprehend. I was in a trial-by-fire of sorts.

I closed my eyes and tried to determine how I would make it to Sooth City alive. I was starting to lose optimism, and my self-confidence was waning. I'd never needed to worry about my well-being. My safety net was disappearing with every new ability I discovered in the Creatures. They were learning faster than I realized was possible. Now that they *were* developing eyesight, it was a brand-new advantage over me and the humans. I would definitely not be able to eat again without interference.

~ * ~

I was determined to make it to Sooth City, incident or not.

I walked at a subdued pace. I surmised I could make it by dawn if I didn't stop.

After several hours, there were voices in the distance. My ears perked up like a hound listening to a dog whistle. To me, the only thing I heard was the sound of an unexpected meal placed at my feet.

But what the fuck were they doing out here?

Entirely motivated by hunger, I walked at a zombie's pace toward the sounds. After a few minutes of clumsy stepping, the shimmering light of a fire in the distance became clear. Not wanting to expose myself, I circled the encampment. Three men were wearing red and black fatigues at the campsite, each heavily armed with weapons I didn't recognize.

Behind me, almost as if signaled, the shuffling feet of the Creatures were audible. Mustering what energy I could, I leaped into the closest tree, hoping they would be distracted by a human meal, and watched the story unfold.

Ten Creatures formed a circle around the camp. The men sitting there appeared not to hear them. I wanted to yell a warning, but I held my tongue because I didn't want to be caught. The Creatures stopped at the edge of the camp and waited.

"Get 'em!" one of the men screamed.

All three men jumped up and faced a different direction, aiming their weapons forward. The first Creature pounced from the shadows and a blue light exploded from the barrel of one man's weapon. The light dissipated, and the Creature on the receiving end of the blast disappeared into a ball of bloody mist.

I stood there on the tree branch with a gaping jaw. Somehow, the Sooth had engineered a weapon strong enough to destroy a Creature completely with one shot.

Shot after shot expelled blinding brimstone on the unsuspecting Creatures, as the soldiers picked them off one by one. Soon, the entire murder of Creatures was nothing more than a pile of smoking dust.

I desperately wanted to know how they'd created such a powerful weapon in their unstable social climate. Resources, especially for Sooth, were limited, and their engineers were not as good as the Noor, so nothing led me to believe they'd made something so advanced on their own.

I needed to meet these men. It was time to make myself known.

Jumping to the ground, I smeared some dirt on my face. I ran once I was fifty-feet from the tree line. I screamed at the top of my lungs, hoping the men would think Creatures were chasing me.

The men had their weapons trained on me.

I stopped dead in my tracks, acting as if fear of being vaporized was paralyzing me.

"Please!" I simpered, "don't shoot!"

The men were pointing flashlights directly in my eyes so it was difficult to see their faces at the time.

I ran into the arms of a man whose name tag read "Warwick" and squeezed him in a bear hug.

Warwick was a tall, swarthy soldier with a kind face. His pleasing features were welcoming in the harsh climate. The push-broom mustache under his nose was black as night. His demeanor was that of a kind grandmother, but it was an act. His steely blue gaze hid secrets his tone betrayed.

"It's okay, bud." Warwick gave me a crooked smile. "We got 'em. You're safe."

"I'm safe?" I asked timidly, hoping to lower their defenses.

"You *are*," he said, softly. "Now, let's get you someplace warm."

They brought me to a canopy tent next to the guard-post, sat me down, wrapped me in a blanket, and gave me some hot chocolate I had to pretend to drink.

Warwick knelt before me so we were at eye level. His comrades, Davidson and Jakovich were behind him, watching me with folded arms.

Warwick peered into my eyes with a hard expression. "Who are you, and what are you doing here at night, son?"

The irony of him calling me "son" wasn't lost on me. Even though I was hundreds of years his elder, I appeared much younger than he did, and I used it to my advantage. All three would naturally assume my naiveté and let their guard down.

"Well," I swallowed, "I've been out here for several weeks, tracking the Creatures' migration patterns with a modicum of success until a few days ago—"

"What happened a few days ago?" Davidson asked.

Davidson was a head shorter than Warwick and Jakovich. He wore black and red fatigues under a flak jacket packed with magazines and handguns. A candy bar wrapper peeked out of his breast pocket. His ginger-orange hair was neatly combed, shiny, and thick. Even through his clothing he appeared to be strong and muscular.

"One of them looked at me." I stared off past all three men.

"Ha!" Jakovich bellowed. "Bullshit. Everyone knows those fuckers can't see shit."

Jakovich was the least attractive of the three. Whereas Warwick and Davidson had what I would describe as "rakish good looks", Jakovich was closer to what one might call "homely". His beard was braided like a Viking's and went down to his belt. His large protruding belly stuck out from under his vest. Acne scars created a mountainous landscape throughout his face. He wasn't ugly, but he wasn't good-looking either.

"Oh, but they can." I turned to Jakovich, maintaining my blank facial expression. "I have no doubt about it."

"How?" Warwick raised an eyebrow.

"A few days ago," I said, "I got lucky and found one of them barely alive, so I stuck around. I stared at it intently, and the Creature looked back at me. *Directly* at me, peering right into my eyes as if it always could."

"Coincidence." Davidson chortled. Clearly, he didn't believe me.

"It's not!" I shouted.

All three men took a pause and stared blankly at me.

"I mean," I said, calming a little, "when I cut it open, there was a clear development of extraocular muscles and a choroid layer hidden behind a shield of flesh."

"Shit." Jakovich turned to the tree line.

"It's fine," Warwick said, cryptically. "What happened next?"

"Over the next couple of nights, I observed them from a semi-safe distance, and I've determined there's a ninety percent chance they developed sight sometime in the last few years but have been keeping it from us."

"What were you going to do with this information?" Warwick

asked.

"I've always been a loyal Sooth," I lied. "I want to tell DeSantos in person, so I've been making my way to Sooth City, hiding in the trees when the Creatures hunt."

"That's quite the story." Warwick paced. He nodded for Davidson and Jakovich to come to a corner where they thought I wouldn't be able to hear. They were wrong.

"What do you think?" Warwick asked the two other soldiers. "Can we trust this prick?"

Davidson put a hand on his chin. "He knows something he's not telling us."

"True." Jakovich stared hard at the ground. "But he does know how to study those fuckers. Who knows? He might be worth something. Maybe Falcone can use him."

"I don't like it," Davidson said, dissenting. "There's something off about this guy. I can't quite put my finger on it, but he ain't right."

"I don't think we have much choice." Warwick looked at Davidson. "We need to tell DeSantos what this kid knows; it could save the Sooth."

"Fine," Davidson turned away from Warwick.

Warwick and Davidson stared at Jakovich for his answer. Jakovich nodded, and the three men turned back around to face me.

"Good news." Warwick put his focus on me. "We're taking you to Sooth City."

My plan was falling into place. It was easier to trick the soldiers than I thought it would be. They'd fallen for my act, hook, line, and sinker.

"What's your name, son?" he asked.

"It's Mason." I extended a hand for him to shake. "Dr. Trevor Mason."

Chapter Three

The next night, we were on our way to Sooth City. I convinced Warwick my research gave me a new proclivity to sleep during the day. They were content with it—many had become insomniacs in recent years from fear-induced paranoia. They wanted to stay alert while the Creatures were hunting.

The men told me they hadn't left their guard post in more than a year. Their sense of direction was better than I assumed it would be.

They were excellent forest-men. They tracked Creature footprints and went in the opposite direction, not wanting to stumble unexpectedly onto a nest. When it was time to rest, they made sure to remove any smell with a unique blend they made using ammonia, rat poison, and good old-fashioned urine. The smell was unbearable and seemed enough to camouflage our location.

It appeared as if we would make it to Sooth City without any Creature attacks.

The sun rose after the first night, and the four of us made a trench in which to sleep. I brought along a foil blanket the soldiers had lying around and used it to cover myself from the sun.

I closed my eyes and made an attempt at drifting off. It was no use. It felt like an ice pick was stabbing my guts. I was starving. I hadn't eaten in more than forty-eight hours, and the hunger was kicking in with a ferocity I'd never faced.

I needed to eat something, but the blood in the vicinity was swimming through the three men's veins. None of them were expendable at the moment, so I bit the bullet and went to sleep anyway.

The next night I woke up with what humans describe as a

hangover—nauseous, aching, sensitive to the amount of light blaring off the moon's reflection. I tried desperately not to eat anyone.

They offered me food, but I didn't accept it. I couldn't. The idea alone made my stomach hurt even more. Warwick, Davidson, and Jakovich gave no mention of how sickly I must have looked as we continued our journey.

Several hours later, we were a few miles away when the pain struck me again. This time, I fell, landing on my knees. I moaned, clutching my belly on the forest floor.

Warwick, Davidson, and Jakovich ran toward me and knelt. Warwick poured water into my throat, but I expelled it immediately. They made separate fruitless attempts to calm me and determine what was wrong. I grabbed at my belly for dear life, screaming indistinguishable phrases.

The pain was unbearable. Daggers shot lightning that stretched throughout my nerves and bones.

I convulsed.

Something rose from my guts and spilled from my mouth onto my chest. Red foam pooled on the ground next to me. I coughed another lungful which sprayed on the faces of the confused men gazing at me.

"It burns!" one of them yelled in complete terror.

~ * ~

The next thing I remember, I was on the outskirts of Sooth City, sans my guides, covered in blood. I had no recollection of how I got there, but between the blood on my clothes and the fullness of my stomach, I surmised what happened. I stopped for a second and contemplated what I could do if I got hungry again. No matter what, I needed to eat, there was no way around it.

I wasn't sure what to do next. Warwick, Jakovich, and Davidson going missing was sure to be noticed. This time, Sooth City knew we were coming, and showing up without my guides would raise more than one eyebrow. I needed to devise a good story, otherwise there was no point in me entering the city at all. It was important I deal with the Creatures stealing my meals out from under me, and Sooth City was the best place to do it.

So, I chose to ignore my blackout and continue to the city walls with or without my escorts.

I arrived at the entrance to Sooth City an hour later, soaked in blood and sweat. I waited there for something to happen. There was no doorbell, so getting anyone's attention would be difficult.

The smell of mulch and copper entered my nose. There was a murder of Creatures closing in on me. I could have saved myself but doing so would have risked exposing myself too soon.

I ran up to the door and started banging on it, yelling as loud as I could. "Help! They're gaining on me!"

There was no response. I kept yelling and slamming my hands on the door, pleading with whoever was on the other side to let me in and save me from my fate.

I spun around and saw ten Creatures running at breakneck speed—lessening the distance between me and them. When they were twenty feet away, they pounced. I closed my eyes, expecting to feel their large teeth biting on my throat or abdomen.

There was nothing. I tried to find the dead Creature I assumed was lying next to me. I didn't see anything. The Creatures simply disappeared from existence.

In a flash, there was a spotlight on me. I shielded my eyes and gazed at the guard post on top of the wall where a full battalion of men was staring down at me, each of them holding the same type of weapon Warwick and his group had used.

"What do we have here?" A booming voice came from atop the tower. "A refugee?"

"My name is—"

"Save it," the voice interrupted. "Come inside and get warm."

Before he finished, the hundred-foot doors in front of me slowly separated from the middle. The sound of rock scraping against pavement filled my ears.

I stepped inside the door, and several men wearing the black and red Sooth City uniforms assaulted me. They stripped me of my bag and my weapons but thankfully left my clothing intact. Immense pressure transformed into pain as a boot made contact with the back of my head.

I had plenty to eat between Warwick, Jakovich, and Davidson, so the blow didn't knock me out right away. The mystery man hit me about a dozen more times, and it became evident he wouldn't stop. The final punch loosened my body enough to fall over. I hit the ground with a thud.

~ * ~

I woke up tied to yet another chair, in yet another interrogation room. I was wet and cold, and I wasn't sure why. A burst of frigid water hit me, and my nerve endings quivered.

I took in my surroundings more thoroughly.

The room was brown, dark, dank, and dripping. Above the door, rusted pipes leaked a brown liquid that dripped into a pool below. There was a bright light in my face making me squint. I was sitting at a metallic silver table with nothing on it.

Right in front of the light was Juan Carlos DeSantos—Mr. Sooth City himself. I'd hunted there before, so I recognized him from his posters around town. His jet-black hair was neatly combed and went to his shoulders. He kept a short beard trimmed cleanly underneath and on the sides of his face. DeSantos was a giant among men, probably somewhere around seven feet, with a naturally muscular torso.

Why was I being treated like a threat? More importantly, did he know more than I did about my journey to the city limits? It was possible. I tried not to entertain the thought and got back into character.

"What's going on?" I mumbled.

A hand slapped its way across my face.

"Quiet you insolent little—"

"Enough." DeSantos put a hand up. "This man is our guest. Let's stop and see what he has to say for himself."

"Where am I?" I asked, keeping up the ruse.

DeSantos chuckled. "You know full well where you are, my boy. You are underneath Sooth City, talking to Juan Carlos DeSantos and his band of merry men."

"Merry?" I asked.

"Yes…merry." He furrowed his brow and peered at me. "Is that a problem?"

"No. Just making sure I heard you."

"What's your name, boy?"

"Dr. Trevor Mason, and I have some crucial information for you, Mr. DeSantos."

"All in good time." He strolled around the room non-threateningly. "For now, Trevor, why don't you tell me what you were doing out there covered in blood and what happened to my men."

Shit. Maybe he *did* know.

"I don't know," I said truthfully. "One minute I was with them, then suddenly we're being attacked by Creatures, the world goes blank, and now I'm here."

DeSantos stopped for a moment then continued strolling around the room. "So, you have no idea how you got here, and no idea what happened to Sergeant Warwick?"

"No, sir," I replied.

DeSantos ran his fingers through his beard. "That's pretty convenient, don't you think?"

"No, sir." I chuckled. "There is nothing convenient about it at all."

He made a grudging half-smile. "Funny."

His demeanor grew serious. After a few seconds, he looked at me. "So, Doctor, what are you truly doing in my city, and what the *fuck* happened to my men?"

I understood he was bluffing. He knew who I was claiming to be, and he knew exactly why I was in Sooth City. Warwick must have told DeSantos I had big news. He was trying to catch me in a lie, but I was way too smart for that. I saw right through his ploy.

"I don't know." I scratched the top of my head. "All I remember is being attacked by Creatures, then I was here. I think Warwick saved my life."

"He did." DeSantos glanced down and shook his head. "I hope whatever you have to tell me is more important than your life."

"It is." I looked him dead in the eyes.

DeSantos waved to the table. "The floor is yours."

I told DeSantos the same thing I'd told Warwick, Jakovich, and Davidson—I discovered that the Creatures developed sight. He was less than impressed.

"Bullshit!" DeSantos pounded on the desk. "Evolution takes millions of years. There's no way the Creatures were able to develop a system as complex as an eye so fast."

"It's true." I kept my head still and locked my gaze on him. "I can show you if you have a fresh body."

He glanced at the two guards closest to the door and nodded. They left the room and slammed the door behind them.

"Tell me, son." DeSantos sat down across from me. "How did you stumble upon this information?"

"There was no stumbling involved." I shrugged. "I've been an evolutionary scientist for many years. I've been studying the patterns of the Creatures for close to two years now. Mostly I've been tracking their migration patterns and the ways they hunt and nest.

"Several weeks ago, I got the chance to dissect one myself, and I discovered extraocular muscles and a choroid layer forming underneath the Creature's face shield. The one thing extraocular muscles can do is control the vestibulo-ocular reflex—the system responsible for involuntary eye movement. The choroid layer of red blood cells and connective tissue provides nutrients to the inner eye. Both are essentially worthless without the rest of the eye's components. The presence of an extraocular muscle means they can, or are in the process of, developing sight."

"That's an impressive story, Doctor." DeSantos squinted at me. "How did you get close enough to kill and dissect one?"

"I came across one in a bunker," I said. "I happened to have a weapon on me. I shot the Creature multiple times in the gut, and he fell and died. It was too heavy to lift to a table, so I brought my tools over and cut the fucker open."

"And that's when you discovered the muscle?" DeSantos asked as if he already knew.

"Correct," I replied.

"Come with me." He stood from his chair and motioned for me to do the same.

As we walked, we passed a room with two large windows. DeSantos ushered me through the swinging doors, in front of which was a large plastic sheet with a slit in the middle large enough to fit a person.

Whatever Sooth building we were in must've been a hospital or research lab at some point.

Inside was a fluorescent light flashing above the metal operating table where a Creature lay motionless.

Whether the Creature was alive, or dead was of no consequence. I was sure DeSantos was going to test my dissection skills.

The two men who'd left the interrogation room were there, wearing dark blue scrubs and white surgical masks. I knew it was the same two men, I could smell them. The larger one came toward me, then pulled out another set of scrubs for me to wear from a shelf next to me. I took the garments then put them on over my clothes.

The other man in the room motioned me to the table with his head. No one spoke. When I got there, he crammed a scalpel into my hand.

I took a deep breath and made an incision on the side of the Creature's head. Translucent red goo spilled from the cut. The guard acting as my assistant held a sponge to the wound to soak the blood while I continued.

When the incision got to be a foot in length, I put the scalpel on the table, grabbed each side of the wound, and ripped the Creature's glossy flesh apart with my hands. Both guards flinched as blood splattered into their faces.

I peeled the Creature's face off and exposed what was behind it.

"Come here." I nodded to DeSantos, who was standing on the other side of the observation glass.

He took a mask from the box on the table next to the swinging doors and held it up against his face.

"See?" I pointed to a blob of transparent substance. "That's the Creature's eye. Somewhere along the way, these guys started to develop the building blocks of sight."

"What made you think to look for an eye?" DeSantos asked.

"Before the Creature died, it looked directly at me," I said. "Its expression haunts me."

"Expression?" He laughed. "Those things?"

"Those things," I repeated.

He and I left. A few moments later, we were in an office far more beautiful than either of the other rooms I'd been in. The wood grain paneled walls and dim bulbs gave the space a warm, cabin-like feel. There was a mahogany desk facing the door with a large leather chair behind it.

"Care for a brandy?" he asked, motioning for me to sit in the identical leather chair across from his desk. I went over and sat. The leather held me in a soft bliss as I made myself comfortable.

"No, thank you." I put my hand up. "Never developed a taste."

"No time like the present," DeSantos replied.

I didn't want to take the drink as I was clueless how it would affect me. The only thing I ever craved was blood, so I'd never tried alcohol, but I needed to accept the glass to maintain appearances.

I begrudgingly took the brown drink DeSantos poured into a clear glass. Putting the glass to my mouth and letting the liquid sit on the front of my lips, I took the smallest sip possible.

"Don't worry, son." He laughed. "You don't have to drink it."

I put the glass on the wooden end table next to my chair.

He produced a glossy wood box on his desk from which he took a cigar out and lit it. He leaned back with his cigar between his teeth. "Why did you come here?"

"I already told y—"

"I know." He waved a hand. "Why did you come *here*? Why not bring this to the Noors? They have far more advanced technology than us poor Sooth. How do I know you aren't a Noor spy? They've tried to infiltrate us, but none of them ever lived to tell the tale. How did you survive out there on your own for so long? What makes *you* so special?"

I wasn't sure what to say. I could tell DeSantos I wasn't a Sooth or a Noor, but it would mean I was the one person alive who would claim such. I certainly couldn't tell him what I really was.

"I'm not a spy," I said. "I despise the Noor with all my being." Then, an excuse came to mind. "I want you to use my information to take down those assholes once and for all."

DeSantos smiled a Cheshire grin, his face shadowed by the dancing smoke of the cigar hanging from his mouth. "Good," he said. "You'll do perfectly."

After another half hour of innocuous questioning about my background, qualifications, and how I was able to know so much at such a young age, DeSantos relaxed.

"Okay." He gave a massive smile. "Let's get you a warm bed to sleep in."

Outside of the hospital/interrogation facility, another security wall led to the general community.

As DeSantos and I approached the structure, I noticed the building material. It was made entirely of Polymer-Xeta.

Poor saps.

"Don't worry," DeSantos said as if he could read my thoughts. "No one's getting sick on my watch."

"How is that possible?" I asked.

On the other side of the gate, there was a wooden guard shack with "Sooth One" written in black and red graffiti. DeSantos grabbed the door handle and took out two pocket-sized boxes, one of which he handed to me.

I raised an eyebrow.

"Like this." He produced a disc the size of a quarter. There was a bright blue dot in the center of the disc that illuminated his face in the darkness of the night sky. He took the device and placed it on his neck under his ear. A circle of light surrounded his head and vanished.

I took the disc he'd handed me and placed it in the same spot on my neck. A brief wave of light surrounded my face, and there was an influx of oxygen in my lungs.

"What is this?" I asked as we walked through the community.

DeSantos put an affectionate hand on my back. "Our engineers designed these several years ago to combat the effects of Xeta Sickness in our population. Make sure you wear it at all times."

"Why not take down the wall?" I asked. "I've seen those weapons in action. Those are a serious force. You could wipe ou—"

"We can never sacrifice the wall," DeSantos looked straight ahead and widened his eyes. "It is the key to everything. Without it, we would be in absolute peril. We don't have the same resources as the Noors, hiding in their ivory towers, perfectly free from the violence we face every day, so we work with what we have. That's why I had our engineers build these devices using tech we stole from those greedy assholes. So we can have safety and have our lives."

The way DeSantos talked about the mass of concrete and Polymer-Xeta reminded me of something scripted. It was more like he was trying to convince himself rather than anyone else. He told the story with such conviction, I could tell he'd given the speech previously, probably a thousand times. He must have done so the first time he showed the community the oxygen discs they would have to wear and any subsequent questions from the townspeople. Otherwise, they faced an excruciatingly slow and painful death.

Something in the moment made me shudder. I couldn't quite put my finger on it, but there was a force in my gut telling me I should never have entered Sooth City.

~ * ~

The hunger had grown in my stomach by the time we got to the house where I would be sleeping. Beyond the inner wall, the city was dilapidated and homely, more like a war zone than a thriving town. The innermost ring of Sooth City was closer to what I would expect from Noor Village.

My new home was a classic ranch house with a red brick exterior and a black door. The lawn was kelly green and soft on my hands when I bent to touch it.

DeSantos produced a set of keys from his pocket, found the one he was hunting for, and took it off the ring.

He unlocked the door, then patted me on the back. "It's all yours, Doc, make yourself at home. Just one more thing. We have a nightly dinner that the whole town attends. I'll make sure there is a seat for you at the head table."

"Sounds great," I said with an upturned inflection.

I didn't know how I was going to fake eating, but I decided to worry about it when the time came.

With a final shove into the room, Juan Carlos DeSantos disappeared like a ghost at sunup.

I stood in the foyer and reviewed the size of the house.

Inside, everything was neat and orderly. The walls were red with black moldings and trim. To the left of the foyer was the living area. In the center of the room, two black couches faced each other with a coffee table in-between. The painting on the wall was General Julio DeSantos, the great-great-grandfather of Juan Carlos, beheading a Noor soldier during the Battle of the Mainland, a battle in which they brutally slaughtered hundreds of Noor soldiers in a nighttime sneak attack.

He was responsible for millions of deaths.

I'd respected General DeSantos for decades. I studied volume after volume of literature—both fact and fiction—regarding his war efforts when I was in what used to be the New York Public Library. Julio DeSantos was a hero amongst the Sooth and a tyrant among the Noor, depending on the history books you read.

To the Noor, General DeSantos was a dictator akin to Adolf Hitler or Saddam Hussein. They believed he completely lacked any moral fortitude whatsoever and scapegoated the Sooth when convenient. To the Sooth, the general was the scourge of the enemy, bravely sacrificing his well-being to annihilate the evil Noor, no matter the cost.

I was in no position to judge. In my time on the planet, I've killed a lot of people, but not as publicly, or theatrically.

I stared at the painting for a moment, then decided to take a tour of the rest of the house.

Across the hall from the living room was a dining area, also painted red with black trim and also with an image of General DeSantos decapitating a soldier.

I followed a passageway from the dining room to the kitchen and looked inside the refrigerator for no particular reason. On the back wall, there was a sliding door leading into an empty backyard, save for a few shrubs and a patch of grass.

My stomach rumbled. It was time to eat again. It was imperative I avoid another blackout if I wanted to blend in. If someone went missing the morning after the new guy arrived, it would certainly raise some red flags. However, uncontrollably killing everyone would also set off alarms. I decided it best to risk not eating for one night. I could make it one night.

I made my way to the bedroom. Once again, the walls were painted red, and there was another picture of General DeSantos killing someone in battle.

It was a nice sized room with a ten-foot window on the wall to the left of the door, to which I fastened a sheet capable of keeping the sun away when it poked through in the morning. There was an armoire directly to my right. Inside there were several sets of red silk pajamas and a black silk robe inside. I took my bloodstained clothing off and put on the pajamas. They were soft and warm around my legs as if I'd recently taken them out of a dryer.

Now what?

Chapter Four

The next night, I awoke to the sound of pounding on the front door. Frantically, I scrambled off the bed and threw on the black robe from the closet.

I opened the door. When my eyes adjusted, Juan Carlos was standing there, arms folded.

"I expected to see you at the family dinner tonight," he said, sounding like a father to his disappointing son.

"Sorry," I replied. "I've been studying the Creatures so long I don't keep normal sleeping hours. I'm pretty nocturnal these days, but I'll make sure I'm at dinner tomorrow."

"See that you are." He squinted and put his hands behind his back.

I knew I should have attended, but I'd been too exhausted.

"Is there anything else, Mr. DeSantos?" I asked after a few seconds more of him staring at me.

"I suppose so." His face appeared to loosen. "I wanted to see how your first day's sleep was."

"It was all right." I rubbed the back of my neck. "It's been quite some time since I've slept in a bed, so that was nice."

"Excellent." He smiled. "Please let us know if there is anything else you need to be comfortable."

"Will do." I grinned.

"Make sure you're at tomorrow's dinner." DeSantos walked away without saying another word.

It was a quick and strange encounter.

My stomach rumbled again; I needed to eat before it grew into a pain.

I took a fresh pair of jeans, a T-shirt, and a black denim coat with a Sooth City patch from the armoire and got dressed.

After waiting a few minutes until the sun dipped below the horizon, I went outside to hunt. Normally, I used extreme caution when scouting such a dangerous new hunting ground. Knowing the risk was not a factor. There was no other choice.

I went through the kitchen into the backyard and walked into the alley. In case anyone was watching, I decided to walk for a few blocks before leaping into the heights of the city.

When I was sure I couldn't hear or smell anyone, I jumped into the night sky, landing on the closest rooftop. I stopped on top of another ranch house and searched for the next open house. I jumped again and made it to the top of a streetlight. There were several voices talking off in the distance.

I went in closer for a better view.

I hopped up and landed atop a one-story maintenance building a few hundred feet away from the voices. I ducked and hid behind an aluminum air conditioning unit.

In a clearing that looked to be an old baseball field, there was a group of ten men standing in a circle. They were armed, but not with the Creature-evaporation guns the rest of the Sooth were holding. Instead, they held archaic AR-15s, which no one had used since before the war.

One man knelt in the middle of the group, pointing to a large piece of paper on the ground. He took the paper, folded it, and got up. The lead soldier said something I couldn't make out to the rest of the men. Each of them nodded and went their separate ways. I stayed hidden until they left.

From my hiding spot, I caught a whiff of the metallic, sweet smell of blood coming from behind me, and my hunger demanded satisfaction. I turned and saw a lone shadow in the distance.

I leaped to another building not too far away from my position. After half a second or so, I went to another, until I was close enough to taste the woman walking alone. She was wearing a soldier's uniform and carrying a Creature-evisceration weapon, and she was going in a clear rotation around the perimeter of the town. She wouldn't be easy prey if she noticed me. The Sooth were good fighters, and she appeared to be stronger than I could handle without my strength advantage. I needed to sneak behind her if I was to succeed.

My saliva glands pulsated under my tongue.

I hopped off the building and landed behind her.

Carefully, I crept closer.

I exposed my teeth. She turned her head just enough for me to see her eyes widening, but it was too late. I sank my fangs into her warm, soft flesh. The crimson liquid shot into my mouth like an exploding grapefruit, draining into my eagerly awaiting stomach. The blood coursed through every vein in my body, replenishing my strength with each flowing drop. My eyes rolled into the back of my head from sheer bliss.

Abruptly, there was a voice yelling indistinguishable phrases at me. There was a loud pop, and a buzzing sound whizzed past my ear.

Not wanting to wait around, I bolted from the area back in the direction of my house. Despite my newly replenished speed, more bullets zipped by me. One caught me in the arm, but I was largely immune to wounds and kept going as if someone hadn't shot me. I jumped into the trees and made my escape.

Using the trees and rooftops, I made it back to my home no more than a few minutes later. The bullet wound through my arm was mostly healed by the time I arrived. The speed at which I heal was directly related to the amount of blood I have in my system.

Crouching behind a bush to wait and see if anyone followed, I'd hoped I was unseen but couldn't be entirely sure.

I dug a hole behind the bushes and placed my bloody clothing inside.

After thirty minutes, when I was sure I was alone, I went into the house.

Walking into the bathroom, I took a quick shower. There was an urgent pounding on the front door as I exited.

I opened the door wearing only a towel, and DeSantos burst in without saying a word. He checked around the house, presumably trying to find the bloody clothing I'd hidden underground.

After a semi-thorough search, he returned to the living room. "Where were you tonight?"

"I've been right here, studying my notes." I pointed to the coffee table where there was a mess of papers and folders strewn about. "See?"

"Okay." DeSantos's shoulders relaxed.

"What happened?" I asked. "What's with the theatrics?"

He went to the couch and sat, placing his head on the backrest. A moment later, he leaned forward and filed through the papers on the table I'd left as an alibi.

"A woman was killed tonight within the Xeta wall." He kept his gaze on the papers. "I wanted to see for myself that it wasn't you."

I forced myself to appear surprised. I wanted to be convincing, so I sat on the couch across from DeSantos and rubbed my eyes. It was probably overkill, but I didn't want to take any chances.

"That's terrible." I closed my eyes. "How did it happen?"

"We're not sure." He put the papers down and stood up. "It appears to be a Creature attack, but none of the men got a good enough look, and it simply isn't possible inside the inner wall."

"Why not?" I asked. "Did you look for holes in the ground? They've learned how to burrow and travel below ground."

"No, we haven't. But let's just say, we've taken precautions to ensure no Creatures ever need to feed on the city's population."

"And you thought maybe it was me who hurt that woman?" I raised an eyebrow.

"We can never be too careful." He glared at me.

The sentence sent shivers down my spine. Somewhere deep, DeSantos must have known it wasn't one of the Creatures. I believed that he simply didn't want to admit it to himself because it would imply failure. He was right of course, it wasn't a Creature, it was me, and I would do everything in my power to make sure he never found out.

He rifled through my files for a few more minutes.

"All right, Doc." He breathed deeply. "I'll leave you to it."

I ushered him toward the front door, confident I'd fooled him into believing a Creature picked off one of his Sooth citizens.

"Be careful." He turned around to leave. "You never know what could be lurking in the shadows."

"Sure thing." I pretended we were both still talking about the Creatures.

"What happened there?" He gestured at the spot where the bullet wound was healing on my forearm.

"Oh, nothing." I grabbed the wound. "I burned myself cooking."

"Make sure you go to the nurse first thing. We wouldn't want you getting an infection now, would we?"

With that, DeSantos left the house and walked down the street.

I decided I'd have to be more prepared for the next hunt. Feeding once every other night would be enough to keep me safe and satisfied. It meant I needed to find another way to eat on the nights I didn't go out.

~ * ~

The sunset left an orange and pink blur in the sky. The ocular discharge and headaches I got were also in direct proportion to how far the sun was down. At its current state, it would cause no more than a headache.

I got myself ready to meet the town at the mandatory citizens' dinner in Sooth City by putting on one of the nicer sets of clothing in the armoire—a black suit with a red tie and a red pocket square. I picked out a black pair of brand new dress shoes on the bottom shelf. Stiff and uncomfortable, I could feel them cutting into my ankle as I walked. I tied the tie in a double Windsor, straightened it then put on the peacoat that was also hanging in the closet.

Nervous about how I would hide my eating habits, I took one last gaze at the mirror in the foyer, then left the house.

The night was cool when the sun made its final journey down the horizon line. The breeze passed gently across my face, moving my hair across my forehead.

I went to the path leading toward the center of town with droves of Sooth sauntering along.

They seemed in high spirits, as if they had no idea of the previous night's attack.

The red and black circus tent was around the block. Lengthy lines of people waited for their nightly meal. I skipped the line, pulled aside the tent's flap then went in.

Inside the tent, the hustle and bustle of the evening was in full swing. Children chased each other mirthfully as their parents struggled to wrangle them to their assigned seats.

At the tables, people sat chatting about their days. The food on their plates was untouched. No one was eating yet. The meal was turkey, mashed potatoes and gravy, yams, and green beans. It looked disgusting. I didn't understand why humans ate the way they did. Humans needed a full host of proteins and nutrients in order to survive, and to get those nutrients, they fed themselves to the point they were fat and lazy.

Juan Carlos was waving at me to come over to the back of the tent. I took a plate of food from the table at the end of the line and headed to the back where DeSantos and three other men were awaiting.

"How was your day, Doc?" DeSantos asked.

"Same old, same old." I shrugged.

He laughed and nodded slightly toward the men sitting next to him. "Come, come, I want to introduce you to my confidants."

He motioned for me to take the seat between the two men dining with him. Obliging without hesitation, I walked around to the empty chair at the round table and sat. Once all the citizens had their plates, a bell rang, and they all started eating.

"This is Captain John Falcone." DeSantos pointed to the man sitting directly to his right.

"Pleasure to meet you." I extended my hand for him to shake.

John Falcone stood slightly to shake my hand. His steady hand had a firm grip that was surprisingly smooth. Like everyone else, his uniform was black and red, with something like a hundred medals pinned to his barrel-chest. His blond hair was naturally curly to the point it was stylish. His short, round nose was home to a bulb at the end which would have looked like a clown's were it colored red. His cheekbones were smooth and curved elegantly into the top of his circular jawline.

"And this is Captain Nathan Caper." DeSantos put his hand out. "But everyone calls him Cap."

"Pleasure to meet you as well, Cap." I bowed my head a little.

"The pleasure is all mine." Cap nodded.

He was taller than his counterpart by a foot. Thin and gangly, he extended his long arms across the table to shake my hand without him having to get up from his seat. Atop his skinny, pointed nose sat a pair of black, horn-rimmed glasses he pushed every few minutes. His short brown hair was neatly combed to the side, and he had sideburns that went to the middle of his ear.

DeSantos sat back in his throne like a king. "Captains Caper and Falcone are interested in the research you've been doing regarding the Creatures."

"What would you like to know?" I asked.

"Everything." Cap closed his eyelids halfway.

"Call my secretary, and we'll schedule a meeting." I grinned, amused at my own joke.

Neither DeSantos, Falcone, nor Cap appreciated my sense of humor. They all stared at me in dead silence.

"How about after dinner?" I wiped my palms on my pants, trying to backtrack a lousy joke.

"That's more like it." Falcone crossed his arms.

"I can't wait." I shifted in my seat.

The rest of the dinner's conversation focused on personal matters. Every few minutes, I secretly took a piece of food from my plate and fed it to an old German Shepherd who'd wandered by and laid down at my feet when I offered.

We talked about what earned each man their medals. You wouldn't know it to look at him, but Cap was one badass son-of-a-bitch. During the battle, he'd single-handedly saved five men from a bombed building, running in face-first each time, ordinance flying in every direction. There were no casualties, though Cap did take a bullet to his right thigh.

Captain Falcone was also impressive. He led the battle of Navy Hill, in which two hundred men fought against two thousand and won a massive victory. Referred to thereafter as "The Hero of Thermopylae," Captain John Falcone was given a house right in the middle of the inner wall and a hero's reward in town credits. He was also an accomplished inventor and engineer. He was the one responsible for the new weapons the Sooth were using.

Both men recounted their tales as I listened carefully.

They were fascinating. Both had read hundreds of historical documents and had no false delusions regarding the state of Sooth City. They were as afraid of the Creatures and their ability to evolve as anyone else in the world, and they wanted to keep everyone safe. I wasn't sure I could make the same claim regarding Juan Carlos. The jury was still out on him.

It so happened that Falcone and Cap were also close followers of General Julio DeSantos and his exploits. Both gave the general the credit for their military prowess. They studied him and followed his example in battle. The battle of Navy Hill was won using General DeSantos's famous "Blister Attack," where a full battalion encircles the enemy and bombards them with Blister Grenades—green cylinders the size of a tennis ball canister. Designed with a nanobot alloy, the grenades create shrapnel capable of burrowing under one's skin and exploding outward, like a bursting blister.

In mid-conversation, a church bell rang in the distance, and everyone stopped what they were doing.

DeSantos stood to address the crowd. "In times like these," he said somberly, as the noise calmed, "we must always look to the future to be our guiding light."

"Our guiding light," the group mumbled.

"Tonight is an extraordinary night," DeSantos said. "We have a new member of our community, and he has important information which is going to help us take down the Noor once and for all."

The Noor? What about the Creatures?

I suddenly understood why I was being treated so well compared to the rest of the citizens. DeSantos didn't want me to save the Sooth from the Creatures—he wanted me to sick them on the Noor.

A few days prior, I wouldn't have minded another Sooth attack on the Noor, or vice versa. This time, however, Juan Carlos posed a threat to my secondary food source. The most important thing to me was that my lifeline to human blood remained unfettered.

I stood and bowed to the crowd, smiling in an attempt to feign enthusiasm. Everyone in the room got up and applauded vigorously.

If only they knew.

They applauded for a full two minutes when DeSantos waved at them to take their seats. I sat back down, hoping I fooled the crowd with my simple gestures. DeSantos gave me an approving pat on the back, and I knew I'd somehow won him over.

~ * ~

In the living room of my house, Cap and Falcone sat on the couches, rifling through my notes, and sipping coffee I'd made for them. I waited in the entrance to the living room with an empty cup in my hands, answering any questions they had.

"How do you know how far they can smell blood?" Cap asked.

It was a good question. I didn't want to answer, but there was an explanation which didn't require a vampire's abilities.

"It was easy," I said, "I dug an elephant-sized hole under a tree whose top they would be unable to reach. I got in the tree, pricked myself, and waited for the Creatures to come. When they fell into the trap, I got out of the tree and ran to a second location where I pricked myself again. Then I measured how much time it took them to get there. I repeated the process ten times before I got it right. I dug somewhere close to fifteen holes."

"Very clever," Cap said, continuing to read, "that must have taken quite a while."

"Months," I replied. "Almost a year of digging every single morning until the sun went down."

I hoped they wouldn't go looking for the holes. The truth was that Trevor Mason *had* performed the experiment, but I didn't know where the holes were and I didn't have the means to recreate the experiment myself. The only available information was in files he kept.

They continued asking questions regarding how I was able to survive without a tribe, how I managed to learn so much, and how I found my way to Sooth City without Warwick, Davidson, or Jakovich.

I told them stories about sleep walking and bouts of bad memory.

After they were satisfied, Cap and Falcone packed and left the house, taking a few of my notes with them. They were surprisingly nice once you got past how intense they were. They'd seen horrible things during their service in the war, and both of them wanted nothing more than an end to the madness.

Through his propaganda, DeSantos had them believing that the Noor were the sole cause of their misery and the Creatures were an unfortunate happenstance of the days.

They lived in dangerous circumstances, neither of them truly knowing what was going on beneath the surface of their lives, all the while following their leader. I felt terrible for them in many ways but killed the thought when I determined they were nothing more than blood sacks I would eventually drain to survive.

I fell asleep around sunrise, anxious for a hunt and a meal.

Though the night left me drained, I believed there was enough energy in me to stave off blacking out the next night.

~ * ~

With my second hunt, I wanted to be more careful than the first. I had to find a way to kill without alerting the guards patrolling the city or leaving any bodies for them to find.

At the behest of DeSantos, people were gluing wanted posters all over town, asking to please contact the elders with any information on the woman I killed. They wouldn't be comfortable until they determined exactly how a Creature had gotten through the perimeter fence. I hadn't taken the time to make it appear to be a Creature attack, they simply assumed it was.

I left that night, planning on observing and waiting for the perfect person to appear. If the coast was clear, I would make my move. If there was anything scurrying around, I would abandon my mission and wait for another chance.

Using the backyard again, I went through the alley. It was a cold night, and the stiff breeze made it difficult to hear what was ahead of me.

As I traveled through the city hunting for prey, I noticed I was back in the same clearing as the first night I'd gone out. Again, there was a circle of soldiers huddled around what I believed to be a map. After the men went their separate ways, this time in groups of two, I decided to follow two of the soldiers to their destination.

They walked their beat, careful not to let anything slip by them. They appeared to be on a high alert and focused. They weren't talking, stopping, or breaking their gaze. I hoped they would do something out of the ordinary, take out a cigarette, unwrap a piece of gum, anything distracting, but neither of them did.

Three hours later, they headed back in the direction of the open field. If they'd given me a chance to feed, then I missed it.

I waited on one of the taller buildings in Sooth City to see where they would go. I figured they were going back to the field to meet their counterparts. They did not. Instead, they both made their way to a house on the north end of the compound near the field, went inside, and stayed there.

The extra protection and security measures must have been due to my activities two nights before. I guessed that they had increased the number of soldiers on patrol and made sure they slept in the same house so they were never alone.

A gunshot rang out from the center of town. I jumped as far east as I could, landing on the spire of the circus tent. I stopped and glanced around to see what happened.

There was another team of two soldiers dragging a Creature into the shadows—a streak of blood left in its wake. The smell of Creature blood filled my nostrils.

After a few minutes, the soldiers and the Creature were gone, lost somewhere in the darkness. I wondered how it had gotten in. Perhaps through their system of tunnels? It was a lucky accident, and it took the suspicion off me. However, I couldn't help wondering what DeSantos would say at the next night's family dinner.

I resigned myself to not eating, knowing I would have to do so the next night, regardless of circumstance. I had to be careful.

I got back home and sat on the living room couch, trying to process the night's events. How had the Creature gotten inside if DeSantos was so convinced it wasn't possible? Were the Creatures able to tunnel far enough to get into the city? Why did they need protection so deep inside a supposedly impenetrable wall? Were there Creatures lurking somewhere in Sooth City?

I decided to join the nightly Creature patrol; it seemed the best way to insert myself into the action without raising any eyebrows. I would be able to discover the inner workings of Sooth City. There was something going on behind the scenes, and I wanted to be a part of it, especially if it had anything to do with the Creatures.

Chapter Five

I woke up at my standard time the next evening, my stomach filled with what felt like rusty nails. I put on my black and red suit, left my home, and headed to the tent for dinner.

Per usual, kids were haphazardly playing and running around, their parents close behind, paying no attention to their surroundings. It would have been easy to pick one of them off and drain them. I had to always keep my hunger in check. I didn't want any more posters around town.

I was nervous to ask DeSantos about joining the nightly Creature hunt. Something in his demeanor led me to believe he liked his secrets, and it was likely he would wonder how I discovered the Creatures inside the city. If he wanted me on patrol, he would have asked me himself. He hadn't assigned me to do anything else around the city, so I could play it as though I wanted to contribute.

I went into the tent and headed directly to the front table without taking any food.

"Not hungry today?" Cap asked.

"No," I said. "I'm not feeling well this evening."

"Why's that?" Falcone chimed in.

I clutched my stomach. "I saw something last night, and it made me uneasy."

DeSantos took a bite from his fork. "You know, no one is allowed outside after dark without a special permit."

"I know." I uncrossed my arms from my stomach. "I just needed to clear my head for a minute, so I went for a walk."

"You shouldn't have done that," DeSantos's eyebrows drew

together.

"What did you see?" Falcone asked before I had a chance to offer a retort to DeSantos.

"I'm not sure I should say." I straightened my back. "I think my eyes were playing tricks on me."

"Probably." DeSantos stared at his food.

The sound of his voice was disconcerting. He was trying to lead me away. Asking him about the Creature-watch probably wasn't the best idea, but I decided to do it anyway.

"I would like to join the city's task force." I made the straightest face I could.

"Don't be crazy, son!" DeSantos turned to meet my gaze. "There's no task force in Sooth City." He lowered his voice and checked to make sure no one was listening. "Not here, come meet me at my office after tonight's meal."

DeSantos took the surprise better than I figured he would. He *was* trying to keep the task force quiet, but not from me. I wondered why he would be so candid, and assumed it was because of my research that he allowed me to talk about something so sensitive.

Dinner ended on a happy note with Falcone, Cap, and I exchanging a few battle stories for each other's benefit. I was enjoying their company. They were good men who had their city's best interests at heart. Neither wanted to see their people harmed by the Creatures, and both wanted to see the Sooth prosper under DeSantos. They were, however, deathly frightened of the Noor.

Never underestimate the power of the brainwashed.

I desperately wanted to be on the right side of history, and I was learning it wasn't as subjective as I once thought. Cap and Falcone were convinced of the guilt of everyone bearing a Noor uniform and weren't afraid to show it. Even though there was unmistakable hatred in their eyes when they spoke of the Noor, it was the kind of hatred that came from a concern for their own. It was simultaneously heartwarming and terrifying.

It was clear the two men were brilliant tacticians, and I wondered whether the Noor had any equivalent minds working on annihilating the Sooth.

The meal concluded, DeSantos saying little for the event's duration, then we went our separate ways. I walked toward the hospital where his main office was located. The dilapidated building was a stark contrast to the meticulously kept office inside.

I let myself in. There were no lights on in the lobby, but my eyes adjusted quickly so it wasn't difficult to see. I headed to the elevator behind the worn-out reception desk and pressed the button, waiting for the car to arrive.

After a few seconds, I pushed the button several more times. The front door creaked on the other side of the lobby, but there was a much louder creak and the clicking sound of a Creature in front of me. Soon enough, I could smell the blood lingering on the Creature. It stalked me, like a leopard in hiding, waiting to leap at its prey. The Creature flew at me, and I jumped to the rafters, landing on one of the wooden support beams holding the structure.

The Creature leapt at me several more times, falling on its back with each failed attempt. Two more Creatures entered the room, peering around as if to gauge their surroundings.

I was trapped. I couldn't get to the ground without being eaten, and there was nowhere for me to go, other than more rafters. Maybe I could have outlasted them for a moment. However, there was the issue of my meeting with DeSantos. Missing our rendezvous was a non-starter, and I couldn't afford to breed more suspicion. I had no weapon on me, and I had no blood with which to distract them.

I waited for a few more minutes. They weren't going to leave while I was in the rafters. There was no other choice.

"Help me!" I bellowed.

I stopped and listened to see if I'd been heard. There was nothing.

"Help!" I screamed again.

This time, there were voices coming from outside the hospital. It sounded like a crew of armed men sprinting toward the building. I let myself fall to the floor so the soldiers wouldn't see me in the rafters and ask questions. I opened my eyes as the Creatures bent their heads and pushed up their shoulders.

Gunshots filled the room. I ducked and covered my head. When the last gunshot echoed from existence, I took in the destruction. To my left lay three Creatures in a pile on the floor, a pool of blood forming around them.

The bell on the lift rang, and the doors spread apart from the middle.

One of the soldiers offered me a hand up, and I accepted.

DeSantos walked out of the elevator, wearing the same outfit he'd worn to dinner—a plain black naval officer's coat buttoned to the top and a red pair of slacks. His shoes, usually pristine and shiny, were scuffed at the top like he'd tripped or kicked concrete.

"What happened here?" He addressed no one in particular.

"Creature attack," said the guard who'd offered me his hand.

"Are you okay, Doctor Mason?" DeSantos asked, with an upward vocal inflection of concern.

"I'm sure I will be." I dusted myself off. "Just a little frazzled is all."

"Come with me." He waved his right hand. "Let's get you upstairs."

I was perfectly calm, but I needed everyone to keep thinking I was human.

DeSantos put his finger on the elevator button, and this time the doors separated right away. We stepped onto the platform, and the door closed behind us before I had a chance to turn around.

After a moment, the doors retracted and I saw directly into DeSantos's office on the top floor of the five-story hospital building. He offered me the seat across from his own. I took the chair from under the desk and sat gingerly.

He took a cigar from the box he kept on his desk. He punctured a hole in the mouth end with a metal stick, put the cigar to his mouth then sparked his lighter and puffed. He leaned back in his chair.

"You want to join our nightly Creature hunts?" he asked.

"I do." I was careful not to offer any information he didn't request.

"And how did you find out about this Creature hunt?" He put his cigar to his lips.

Thick vanilla and tobacco scented smoke filled the room and lingered in my mouth every time I exhaled. The room grew hazy as he let huge clouds of smoke out of his mouth.

"I was going for a walk last night," I said slowly, "and I noticed your soldiers dragging one of the Creatures away. I didn't think any Creatures could get in, and I want to make sure that remains the case. Sooth City is my *home* now, and I would be remiss if I didn't offer my services to help defend it."

"You weren't supposed to see any of that." DeSantos let out another mouthful of smoke.

His demeanor changed from inquisitive to accepting in seconds, and I couldn't determine what I'd done to alter his mood. In any case, he no longer seemed interested in how I discovered the task force or why I wanted to include myself.

"I know." I stared at my feet. "It won't happen again. I promise."

"Okay, good." He put his head back a little bit. "You can start training tomorrow."

"I can?"

"Of course." He smiled. "We need all the citizens we can get."

"In that case," I returned his grin, "I'd be honored to join the group."

He motioned for me to make my exit, so I got up from the chair and went to the elevator. I pushed the button, expecting to wait for the car to arrive. I stepped inside, took a deep breath, and exhaled when the doors closed.

When they retracted, I thought I'd see the lobby. Instead, I was in the basement where the interrogation room was. On the other side of the elevator, the soldier who helped me in the lobby was there to greet me—I hadn't paid attention to it before, but this time I took a look and his name tag read "Williams."

Williams was tall and scrawny, and simultaneously athletic. He had strawberry blond hair and freckles, but there was nothing childish in his face. There was a lengthy, jagged scar that went diagonally from the top of his forehead to the bottom of his chin, likely the result of a Creature attack. Though he appeared to be a hardened criminal from the outside, there was a softness to Williams that was difficult to ignore.

He glanced at me and gave me a toothy grin. "So, we need to get you geared up?"

"I suppose so." I gave him a half smile.

Williams chuckled and led me down a dark hallway with a few fluorescent lights buzzing overhead that barely illuminated anything. A hundred feet down the corridor, there was a locked cage with a cache of weapons in it. He took a ring of keys off his belt, fumbling through them for a second until he got to the right one. He opened the cage with a booming scrape of metal, slamming once it got to the other end. The noise echoed through the empty hallways.

He gave a half-grin and nodded his head for me to go inside. I glanced around, slack-jawed, at the armory of weapons the Sooth had at their disposal.

"Impressive, no?" He walked backward down the hall as he spoke to me.

"Yes." I looked at him but tried not to make eye contact for too long. "Yes, it is."

He went to the east wall and took down one of the rifles. "I know you've already seen these in action. It's an X8, long-range disintegration ray."

He pulled back on a lever at the top. It made a clicking sound followed by a metallic buzz. A blinking light next to the trigger flashed three times and stopped.

"Be careful." He handed me the gun. "That's the most powerful weapon we have to use against the Creatures. Bullets, we've found, don't do much to harm those fuckers, but you knew that already, huh Doc?"

I nodded as I inspected the gun in my hand. The lightweight rifle was well-balanced and as natural as a handshake. "Nice."

"The rifle holds a one-hundred-thousand-watt charge that should last up to six hours at a time, depending on how many bloodsuckers you encounter in any given night. You'll need to carry at least two additional charges with you per shift."

"Got it."

"Meet me here after dinner tomorrow, and we'll get you trained up." Williams gave me an approving pat on the back before he put the rifle in a bag for me to hold onto.

"See you then." I bowed my head a little.

Williams handed me a uniform to wear and a few more pieces of equipment I'd need, including a knife, modular vest, and a comms device, placing them into a knapsack for me.

As we went to leave, I caught a whiff of something familiar—a coppery tinge covered by the smell of rubberized plastic.

There was packaged blood somewhere close.

Peering around, I desperately tried not to change anything about my behavior. After a few seconds, I noticed several white refrigerators with a red cross on them in another caged-off room.

My mouth watered.

Hunting in the city was far too dangerous, and if I was going to survive in Sooth City, I needed a better plan. And right here before me, one had presented itself.

There was no way to steal the whole refrigerator at once without someone noticing, so I needed to determine a way to access it without arousing suspicion.

I had an idea—a terrible, terrible idea. I decided to lure one of the Creatures to the room so it would dig a hole underneath and build me a tunnel I could use. Using one of the X8 rifles, I would annihilate anything which entered the room behind me.

While formulating the plan in my head, I switched my focus back to Williams, who was taking me back to the elevator. When the elevator got to the lobby, I saw there were no more Creatures laying on the floor. As I walked out of the elevator, I was expecting Williams to follow me, instead he looked at me, tipped his head slightly, and stayed in the car.

Leaving the hospital building, I was confident I wouldn't have any issues getting home.

I was excited to start training, but more importantly, I was ready to go deeper into Sooth city. There was something off about the way

DeSantos was treating me and getting closer to his inner circle was the best way to determine what was going on behind closed doors. All that was left to do was sit back and wait.

The prospect of having to hunt again within the city limits was not one I was looking forward to, so I was excited I'd found blood to eat. With access to the fridge, my problem was solved. I wouldn't have to hunt, and I wouldn't have to risk being caught by anyone in town.

Chapter Six

In order to find my way into the blood fridges, I planned to sneak in through the basement, open one of the bags, and wait for a Creature to dig a hole into the room. There were plenty of risks involved, and there was no way I could sustain a nightly hunt without eventually being caught by a Creature, or even worse, a guard. DeSantos wouldn't let me get away with murder twice.

After I met with him the next night, my original plan was to head toward home and double back. Instead, I found that there was no one around so I darted to the rear entrance of the hospital building to scope the situation.

The hunger was unbearable, growing from a short pain to a sharp stabbing that caused me to double over and clutch my stomach. No matter what, I *had* to eat. Whether it be fresh or packaged didn't matter; it was too dangerous for me to go another night without any blood.

Having arrived shortly before the guard's shift change, I needed to hold out for a window in which I could avoid the guard who relieved the early shift.

Sitting in the shadows, I waited for my moment to strike.

Twenty minutes later, the first guard was leaving through the rear door, so I ran toward it. I crossed the threshold before it closed fully. In the blink of an eye, I was through.

On the other side of the door, silence blanketed the room. I was in the hallway leading to the interrogation room, the armory, and my prize at the end.

There were footsteps in the distance. I ducked behind a stack of wooden pallets and held my position. After ten seconds, the sound dissolved in the opposite direction, so I continued my way east to the fridge room.

I approached the cage that held the blood fridge; it was tall and metal with a diamond pattern which made it look like houndstooth fabric. I took the handle, pulled it to the left and let the door swing open, all the while hoping no one would hear the clanging metal scraping against itself.

There were four total refrigerators in the room and a dusty looking brown rug that someone had haphazardly thrown to the corner. I went to the closest one and opened the hatch. A bright light illuminated the contents of a fridge packed to the gills with IV bags of blood— enough to last the foreseeable future.

Lifting one of the bags from the fridge, I stared at it intently. The bag read, "Test-Blood: TB-456; Source: Human; Blood Type: O-Negative; Notes: Treated for Creature Consumption."

The last line made me do a double-take. I wasn't sure what was in there, and I didn't need to ask. It was easy to infer what "Treated for Creature Consumption" meant. It occurred to me DeSantos was likely keeping Creatures to experiment on with some kind of blood derivative.

"What do we have here?" I said as I examined the contents of the bag under the light.

The color of the blood inside the bag was a much lighter red than the blood I was used to drinking—clearer and less opaque. It appeared to be blood, but I wasn't sure what was actually in the bag, so I was wary of opening it. However, I was hungry, and I needed to eat. I'd wasted a lot of time finding the bag I held in my hands.

I didn't trust DeSantos. However, my curiosity and drive to survive were greater than my mistrust, so I decided to go against my gut and try whatever was in the bag.

Opening the bag with my teeth, I caught a whiff of the contents. A sour smell stung my nose and made me flinch.

"Jesus Christ," I said under my breath.

With my forefinger and thumb, I plugged my nose. I tipped the bag upside down and drained the contents into my open mouth. When the bag was empty, I carefully crumbled it and jammed it into my pocket to throw away later. Despite the spoiled-milk taste, it did the trick. My stomach stopped growling immediately, and my limbs loosened. It rejuvenated me in a way I'd never experienced from human blood. My entire body was focused and ready to spring into action at the drop of a hat.

The ground rustled beneath me, each dirt molecule being pushed aside with each movement through the dirt. The Creature's nails scraped the sides of the tunnel, and the moment it got there, there was a rhythmic pulsing that sounded a lot like a heartbeat.

I stared where I somehow knew the Creature was going to create a hole and shot my X8 directly into the ground. When the dust settled, there was no Creature there. It had simply disappeared under the bright light of the weapon.

I went into the hole, covering it behind me with the brown rug. The tunnel was dry and dusty, and it was difficult to see more than a few feet in front of me.

Crawling through the tunnel, I felt every atom I touched. I smelled the musk of the Creature who'd made it; it was not unlike the mulch I smelled in the blood bag I'd drank. I felt the earthworms crawling underneath my hands. I was aware of everything in the immediate vicinity. My senses were at the top of their game, and nothing escaped my purview.

After ten minutes of crawling, I was at the end of the tunnel. To my surprise, I was still inside the city, between the inner and outer walls. There was a commotion of clicking sounds from the vibrations in the ground, and I blindly headed toward it.

I saw everything as if it were clear as day. Every detail of every building, person, and leaf was sharp and in perfect resolution.

A hundred feet in front of me there was an enclosure the size of a shipping container. I looked more closely and saw there were Creatures inside. The pen was packed.

There was a brawl going on between two of the bigger ones. Two guards holding cattle prods went to the cage and jammed the long sticks into the bodies of the arguing Creatures. Each bellowed a shrill scream, then slumped to the ground.

Before there was a chance to process why the Sooth were holding a cage full of Creatures, a wave of exhaustion encircled my entire body. My heart thumped in my chest. All the pores in my body secreted saline. A ball of nausea rolled in my stomach, creeping up into my throat. I didn't know what was happening. My pulse raced harder in my head until I could almost hear it. My eyes burned and watered at the sight of the halogen lights in the distance which made it hard to see. I blinked several times, then a tear rolled down my cheek.

I dropped to my knees and clutched my stomach, covering my mouth with my sleeve to stifle the scream.

"What the fuck was that?" one of the guards asked.

Not wanting to expose myself any further, I got up then headed toward my domicile.

As I ran, the nausea became more intense. The rising bile made it difficult to run at a rate I would have liked, so I slowed to a jogger's pace when I was sure I was no longer in range.

I got to the back of my house two minutes later, slid the door open, then went inside. I slumped onto the wall to the left of the kitchen. I took a deep breath and closed my eyes. Turning to the trash can, I expelled red vomit from the depths of my stomach into the can, leaving some dangling from my lips.

~ * ~

Whatever the Sooth had added to TB-456 was powerful. It didn't last more than half an hour, and as soon as it wore off, I felt like I was dying. I'd never taken a substance which heightened my senses or gave me such euphoria, and there was a voice in the back of my mind telling me I wanted more.

There were so many questions, and no one to answer them.

What the fuck was that? Why were they keeping a stockpile of Creatures? Who would engineer blood designed to enhance the Creatures? Does TB-456 have the same effect on them as it did on me? Do I keep drinking it, or do I go back to hunting? How many people knew about this?

I considered whether Falcone and Cap were aware of the Creature-zoo, but decided they were both too noble to go along with something so illogical and dangerous. Or perhaps they *did* know and were putting on an act to trick me into thinking they were reasonable men.

I wasn't sure who to trust anymore. DeSantos was doing something far more sinister than I initially assumed. Sure, he was a little off, but I wouldn't have guessed he could put his people in such monstrous peril.

My best bet was to play along and keep building working relationships with DeSantos, Falcone, and Cap. That way, I could use the nightly watch to continue investigating what was truly going on in Sooth City.

The sun was peeking over the horizon—pink and orange hues illuminating the foggy morning sky. My eyes were like two marbles in my head, and my eyelids were closing involuntarily. I extended my arm and took an afghan off the back of the couch, covered my head, and closed my eyes. I did my best to fall asleep, though my pounding brain made it difficult.

~ * ~

I woke up confused. I had no idea how much time had gone by. It felt like I'd slept through at least one night.

There was a knock at the door. I could smell DeSantos's cigar through the wall. I jumped up, sped into the bedroom, put on my clothing to avoid suspicion, then got back in between knocks.

I turned the handle. "Good evening, sir, what brings you by?"

"You missed dinner last night." DeSantos peered at me through squinted eyes. "Why?"

"I'm sorry." I rubbed the back of my neck. "I came across some research I thought I'd lost, and I couldn't put it down. Next thing I know, you're knocking on my door."

"How long have you been awake?" he asked with a hint of concern in his voice.

I pretended to look at my watch. "Holy shit—three days."

"Okay." DeSantos closed his eyelids even more. "Get to dinner, and make sure you're ready for training. You missed your first day."

"Fuck." I was disappointed. "Do you think Williams'll forgive me?"

"Of course, he will, son." DeSantos's face relaxed. "Just get to dinner."

He patted me on the shoulder once and left. I breathed a heavy sigh of relief that I'd created a plausible excuse.

I went into the washroom and inspected myself. My face was withered and wrinkled like I'd aged a decade overnight. My pupils were each the size of a needlepoint, so I rubbed my eyes in the hopes they would reset. They did not. I must have looked like a crazy person. I barely recognized my reflection.

TB-456 had done a number on me. Drinking more would be a mistake. I couldn't silence the voice telling me how badly I wanted another dose. It was a difficult feeling to shake. I knew it was bad for me, and it was all I could do to stop myself from running out of my house for another bag.

No. Despite how much I wanted to, I wouldn't go down that road. It wasn't worth it.

~ * ~

Later, still hungover, I prepared to head to the tent for dinner when the dog greeted me. Each night he met me at my table and sat at my feet for food scraps and scratches behind the ear. It was a mutually beneficial relationship. Since I had no need for food and he greatly did, he was happy to be at my disposal. I named him "Scraps" for obvious reasons.

I'd asked around, and no one wanted to claim ownership of the mutt, so for all intents and purposes, he was mine to do with as I saw fit. This was the first time he'd met me before dinner, and I was happy to see him waiting for me. I bent over to pet him, the way he preferred, and he whined an approval.

I went to the center of town with the rest of the citizens, Scraps at my side the entire time.

Arriving at the tent, I skipped the line in my usual fashion, took my food, and sat at the head table with DeSantos, Falcone, and Cap.

"Looks like you have a new companion." Cap smiled at the dog following me from outside instead of meeting me.

"Looks like it," I responded.

Out of the corner of my eye, I saw someone coming to the head table.

It was Williams, approaching at a calm pace. His face was bright red, and he was sweating. When he got close enough he whispered something in DeSantos's ear, then walked away without saying a word to anyone else.

DeSantos took the napkin off his lap and threw it onto the table. He left without saying a word.

After picking at my food for a while, I gave the last of it to the shepherd and made my way out the tent for my first night of training. Along the winding sidewalk to the facility, Scraps stayed at my side. I liked having a follower who gave me something to care about other than myself, something other than blood and Creatures.

When I got to the east end of the compound behind the outer wall, I walked into the single-story building and stopped for a second. Scraps went off to the side and wandered around until I couldn't see him anymore. I was sure he'd be there waiting when I finished.

Inside the door was a large, open room with mirrors on two of the walls. In the middle was a boxing ring with a gray floor covered in brown stains. Frayed ropes dangled from the turnbuckles. There was a single light coming from the ceiling above the ring which illuminated the area.

I didn't see Williams. I walked around to inspect the gym. There was random equipment splayed about. Nothing appeared to be in working order save for the jump ropes laying like dried-up worms stranded on hot pavement.

On the other side of the ring, there was an old pair of boxing gloves hanging above one of the wall mirrors. I took them off the hook then slipped them on.

I put my hands in front of my face and threw a couple of quick jabs at my reflection. There were footsteps coming from outside of the room. From the smell of his cologne, I could already tell it was Williams, running late for our session—I assumed because of whatever news he'd given DeSantos at dinner.

"Good form," Williams said as he entered.

"Thanks." I chuckled.

"Have you boxed before?"

"Not that I can recall."

The truth was, I *had* boxed before. In the 1920s, I had a brief career in the industry that helped me find prey. I went by the name of "Boxcar Bobby." It was a stupid one I'd made up for myself to blend in and ensure the citizens of New York City thought I was a hobo. Back then, it was easy to lack an identity. There was no electronic database of information on people, so if you wanted to make a name for yourself, you had to do it yourself.

I never made it big, but that was by design. I cruised right down the center, enough to make a few bucks and taste some boxer blood.

"Looks like you're a natural." Williams smiled.

As I smiled back at him while he walked to me, he threw a gym bag at my feet. "This is for you. Go put it on and meet me back here in ten minutes."

Unzipping the bag, I saw there was a brand new pair of black and red boxing gloves I pushed to the side to reveal the rest of the contents. There was a black pair of shorts with red trim, a black and red pair of boxing shoes, and a wheel of black tape to wrap my hands.

"Go ahead." Williams nodded toward a closed door that read "Men's Locker Room" in bold black letters. "This'll be fun."

The door creaked at the hinges, making a metallic scrape which filled my ears and caused me to pull back a bit.

The state of cleanliness in the locker room was the same as the hospital building, rundown, yet somehow functional and efficient. The brown walls were wet, and the smell of mildew filled my nostrils.

I chose one of the many lockers and pulled the handle. There was nothing inside. I unbuttoned my shirt and gently hung it on the hook, then did the same with my pants. A chill ran from the base of my spine and crept to the top of my neck, but I wasn't sure why. I hadn't heard anything or sensed I was in any danger, yet something in the back of my head was telling me to be cautious.

I put on the shiny shorts and tied the string until it was snug. I slung the gloves over my shoulder, picked up the roll of tape, and walked toward the locker room door.

Beads of sweat formed around the base of my hairline. I wiped the moisture off my forehead with the back of my hand, took a deep breath then exited.

Williams was waiting for me in the center of the ring, wearing a hooded black and red sweat suit. He held two focus mitts in his hands which he playfully slapped together when I emerged.

"Everything good in there?" he asked.

"Oh yeah," I said. "I couldn't figure out how to get this tape around my hands, so I figured I'd have you do it."

He chuckled and dropped the focus mitts on the ground where he stood. He jumped from the ring and approached me, taking my hand when he got close.

"How's that feel?" he asked. "Not too tight? We don't want to cut off your circulation."

Williams winked at me like he was fully aware I had no circulation. I squeezed my hands twice to loosen the tape a bit.

"Yeah." I gripped the air several times with my fingers. "It feels good."

He took the gloves hanging off my shoulder, untied the knot, then slid them onto my hands.

"Come on." He headed toward the ring.

There was a three-step wooden staircase in the corner that led to the platform. Williams pulled the top rope, stuck his foot on the bottom one, and invited me to enter.

"Hands up," he said when we got to the center.

I put my hands up.

He bounced about in the area, making half-circles around me. "Don't forget to breathe. Make sure you're covering your face. Keep your feet moving. Never lock your knees."

I already knew the proper stance, but to make him feel like I was starting from scratch, I adjusted my feet so they were facing the same direction.

"All right, loosen up a little." He grabbed my arms and swung them around like ropes.

He walked behind me and kicked my feet until I was forced to place one foot behind the other, rotating my equilibrium to where I was more flexible.

When I was in what was an acceptable stance, it was time to start throwing punches. I followed him around with my fists and my feet, careful not to take my eyes off him.

"Let's see what you got." He stood in front of me and put his arms up. "Throw a punch. Concentrate on making contact."

Throwing a fast right-jab, my glove landed squarely in the middle of the pad.

"Good." He nodded quickly. "Again."

I punched the mat again, this time a lot harder.

"Perfect," he yelled. "Now, give me a left!"

As I hit the mat with my left fist, it started to feel normal.

"Okay, here's what I want you to do. Right, right, left, duck right. Then left, left, right, duck left."

After throwing two right hands, and a left, Williams waved his hand at my head with the focus mitt and hit me directly in the face. The force of the pad was enough to knock me off my axis a bit, but I pointed my left foot out and regained my balance before I fell.

"Again!" he yelled like a drill sergeant.

My next two punches connected perfectly with the white square in the middle of the mat. Lifting my left arm, I put the force behind my shoulder, and landed my hand gracefully to the mitt. This time, I bent my knees, lowered my torso, then ducked out of the way as soon as Williams whipped the mitt over my head.

"Good! Again! Faster this time!" He continued to bark orders at me.

We went through the routine for an hour, each time going faster, until I was back to my old self in the ring. By the time we were done, the muscles in my arms were like noodles dangling off my clavicle; wet, loose, and thin.

Knocking the dust off was easier than I thought it would be. Being in training again gave me a sense of accomplishment. Fending off Creatures made it difficult to focus on anything else, and I was glad to have an outlet to expel energy not spent on worrying about monsters or blood.

Blood. I could absolutely go for some of that packaged blood right now.

I was craving more test blood. I told myself I wouldn't go down that road, but it was difficult to deny the boost it gave to my senses.

As we finished our first night of training, I couldn't help but notice the slightest amount of acceptance from Williams. He taught me with a soft hand, and he was more than patient with my purposeful missteps in the ring.

"You know," he said as we changed our clothes in the locker room, "DeSantos has extraordinary plans for you."

"He does?" I asked with an upturned brow.

"Oh yeah. You may be the most important person in this town right now."

"Shucks." I rolled my eyes a little. "I'm just one guy."

"Yeah," Williams said with a hint of snide. "The one guy who can finally help us rid the planet of the Noor."

"I can't wait," I said with a quiver in my voice.

I was so entrenched in the Creatures, and establishing myself in the city, I'd almost forgotten DeSantos and the rest of the Sooth expected me to be planning a takedown of the entire Noor population. I didn't want to get rid of the Noor as much as I wanted an end to the Creatures, but if it helped the Sooth help *me*, I would play along.

The Sooth's irrational fear of the Noor above the Creatures was astounding to me. How did DeSantos so perfectly convince everyone the Noor were more important? I reminded myself once again how powerful brainwashing can be.

Williams and I went our separate ways. He told me he was going to a meeting with the town elders but wouldn't tell me what it was in regards to when I asked. Scraps was outside when I left the training facility.

We took the long way through the center of town. On the way home, there was a growl in the pit of my stomach. I wouldn't be able to eat, and even if I did, I wasn't sure whether TB-456 remained a viable option. The idea of taking something with addictive effects gave me an uneasy restlessness in my chest.

Could I control myself on such a substance? Was it worth it simply to avoid hunting? Was it better to steal the bags and keep the population intact?

It wasn't easy to decide. I didn't have a lot of options when it came to meals, and there were a lot of variables to consider. Obviously, the less time I spent hunting, the better. The fewer people killed, the more my safety was guaranteed. Perhaps someone would notice missing blood bags, but I had to assume it wasn't as much of a risk as someone catching me killing a person.

I chose not to make my final decision until the next night, though something was gnawing at the back of my neck, telling me it wouldn't be the last time I would taste TB-456.

Scraps and I got to the house. I invited the dog in, but he was content to sit and hold the porch. I went inside and got a bowl, then filled it with water before placing it outside for Scraps.

It was late and the sun was rising, so I went directly to my bed. The moment my head hit the pillow, a calming wave washed over me, whisking me to instant slumber.

~ * ~

The next night's routine went the same as the previous one. Scraps and I went to dinner, then to the training building.

After the session, the rumbling rose in my gut again. There was no getting around eating, and I had to think of something.

TB-456 it was. At least it'd be fun.

After a lot of thought and inner conflict, I decided to go back to the room where the blood fridge was.

I went home with Scraps, left him some fresh water, then headed back inside to change into some clean clothing. I put on a black turtleneck with a Sooth insignia sewn into the chest. Looking at myself in the mirror I couldn't help but feel like I was becoming a Sooth.

No. I'm there to make sure my food source was safe.

When I was done dressing, I left my house in my usual manner through the backyard, then through the alley behind the neighborhood.

It was particularly dark and the lights in the alley were dead, so I was able to move with less risk of being seen by anyone.

With a slight pounding in my chest, I traveled the path to the hospital wing. Part of me was feeling excited I was going to eat; however, instincts were telling me I should be wary of getting high again.

At the back door of the building, the guard was leaving for the evening's shift change. Slipping a foot in the crack before the door closed, I let myself into the hallway.

Making my way past the interrogation room, I got to the cage where the blood fridge was and made sure no one was coming.

There were no Creatures in there and the room was as I left it, the brown rug covering the hole. I was sure someone had likely been in there at some point.

Standing at the fridge, I opened the top then removed a bag of blood.

Nervous to use an entire bag of TB-456, I drank only enough to make my stomach stop growling. To my relief, it didn't affect me the same way it had the first time. My senses were still heightened and there was still a euphoric sensation, only this time I was able to control myself, and my movements were more natural. I took a couple of bags and put them in the pouch I was carrying.

I pushed aside the filthy brown rug, and it dropped into the hole below. On the other end I was hoping to continue investigating the pen of Creatures DeSantos was hiding. The moist tunnel smelled like fresh soil underneath me.

I emerged from the tunnel fifteen minutes later. There was no one in the vicinity. The pen holding the Creatures was no longer there. In its place there was a brick structure, inside of which nothing moved.

Jumping into the trees to get a better view of the surrounding area, I noticed there were no doors or windows for anyone to enter or exit through.

"What happened to those Creatures?" I murmured.

Something was wrong.

How did they move them all in two nights? Just as importantly, *why* did they move the entire pen? Had they seen me the first time I exited the tunnel?

While I waited to see if anyone came by, a cold feeling in my gut rose, then I took a sip of blood, hoping it would provide some relief. The pain in my stomach and head subsided.

I stopped for a second to make sure no Creatures smelled the bag, and when I was satisfied they hadn't, I closed it then leapt down from the trees, landing on the dewy grass below.

Done taking risks for the evening, I decided it was time to get back home.

Chapter Seven

Over the next couple of weeks, I found a third of a bag of TB-456 was enough to keep me sated without getting me too high. I remained clueless as to what was *in* the blood that made it so hopelessly addictive, but as long as I held my middle ground, it did the trick, and I didn't have to hunt.

The fridges were replenished weekly, and no one seemed to be keeping track or noticing a few bags missing here and there.

Several nights a week were spent talking shop with Falcone and Cap before the daily dinners. We mostly discussed the Creatures and their evolution. Both men were intensely fascinated with the Creatures's ability to develop secondary characteristics in such a short amount of time.

Every day, Williams and I worked out and sparred for ten rounds at a time. He was an impressive boxer. Even though I was downplaying my incredible speed, he could land hits without issue, avoiding mine like he could see into the future.

Something was calming in having a strict regimen of exercise and work which made it easier to accept my circumstances in Sooth City.

I was also having a good time in the company of Scraps. Eventually, he grew comfortable and took up residence in my home. He followed me around, happy to no longer be sleeping outside on the porch. I acquired steaks for him to eat, which helped me continue the ruse that I ate every night.

Blending in was getting easier. People were starting to recognize me, and I even believed some of them to be friends. The citizens of Sooth City were growing on me. Despite their secrets, there was a quaint simplicity to the daily life of the people. They made me yearn for a life in which the Creatures and the Noor were a non-issue, and I could continue hunting and draining people without worry.

I kept a close eye on the brick building that had caged the crew of Creatures. There was no change. I gathered they must have moved the cage to a less visible position.

It was our last night of training before my first night's watch, and Williams was excited.

He straightened his back and puffed out his chest. "Looks like you're going out tomorrow night."

"I suppose I am." I returned the gesture.

"You're not excited?"

"Don't get me wrong." I rubbed my neck. "I am. I'm going to miss our nightly sessions."

"Don't worry." He tapped my arm with his glove. "You'll be back in the ring soon enough. Now let's go."

We tapped gloves and went to our separate corners.

"Ding, ding." Williams hit an invisible bell with an invisible hammer.

He swung first—a stiff arm which landed squarely in the middle of my face. I shook it off and kept going. I jabbed at him with my left hand, hitting him in the ear. He backed up from the force, slapped his gloves, and came back at me. He threw a left hand that landed against my ribs. It was a light tap, so I didn't react much. I retaliated with a left hook that caught Williams in the jaw, causing him to spit blood in the air and onto the floor.

"Nice one." He hopped in place.

Too busy concentrating on beating him, I chose not to say anything. He wasn't faster than me. However, he did have a much stronger aptitude for boxing than I could ever have.

Williams approached me. He lifted his left hand and jabbed me with his right. I ducked out of the way and came back up, extending my arm in an uppercut, hitting him directly under his jaw. The blow caused him to spit his mouth guard onto the floor. He bent to retrieve it, then put it back in his mouth and went to his corner. I went to mine.

This time, we came out swinging our fists in full force. Several left hands hit me in the glove. I gave him another uppercut with my right hand but was denied by a block from his forearms. I put my hands to my face. He threw a right hand toward my head, I stepped to the left and dodged.

It was more like a street brawl than a boxing match. The both of us let loose and punched at each other as fast as we could, neither of us taking the time to rest in between. We were playing, and I had to admit I was having fun.

When the buzzer stopped a minute later, the two of us tapped gloves. We went to the edge of the ring, sat, and rested our backs on one of the ropes.

"I'll miss this too," he said.

After a few minutes of silence, we got up, headed to the locker room, then got changed out of our training gear. We said almost nothing to each other. There was an awkwardness between us, and I didn't want to address it.

We left saying little else save a brief farewell while I waited outside for Scraps.

~ * ~

It was time for me to officially join the patrol. Before dinner, Williams dropped off a box with a new black uniform with red trim, which I inspected. There was a patch on it which said "Mason" in the same font as the rest of the town's soldiers.

I put the shirt and pants on and stared at myself in the mirror. I looked like a soldier, ready to kick ass at the drop of a dime. It was a far cry from what I normally wore, even when I was going to be fighting, and I couldn't help feeling purposeful with it on.

Scraps whimpered at me.

"I know, boy." I looked at him. "I don't like it either."

I changed back into a clean suit, because I was only supposed to wear my uniform when I was on patrol.

Accompanied by Scraps, I took the fastest route possible. I didn't want dinner to last any longer than it needed to.

When I got to the tent, I picked up some food for Scraps then sat at the table. I was too distracted to talk. I kept thinking about what was going to happen tonight. I would have to wait a long time before DeSantos let me in on the city's secrets, and I was happy to get started.

Dinner went by at a snail's pace. Per routine, Falcone and Cap talked about tactical strategies and the philosophies behind them. I fed Scraps while DeSantos sat there eyeing his servants.

Anxious to get into the field and determine what was going on behind the scenes in Sooth City, I spoke little for the rest of the evening. I wanted to ask about the brick building but couldn't do so without giving away that I'd been in a restricted area.

After the meal concluded, Scraps and I went back to the house. I changed into my new uniform and equipped myself with my new gear. I closed my eyes for a second, and when I opened them, I made sure my game face was on.

I went to the front door and as I left to rendezvous with the rest of the Creature patrolmen and women, I tried to get Scraps to stay behind, but he refused to leave my side.

"Oh well." I scratched his head. "I guess you're coming too, huh boy?"

Scraps perked his ears all the way and crooked his head as if to say, "no shit."

"C'mon." I nodded to the door.

The two of us left the house and walked down the street.

There was a distinct lack of people outside, which was odd because a beautiful night in Sooth City was typically a bustling scene of citizens going about their business. A breeze wafted in the summer night's air, cooling the beads of sweat resting on my clammy forehead.

I arrived at the training facility where Williams, Falcone, and Cap waited with the rest of the team. They greeted me quietly while they continued running diagnostics on their equipment. There were five new bodies in the crew I'd be working with—three men and two women.

"Everyone," Williams addressed the room. "For those of you who have not been formally introduced, this is Dr. Trevor Mason. He's a close personal friend of General DeSantos, and you are to treat him as you would any superior."

Everyone nodded.

"Okay." Williams looked at me. "Introductions. This is Deborah Cushing, Cyrus Davenport, Francois LaRue, Marina and Dustin Vander. These are the best of the best any Sooth territory has to offer. Each of these impeccable soldiers has taken down a Creature with their bare hands...in front of witnesses."

"It's nice to meet you all." I greeted each of them with a handshake.

They all wore the same uniform and, on paper, shared the same description—dark hair, six-feet tall on average, blue eyes, and strong as fuck. However, some of the specifics were different.

Cushing was the tallest and thinnest of the five by six inches. Her face was long and thin with the nose and cheekbones to match. Under her eyes were two streaks of black paint which went from the bridge of her nose to her earlobe. Her hair was in a tight bun atop her head, and underneath her hairline was a red bandana, folded into a headband.

Davenport was the shortest at around five-foot ten-inches. His black hair was buzzed to a one. His build was stocky and strong, like he could win a hugging contest with a bear. His long black beard gave him the appearance of a warrior dwarf from a fantasy novel.

LaRue was from New Orleans and spoke with a Cajun accent. I later learned from Williams that LaRue's mother and father fled during the Battle of Tremé and sought refuge in Sooth City after they were declared enemies of the state by the Council of Noor. He was of average height and build, taller than Davenport, slightly shorter than Cushing. His hair was short and neatly combed to the side with pomade.

The Vander twins, Marina and Dustin, were roughly the same height as LaRue but carried themselves like they were twice as tall. Marina was bucksome, full-figured, and covered in lean muscle. Her black hair was cropped short and spiked on top, and underneath her hairline, she wore the same red bandana as Cushing.

Dustin looked almost exactly like Marina. His build was lean and muscular like an Olympic swimmer. He, however, did not wear a red bandana. Instead, he wore a black knit hat with a red Sooth crest sewn onto the front.

They were a hardened group of soldiers who looked like they'd seen more battles than a battle could shake a stick at. Glancing at their stern faces and stalwart, deliberate actions, it was easy to see they were a well-oiled machine. Clearly, DeSantos had done a thorough job hand picking them.

"Here are your assignments for the night." Williams took a paper map from his pocket and placed it on the ground in the middle of everyone. He knelt and pointed to specific locations. "Vander and Vander —you two are going to take the northeast quadrant. Davenport, Cushing, and LaRue, you three will take northwest. Falcone and Cap, you'll be in southwest, and Mason and I will be patrolling southeast.

"Those of you going to northwest...be careful. Scouts have reported Creature sightings on the last two patrols. Make sure you three watch each other's sixes and *call for backup* if you see one of those shitheads. We don't want any heroics tonight. Understood?"

"Sir!" the team yelled at a surprisingly high volume.

We departed for our assigned locations a few moments later, each group headed in opposite directions.

Williams and I said nothing on the way to our patrol. Our first order of business was to make our way around the perimeter and survey for any potential breaches. We found nothing.

After an hour, we climbed to a hunting blind in a tree at the center of southeast. From our position, there were three identical locations that were hundreds of feet in the air above the forest line. Even though it was dark I could still see each of the massive trees in the distance.

Williams offered me a cup of coffee from a thermos already in the blind. I refused with a wave of my hand.

"Suit yourself." He took a sip from the thermos. "But it's gonna be a long one, and I smell Creatures in the air tonight, my friend."

He wasn't lying. I smelled them also—the stench of flatulent goo emanating from almost every direction. They were outside the city walls, dozens of them. Maybe hundreds.

Something was even stranger than usual—they weren't moving. I waited and listened for a moment to try and discern what they were doing, but they remained sedentary and showed no signs of going in any particular direction.

Sooth City was surrounded by a circle of Creatures.

"Something's wrong." I put a hand behind my ear and listened intently. "Can you hear that?"

"Yeah." Williams put a hand on the pistol at his hip. "I can."

The clicking sound of a thousand Creatures descended, filling the night's air like a swarm of cicadas, covering the city in a blanket of relentless static which hung onto every soundwave.

Williams lifted his radio to his face and pressed the button. "Quadrants...report."

There was nothing but static coming from the other end.

"Quadrants...report," he repeated, this time louder.

Again, only static.

"Shit." He glared into the distance. "They can't hear us. Those fuckers are too loud."

"I don't think that's it." I pointed to the northeast.

Off in the distance, the radio tower outside of Sooth City was bending in the center. A loud creak rang out over the sound of the Creatures clicking as they destroyed it. A few more seconds went by, and the tower fell into the surrounding trees, taking many of them with it.

"Shit, shit, shit." Williams barely broke his concentration. "Stay here, Mason. That's an order."

I nodded.

He took a carabiner from his belt and attached it to a metal line. He got onto the ledge then jumped off. The zipline took him to the ground, a few feet inside the outer wall. He raced off to the southwest quadrant, where Falcone and Cap were stationed, presumably to make sure they were alive and no Creatures had penetrated the wall.

As Williams disappeared into the tree line, the clicking grew more intense.

I was a few hops away from the wall, so I decided to investigate. I took one of the carabiners off the table in the west corner of the hut then stepped up to the zipline like Williams had. On my way I glanced at the other side of the electric fence.

Sure enough, hundreds of Creatures stood on their hind legs outside the wall, alligator mouths pointing to the sky, clicking as if to accomplish something. They were lined shoulder to shoulder in each direction.

Sooth City was doomed.

I wasn't sure what they were doing, but my best guess was that it had something to do with the Creatures DeSantos kept locked underneath the city. Perhaps the caged group was able to communicate to the larger hive that they were in trouble and needed to be rescued.

Suddenly, it hit me. The larger group of Creatures was creating a diversion while a rescue team went to free their imprisoned comrades.

The Creatures were showing an entirely new level of intelligence not even I could have imagined. They were evolving like nothing history had ever seen; they were formulating cogent plans.

Sooth City relied on the radio tower for more than communication between soldiers. It was how they relayed the news, Creature migrations and food supply lines with other Sooth communities throughout the region. The Creatures must have destroyed several towers to ensure no one contacted Sooth City to alert them.

I needed to get to Williams.

After I landed on the ground, I ran to northeast quadrant.

The risks of running full-speed to the next quadrant were great. However, I needed to hurry or I wouldn't get there in time to warn the rest of the team about what the Creatures were doing.

I decided to take the chance and run as fast as I could to Williams.

It didn't matter, by the time I got there, it was too late. The clicking had stopped, which meant the Creatures had accomplished their mission. I guessed that somewhere in the compound there was an empty cage and a hole in the floor.

"What the fuck are you doing away from your post?" Williams asked harshly.

"I needed t—"

"I don't give a shit what you *needed* to do!" he snapped back. "You *do not* abandon your post for *any* reason."

"Yes, sir," I said.

"So…what in the absolute *fuck* was so important you disobeyed a direct order?"

I didn't answer.

~ * ~

We got back to the training center two hours before sunup. Our relief team came to excuse us from duty, and by the time they did, I was ready to get home and have some blood. It would have been a nice way to end the evening.

Williams asked Falcone, Cap, and me to stay and sent the rest of the team home.

They brought me into the breakroom. Williams and Falcone poured themselves coffee and took a seat at the large round table in the middle of the room. Cap was leaning against the counter with his legs crossed.

"Okay." Williams took a sip of his coffee. "Let's start from the beginning. How do you know the Creatures were creating a distraction and not trying for weak points in our security system? How do you know they weren't trying to freak us the fuck out?"

"It's hard to explain," I hedged.

"Try." Falcone squinted, and his lips tightened.

"How did you get to us so quickly?" Williams asked.

"I'm *extremely* fast," I said.

"No shit." He chortled.

Falcone used a dark voice. "Not funny."

Unsure of what to say next, I put my hands on my lap and rubbed my thighs. Since I hadn't had time to think of a good excuse before running headfirst toward northeast quadrant, I didn't consider whether anyone saw me jumping from the wall.

I was off my game.

Garnering sympathy for the Sooth was something that needed to change. Keeping in mind that I was helping them because the Creatures were threatening my food source, as far as I was concerned, it was a mutually beneficial arrangement. I wasn't sure Williams, Falcone, and Cap would see it the same way. I *knew* DeSantos wouldn't.

It didn't seem like there was much of an option, so I decided to tell them the truth and see how they reacted. If I was going to kill the men and flee Sooth City…so be it.

"All right," I said eventually, "but it *truly* is hard to explain in a way you might find satisfying."

"We'll judge that." Cap broke his silence. "You just worry about telling us the truth."

I closed my eyes and took a deep breath through my nose. "For lack of a better word, I am what you would think of as a vampire."

My eyes opened and the three men were peering at me like I told them their mothers died.

"We're not amused." Falcone kept his gaze directly on me.

"I'm not trying to be amusing." I exposed my fangs to the room and made the hissing sound I'd seen in movies. I'd never actually hissed at anyone out of anger.

Williams and Falcone jumped from their seats, knocking their chairs to the ground, and took their sidearms from their holsters.

Cap did nothing.

"What the fuck?" Williams yelled into the room.

"Calm down, gentlemen." I used the most soothing tone I could muster. "Don't think for a second you've maintained any advantage since my arrival. I am faster and stronger than you, and I can sure as shit get those pistols out of your hands before you have a second to put pressure on the trigger."

Using all of my speed, I got up and took Williams's weapon from his hand before anyone had a chance to blink. Then I turned him around and pointed at his head like he was a hostage. "You can trust me when I say this, gentlemen…if I wanted you dead, you would be."

I let Williams go and gave him back his firearm, which he accepted graciously.

Apparently, it was enough for him and Falcone to stop. Cap, on the other hand, remained exactly as he had the entire time.

"I don't understand." Williams holstered his pistol. "What are you doing *here,* of all places?" He picked his chair from off the ground and set it at the table across from me.

I paced slowly around the men. "For some time now, the Creatures have been a threat to my food supply—humans. I noticed several months ago they were hunting more frequently and in larger numbers. When I discovered them originally—"

"Wait," Williams said. "*You* discovered them? That's bullshit. What about Avery Swanson, the archaeologist? He discovered them on an expedition into the Grand Canyon."

I stopped in front of him. "I discovered them in the Adirondacks almost twenty-years before Swanson's expedition," I replied. "Yes, he *was* the first human to see a Creature and survive to tell the tale, but he was *not* their finder. That was me.

"As I was saying, since I discovered them all those years ago, I've been tracking their patterns, and mostly we've been staying away from each other. However, they interrupted several of my meals and were starting to encroach on my ability to eat properly."

"What happens if you don't eat properly?" Williams raised his right eyebrow and furrowed the other.

"Then you get what happened to Jakovich and his team," I said. "Instead of hunting quietly and discerning what I eat, I kill whoever is unlucky enough to be around me at the time."

"Why tonight?" he asked. "What happened to make you risk being caught?"

I started pacing again. "In the morning, you will find out from DeSantos his lab has been broken into, and the Creatures he was keeping captive have been emancipated. That's what I was coming to tell you. The clicking outside was a distraction meant to hold our attention long enough for a team to get inside. By the time I got to you, they'd stopped, so it's safe to assume their mission was a success."

"How can you possibly know any of this?" Falcone squinted at me.

"I can smell them." I stopped at the head of the table and put my hands on it. "I know how they move. I know how they operate. I've been tracking them for years now, and I am certain they are intelligent enough to plan something as complex as what I've described."

The three men stopped talking for a moment, undoubtedly contemplating whether what I'd told them could possibly be true. They understood Creatures existed, and I hoped vampires wouldn't be too far a stretch.

"I guess *that* explains why you only sleep during the day." Williams sat down.

Cap took a seat at the far end of the table. "So, we need you to help us defend against the Creatures, and you need us to help keep your food supply safe?"

"Essentially." I lifted my hands off the table and sat.

"How the fuck can we know you're telling the truth? And what makes you think we are just going to let you feed on the citizens we're trying to protect?"

"I suppose you'll never truly know. As far as feeding me goes, that's something we'll have to discuss. But…how about this? In the morning, if DeSantos reports everything is fine, then you can drag me into the sun and watch me burn like a bonfire."

Williams, Falcone, and Cap nodded at each other.

"Until then," Williams said menacingly.

Chapter Eight

Williams escorted me to my house and made camp in the living room to stand guard. Falcone and Cap went to DeSantos to debrief him on the evening's events.

I was positive he would tell Falcone and Cap the next morning that the lab was broken into and the Creatures inside were freed. I *was,* however, concerned they would also tell him I was otherworldly. If they did, there was no possibility he would let me live. I'd have to seek shelter in the nearest Noor-occupied town and convince them I was human. If they said nothing, I was unsure of what they would do next. Either way, my death was on the table.

I woke up the following evening, which meant they'd chosen *not* to kill me and that DeSantos had told them about the Creature's liberation.

Falcone and Cap joined Williams who was sitting on the couch in the living room.

The trio had been there since noon.

"So, you're a legitimate vampire," Cap said when I entered the room.

"For lack of a better word," I replied.

"The three of us have been talking all day," Williams stood from the couch. "We've concluded you'll be more of an asset to us alive."

"Meaning, you didn't tell DeSantos?" I asked.

"No." Falcone clenched his fists. "We didn't. He told us about the Creatures, and we wanted to wait and see what exactly it is you bring to the table before we put you on one and dissect you."

"All right, let's start from the top." Williams sat back down, leaned forward then rested his elbows on his legs, interlocking his fingers. "What's your real name?"

"I don't exactly have what you would consider a 'real name.' I've never interacted with humans to the point I'd need a permanent one, and I don't recall having parents or a birth name. I've never even thought about it. Let's say for now, you continue calling me 'Mason,' or 'Trevor.'"

"Fair enough." Williams said. "What else do we need to know? You said you were uncontrollable when you grew hungry enough, and *that's* what happened to Jakovich and his team?"

I took a seat across from them. "On a normal hunt, I drain enough of a person to fill me up—sometimes it kills them, sometimes it doesn't—and I repeat the process each night. Ninety percent of the time, no one ever knows I was there. Lately though, the Creatures have been getting in the way of my eating every night. I've slept in the ground, I've foregone meals, and I've awoken covered in blood I didn't recognize."

"Their evolutionary timeline is accelerated to the point that each day could yield a new ability." I sat forward and rested my elbows on my knees. "They are getting in my way, and it's becoming dangerous for everyone.

"From what I glean…I can go up to thirty hours without eating, but any longer and I indiscriminately eat whatever human is around, without remembering I've done so. And yes, I believe that's what happened to Jakovich, Davidson, and Warwick. I must have drained the three and left the rest to the Creatures."

I leaned back. "You should know I don't feel good about it. It's not my prerogative to kill anyone in such a violent and barbaric manner. If it were up to me, I would have quietly drained one of them and left it at that."

"Thanks." Cap snorted.

"So," Falcone took a deep breath and his eyes widened for a brief second, "we'll need a supply of blood for him to drink three times a week."

"Shouldn't be an issue," said Williams. "We have a full supply of TB-456 we can u—"

"No!" I snapped. "It absolutely *cannot* be altered blood."

"Why the hell not?" Cap raised an eyebrow.

"Its effects are far too strong for me to use as sustenance. It's like being on acid, but it's far more addictive. I can drink a little at a time, and no more."

"How do you know that?" Cap crossed his arms, squinted, and pursed his lips a little.

"Let's just say I've tried it, and it's more than I can handle on a daily basis."

"Then the blood has to be from a human?" Falcone was seemingly unconcerned with how I had acquired the test blood in the first place.

"I think so, but I'm not saying that. I *am* saying TB-456 is in no way a permanent solution."

Falcone wrote something on the pad of paper he was carrying. "All right." He didn't look up. "What else?"

It took an hour to get it right, but the four of us figured a way to keep my identity under wraps, simultaneously making sure I was able to feed on something other than TB-456 or the population of Sooth City. They would supply me with the human blood I needed each day and in return, and I agreed to help them whenever I was asked.

The deal was fair. It kept me away from the Creatures and allowed me to make sure I could protect my food source. They also gave me a home base with resources I could employ in my study of the Creatures. Falcone helped me move some equipment into the basement of my house where I established a laboratory of sorts. There, I was able to do as I saw fit, without having to bother Falcone while he worked on new technology for the nightly patrol.

Falcone, Williams, and Cap told DeSantos during their debriefing that my first night on patrol was successful, given the circumstances. They could have told DeSantos what I actually was, which would have been a huge error on their part. I needed the people in Sooth City as much as they needed me. For the time being, I was willing to accept that our arrangement was mutually beneficial.

It would have been much easier to drag me into the sun and watch me burn. During the day, I had far less in the way of strength.

There was a part of me that was excited. I'd have a chance to rip a few Creatures open with fancy tools.

I told the team they would have to keep at least one Creature a night from being totally disintegrated, so I could spend the next night researching whatever new evolutionary ability they'd acquired.

The plan was pretty clear: keep my identity hidden and learn as much about the Creatures as I could in the meantime.

~ * ~

It had been a few weeks since I'd told Falcone, Williams, and Cap what I was, and the plan was going smoothly. During that time, I'd dissected several new Creatures, and the tests were starting to yield positive results.

The first two on which I performed autopsies showed no signs of alteration—or at least none large enough for me to detect. However, in the third week, I was able to prove my hypotheses were correct.

They *had* fully developed sight. Prior to this dissection, I only saw the parts of the eye that would evolve. This time, I was looking at something different.

Hovering above the table, I peered into the open cavity I'd made in the Creature. Since I'd last dissected one, they'd developed a cornea, aqueous humor, an iris, a lens, vitreous humor, cones and rods, a sclera, and a retina—in other words, a complete working eye the size of a damn watermelon. The sight was like a painting to me. Something I could look at and interpret the meaning of. Their evolutionary skills were a thing of beauty matched only by my own.

I continued the procedure by cutting into the skull.

They *were* growing in intelligence.

Staring at the Creature's cerebral cortex, it was easy to see it was larger than the previous one I examined. Parietal lobe and diffuse brain functionality were clearly visible when dissecting their brains. This meant they were a split second away from developing tools of their own. I compared the weight of the first brain I studied to the most recent and recorded in my notes; the latter was close to double in size.

The news was bad. The Creatures could see their prey, and they were also intelligent enough to develop a language they could understand and use effectively enough to gather troops, give orders and follow them, and even determine when one of their own was in danger, whether a building was filled with Xeta or not.

Polymer-Xeta was no longer of any use.

An amount of good news. The results meant Polymer-Xeta could be removed from the buildings which would help save a lot of the population from lung defects.

DeSantos was expecting a report on the state of the Creatures, and I was not looking forward to delivering the news about my findings.

~ * ~

Later, in the training facility, I prepared the presentation for DeSantos, Williams, Falcone, and Cap.

I connected the holo-drive to the port on the table in the middle of the presentation room, and the holographic image of a Creature in attack position floated three-feet above the table.

Williams entered the room fifteen-minutes before I planned to start the presentation. "Jesus Christ."

"Hopefully *he* had nothing to do with *this*." I nodded toward the Creature with my head.

"I should hope *not*," he replied. "How's everything going in here?"

"As well as can be expected. But this is the easy part. DeSantos is the hard part. How did he seem this morning?"

"His usual self—ornery, strange."

"Shit. That means this could go either way." There was a bit of worry sticking in my chest that DeSantos may react poorly to finding out his plans for the Creatures would have to change.

Williams smirked. "Pretty much."

He was starting to trust me again. He was the one bringing me bags of blood to drink each night, and though he refused to tell me which man each bag came from, he, Falcone, and Cap were on a rotation. They *did* tell me they would be using their own blood. Due to their varying blood types and diets, each man's blood tasted different, and it didn't take me long to guess who was donating which meal. For reasons I didn't understand, the one I determined was Cap always gave twice the amount the others did. I needed a pint a night, and he was donating more than he needed to.

Falcone, Cap, and DeSantos entered the room—also early for the occasion.

"Gentlemen," I said. "Welcome."

"Dr. Mason." DeSantos nodded at me as he took his seat. "I hope you have some good news for us."

"I wish I did." I snapped my gaze to the side for a brief second.

He stared at me with dead, expressionless eyes.

I didn't wait for a response. "It would appear that I was correct in my original hypothesis. The Creatures have developed a massive cerebral cortex and a fully functioning ocular system, incapable of depth perception, but extremely capable of detecting and honing in on prey."

I pressed the button on the remote I was holding, and the holographic image zoomed into the Creature's brain and eye system.

"I believe they are now able to divide themselves into leaders and soldiers," I continued. "The evening they circled our camp was the result of intense and meticulous planning which must have taken days to assemble."

I pushed the button on the remote again, and the image changed to bodycam footage of the radio towers coming down.

"They destroyed our radio communications with simultaneous attacks. This *also* means we can expect they are now able to communicate with each other in a way I'll need to study to understand. As far as I can tell, it's a series of clicks and screeches, but we'll need at least one male and one female to be live specimens to precisely determine what they might be saying to each other."

DeSantos's face relaxed, and he smiled a little. "That sounds like great news to me."

Williams, Falcone, Cap, and I glanced at one another, careful not to break our facial expressions. What I delivered was definitely not good news.

"I'm afraid I don't follow." My back tightened.

"This is perfect." DeSantos clapped his hands together. "With the new test bloods we've been working on we'll be able to use this new information to manipulate the Creatures into fighting the Noor for us."

As soon as he mentioned the Noor, I knew he would never stop his quest to destroy them. Nothing I could say to him would convince him the Creatures were the incipient threat.

If anything, the Creatures were far more dangerous to experiment on than before. They were more cunning, and their ability to see was an entirely new game. There was so much more we didn't understand about them now, and he was mainly concerned with how he could use them to annihilate the Noor.

I wasn't sure anyone else in the room cared whether they were obliterating half of Noor Country. They cared more about protecting the people who resided in Sooth City from Creatures. I took the defensive route.

I glanced awkwardly at Williams, Cap, and Falcone, respectively. None had changed their facial expressions. "But—"

Williams shot a razor-sharp look at me as if to say, "*shut the fuck up, you dingus, we'll discuss this later.*"

"Your next task," DeSantos pretended he hadn't heard me, "is to alter our test blood to use as a mind-control serum for the Creatures."

"Yes, sir." Cap wrote something on the pad of paper in front of him.

Falcone and Williams nodded. I did the same for fear Williams might give me another look of scorn.

"Excellent job, gentlemen." DeSantos got up. "I'll expect a full plan by next month's meeting." He left the table then exited the room, walking with his head held high.

"I don't get it," I said when I was sure he was gone. "Is DeSantos *that far* beyond convincing?"

"You have no idea." Cap folded his hands behind his head and put his feet up on the table.

Williams looked at his shoes for a moment, his brow furrowed. He placed his hand on his face and stroked it. He ran his fingers through his hair twice, pulling it back as far as it would go.

I wondered what he was thinking.

"Listen." He turned his head up. "I have a plan." He tapped a few keys on the station, and a new holographic image hovered above the table, this time of a Noor encampment on the southern outskirts of Wisconsin. "If the four of us want to make sure humanity can survive long enough to fend off the Creatures indefinitely, then one of us has to infiltrate the Noor and warn them about these new developments without alerting DeSantos."

"That's insane." Cap frowned.

I kept silent. I wanted to know where this was going before I interjected with doubts.

"I know," Williams replied. "But I can't think of anyone else with the resources to help keep the Creatures at bay, and I believe Mason here can be of some use to us. We need him to go undercover to Noor Village and get a message to Raymond Harrington about what Mason's discovered."

"It's a suicide mission." Falcone gave Williams a short grin. "Harrington is ruthless. There's no way he's going to listen to a Sooth."

"That's just it." Williams stood up. "Mason isn't really a Sooth, or a Noor, which gives us an advantage. You're right, Harrington isn't likely to hear out a Sooth, but he will listen to a neutral party. For all he knows, there's no such thing as a neutral party. His curiosity will be piqued for sure."

He then spoke directly to me. "Make sure you tell them what happened here and show them the footage you've acquired. Don't hold anything back, and make sure you tell no one other than Raymond Harrington. He heads Noor Village. You got that?"

I was not ready to go on a solo mission into Noor territory; I also didn't have much choice. They made sure I was fed and kept my identity a secret, so I was obligated to help them. Cap, Falcone, and Williams were my food supply. I owed them a lot, and I didn't want to kill them. If I wanted to continue using Sooth City for shelter, proving my worth to them was a necessary evil, whether I liked it or not. It was definitely an incentive to return.

After all, Sooth or Noor, it didn't matter to me. Both were humans, and more humans meant more food. My main concern was the Creatures. I wanted them destroyed or driven back underground where they belonged, and if Harrington possessed the resources to keep them safely away, it was worth it for me to try. He might attempt to execute me, but there was no way he would succeed.

I decided to accept the price to keep my place at the table.

"Got it." I nodded.

"Then," Williams continued, "return quickly. We don't want

you getting too hungry out there, and you certainly can't explain what you are.

"They're going to search you when you arrive, so we can't give you any blood. That means the mission has to take no more than forty-eight hours, after which we won't have any control over what happens. Be sure to get your ass back here, so there aren't any unnecessary casualties."

"Agreed." I folded my hands on the table. "What's the plan for infiltration?"

"You tell us," he answered.

I sat and thought about it for a few minutes. "Hmm…to infiltrate the Sooth, I played on your sympathies, but the Noors have almost none, so I'll have to come up with a different approach. Give me twenty-four hours, and I'll have a plan."

"Fine." Williams peered at me. "Remember, DeSantos wants us to present some form of this plan to him in four weeks, so get back to us A-S-A-fucking-P."

"Twenty-four hours," I repeated.

~ * ~

I spent the next day devising a plan to infiltrate Noor Village and get the message to Harrington without being hanged. I came up with a clever way to get through the gates. I also decided to make sure I was sent directly to Harrington by getting captured at the entrance.

He was notoriously single-minded. I knew from studying the Noor that anyone affiliated with the Sooth was publicly executed in what they called a "regression," whether or not they were defectors. The Noor described it as a way in which the Sooth could become more than the sum of their birthplace. They saw it as a kind of mercy.

I disagreed—such a waste of blood.

However, it was of no consequence. The most important part of the scheme was them believing I was a Noor, and the information I carried was enough to warrant a meeting with Harrington. That way, I wouldn't be beheaded.

No matter what happened, I absolutely needed to be sure I was back in fewer than forty-eight hours. I didn't want to draw any unnecessary attention to my behavior, and no one was going to die unless it was necessary.

They couldn't find out how closely affiliated with the Sooth I was. I'd spent several weeks blending in with them, and my mannerisms were involuntarily changing to reflect it. I was using their slang terms, and I was even getting to enjoy the company of my compatriots. It gave me a strange feeling in my chest which ran slowly through the rest of my body.

Humans were starting to grow on me in a way I hadn't experienced in the years I spent avoiding contact with them. For centuries, they were nothing other than food, and now I was ready to go to bat for them with their full support.

The Creatures were way too close to wiping me out, and if I did nothing, there was a better-than-good chance they would destroy me before I destroyed them. For the first time in my history, I required actual human connection.

The Creature's inconceivably fast evolution made it possible that, by the time I got to Noor Village, my information would be dated.

The way Creatures developed new traits was the result of something introduced into their environment—something I overlooked along the way or brushed off as inconsequential. I'd hoped it might help me think of something better than running headfirst into one of the world's biggest Noor territories, but it didn't.

No matter. I knew what I was going to do, and I was prepared to ensure my survival.

Chapter Nine

After dinner the next night it was time to present my plan to the team. Once again, I was at the training center's conference room setting up my hard drive. This time, however, it was Cap who came in five minutes early.

"Cap." I nodded in salutation. "What brings you here so early?"

He gave me a hard stare.

The man rarely spoke and when he did, it was deliberate, blunt, and poignant. To say he was aloof was to put it lightly—an absolute-fucking-mystery was closer to accurate.

"You *may* have Falcone and Williams fooled, but I'm not as easily convinced." He tapped a finger on my chest. "You *say* you're hundreds of years old, but you sure as shit don't act like it. I can't imagine something so old would be as naive as you're pretending to be.

"I've seen vampire movies. I've read all the books—and I mean *all* of them. I've been into that shit for damn near thirty years, and I realized something this afternoon. All the stories, all the lore, all the canon, they're *all* about you, aren't they, *Trevor Mason*?"

"It's entirely possible." I shrugged. "I've had a lot of run-ins with a lot of people over the centuries. I wouldn't be surprised to hear some of them lived to tell the tale, or there was a bystander or two who happened to notice."

"Well...here's the thing," he paced with his hands behind his back. "I'm having a superbly difficult time believing you're anything other than a bloodthirsty monster who's concerned with humanity because its food source is in danger. But I also understand one of *you* is far less dangerous than ten million of *them*.

"So, here's your chance, cowboy." He stopped in front of me. "Show me you are more than the voodoo queens' and witches' campfire stories. If you come back here in two days, you can consider me a whole new man. Hell, you and I are going to have a long conversation about vampires which I am very much looking forward to."

His face darkened. "But if you don't return, and I discover you've betrayed these stalwart, trusting, goodhearted people, I will sell you out to this whole camp. I *will* hunt you to the ends of the earth until my face in the sunlight is the last thing you see. Before my dying breath, I promise you this."

It was more than I'd heard him say all at once in the time I'd been in Sooth City, and he made some extremely good points.

In my "heart," I was self-serving. However, Cap was correct: one of me *was* far less dangerous than ten million Creatures. His seeing the true benefit of our relationship was a breath of fresh air. He was the one thing standing between my success and failure.

The others entered the room before there was a chance to respond to him the way I wanted to—I'd have agreed and lectured him about how I don't call myself a vampire.

Falcone and Williams took their usual seats across the table from each other. Cap placed himself on the stool in the corner per his routine, and I got ready to present.

"All right, Doc." Williams sat at the head of the table. "What have you got for us?"

"The plan is simple," I answered. "When I get to Harrington, I'm going to tell him the truth, or most of it, anyway. That's the easy part. The hard part will be walking right up to the compound with a dead Creature's head strapped to my back."

Falcone and Williams both gave me the same upward eyebrow.

"Are you sure about that?" Falcone clasped his hands and planted his elbows on the table. "It sounds risky as fuck."

"It is, but there's no other way." I moved to one of the chairs and sat. "Hear me out. If I go in scared because a Creature attacked me—like I did with the Sooth—they are going to shoot me on sight. We already know this. They are definitely going to wonder how I accomplished such a feat. I'll tell them I am only willing to speak with Harrington."

"After they take me to Harrington, I'll show him the Creature's brain map and tell him what we've discovered."

"Sounds easy enough." Falcone's eyes widened a little. "What's the catch?"

"There are a couple," I said. "I'll need a uniform from Noor Town or some kind of replica and the proper transfer documents. I don't want to be stopped by any Noor without them."

"Shit." Williams turned his head toward Falcone. "Those are not easy to come by...Falcone?"

"I can have the uniform made by our seamstresses." He ran his fingers through his hair. "The color-matching will be a challenge, but not impossible. The credentials are going to be more difficult to get within the next four weeks, but that's also not impossible."

"Good." Williams wrote something on his pad of paper. "And the second?"

"The second catch is," I continued, "we have a finite amount of time before the Creatures see or smell me walking around with one of their heads."

"How much time?" he asked, rubbing his hands across his face.

"Ten minutes."

"How are we going to pull *that* off?"

"We're going to take a cargo ship, land it no more than fifty miles away from the closest entrance to Noor Village, and I'll run the rest of the way."

Falcone raised a hand. "There are a couple massive issues with that. The first is, it's nearly impossible to get a ship close enough to Noor grounds without setting off their pressure systems the moment we hit the ground. The other issue is...can you run fast enough?"

"Even carrying a Creature's head, I should be able to make the run and get inside before the Creatures catch up. It has to be fifty miles though, and no more."

"I guess you can call it a plan." Cap shifted his legs.

"I don't see any other way around it." I leaned back in my seat. "The Noor have specific philosophies, and the best chance we have is to play to their sympathies which are power and hating the Sooth. I may also end up saying a lot of things about the Sooth I would rather not, but sometimes getting into their psyches means selling out some people."

"I don't give a shit about that." Williams rubbed the stubble on his chin. "Just make sure it works...say whatever you have to get through the doors. If you think you can make it to the gates before you're devoured by Creatures, then we can get you close and make it happen." He looked back to Falcone. "Can you figure out a way to get us near Noor Village without setting off their perimeter alarms?"

"They have a hundred miles of pressure and proximity sensors surrounding the city." Falcone pulled on his earlobe. "So, as you mentioned, it's going to be difficult to get a ship nearby. However, I can work on modifying our stealth tech to get Mason low enough to hit the ground running. I'll have to determine how to get around the pressure sensors…"

Falcone was already in his own world of technological innovations and engineering ideas.

"Cap." Williams tilted his head. "Can you get a Creature head without drawing too much attention? I don't think DeSantos is going to like that part."

"We're going to tell DeSantos the truth?" I asked before Cap could answer.

"Most of it," Williams said. "He wants us to infiltrate a Noor community, but he doesn't need to know how we're going to get inside. At this point we'd have to divulge too much about you. We'll think of something to tell him in the next few weeks while we continue planning."

"Yeah." Both of Cap's eyebrows lowered. "I should be able to pull it off."

"Remember…," I turned so I was fully facing Cap, "the head has to be fresh. So be sure you take it no more than a few hours in advance."

"That's cuttin' it pretty close." Williams sounded uncertain.

"Unfortunately, it's the only way we're going to convince the Noor Village guards I'm legitimate. Otherwise, we can kiss my ass goodbye at the first sunrise."

"We'll figure it out." Cap had a tinge of hatred in his voice. He stood up from his stool and stretched his back.

"All right, gentlemen," Williams addressed the room. "You have your marching orders. We have three and a half weeks to get everything in motion, so we can accomplish DeSantos's goals and our own. I won't lie to you, fellas. This ain't gonna be a cakewalk with your grandmothers. There's a lot of risks involved. We have to be meticulous, careful, and above all else, incog-*fucking*-nito."

Falcone and Cap nodded.

"We have a lot riding on you, kid." Williams looked at me. "You'd better not be fucking with us."

With the final threat of the night concluded, the four of us went our separate ways.

Cap had no intention of trusting me until I got back from Noor Village without a scratch. However, it didn't mean he would hinder the scheme. No, if anything, he would craft his part of the project to be the most concise of the three.

Our marching orders *were* clear.

Falcone was to think of a way to get me close enough to Noor Village and low enough to the ground without setting off any of their millions of sensors.

Cap was in charge of sneaking a Creature head from the science wing without alerting DeSantos or any guards.

Williams needed to determine a way to present an extravagant plan DeSantos would be happy with.

I had to decide what to say when I got to Noor Village. There were going to be a lot of holes to fill in, and I needed my bases covered.

Our work was cut out for us, and the advantage of a four-week turnaround gave us plenty of time to think about it. DeSantos was not known for his patience, so I was surprised he gave us enough time to devise a plan instead of making one of his own.

We did have *that* going for us.

~ * ~

The next month went by effortlessly. I ate dinner with the town every night, though I didn't spend time conversing with the rest of the team. They weren't exactly thrilled with me, and I didn't want to force a relationship or feign an apology. They wouldn't have accepted one anyway; they were too proud and far too cautious.

Falcone didn't show up to dinner most of the time. He was busy devising new ideas for tech to help us in our mission to get to Noor Village.

Cap didn't talk much, as expected. He was keeping a close eye on me and my movements. After dinner, I went straight home and to the patrol. He always made a point of letting me know he was following.

Williams was the least concerned with me. He was determining ways to fill in DeSantos with what we were doing in a way that was palatable for his specific kind of desires.

During the weeks, I mostly kept to myself—either sitting outside on the porch with Scraps or performing my duties for the nightly watch.

The patrol was always quiet, and there were no further incidents with the Creatures. At the time, it seemed they were content that they got their point across regarding the raid on Sooth City. No other Sooth sectors reported any activity other than the two who saw their radio towers destroyed in the first attack.

I was on edge during the dark hours. I knew the monsters well enough to know they never went long without striking. Not anymore. Especially now, since their ability to think was on par with a toddler. A month gave them a lot of time to develop new attributes.

I was prepared with my part of the plan—both in what to tell DeSantos when the moment came and what I would have to say to get into Noor Village.

The rest of the team wasn't having much luck.

Falcone found the correct height and distance at which to fly. However, he couldn't determine how to safely put me on the ground and give the ship enough time to make a getaway. The best he came up with was for whomever was piloting the ship to hoof-it-the-fuck-out-of-there. It appeared as if hoofing it was where we landed on *that* part of the plan. He did have thoughts to alter the ship to increase its maximum speed enough to outrun any Noor ballistics. Still, it was hypothetical until he could make the prototypes and get his hands on a ship to modify.

Williams had decided what he would say to DeSantos. He was debating with himself so many potential outcomes and how he could respond to them it was driving him mad. He stopped going to meals and was rarely seen outside of the training facility where his office was.

As predicted, Cap's part of the plan was nothing short of masterful. He knew exactly how to sneak a Creature head from the wing and into an airtight container so the other Creatures wouldn't be able to detect the smell. All he had to do was walk out normally and put the crate on the ship he'd helped requisition as part of the DeSantos-version of the plan we were calling *Operation Horizon*. The full project was actually called *Operation Phantom*.

The rest of the teams knew of Horizon. Even then, we kept them on a need-to-know basis as it was difficult to know which of them to trust. We did, however, enlist Dustin Vander to co-pilot the ship into Noor territory along with Cap, both of whom were among the best pilots in any Sooth sector. Whether it was Horizon or Phantom, we needed two good pilots to man the cargo ship, so we didn't exactly have to clue Dustin in on Phantom.

There were a few times during the month when I thought Dustin might have been onto us, but it was nothing other than paranoia. Aside from a few hiccups, the plan was going well.

~ * ~

The time for the four of us to present our plan to DeSantos had finally arrived.

I was certain we'd covered every angle of both Horizon and Phantom, and the meeting would be an easy one, depending, of course, on DeSantos's mood.

This time, I wouldn't have to present anything or even talk if I wasn't directly asked a question, though I was prepared to do so.

Falcone, Williams, Cap, and I were waiting patiently when DeSantos arrived after dinner.

"Good evening, gentlemen," he said in an almost Hitchcockian tone.

"Sir." Williams nodded his head—a sign of respect.

"I hope you have something good for me tonight. I want to see some Noor dragged through the mud."

"We think you'll be pleased, sir."

Williams pressed a button on the station's panel, and a three-dimensional image of the Noor Village compound hovered above the table. He pointed to a spot on the map. "The plan is to drop Mason off here."

The map zoomed into a field fifty yards away.

"Falcone has drawn up blueprints for a special engine fast enough to outrun any Noor ballistics they can throw at it. He has also theorized a way to decrease our radar detection for a short amount of time. If any Noor spots the vessel, it'll be far enough away from Mason that he won't have to explain why he arrived on the same day as a Sooth attack.

"When he gets inside, Mason will plant specialized pyrotechnic grenades—also developed by Falcone and his team—in several locations. Targets include the homes of Raymond Harrington and his right-hand and left-hand men, John Mansen and Bruce Lincoln. At approximately five hundred hours, Mason will push the proximity trigger. Then Cap and Vander will extract him using the same ship."

DeSantos stroked his beard thoughtfully.

We all waited with bated breath to hear whether he liked the plan or would put the kibosh on the whole thing.

"How are you going to get around the security measures?" he asked after several seconds.

"To get past the proximity alarms and underground sensors," Williams replied, without missing a beat, "Falcone has developed a signaling device that will disable the sensors below with each step. By the time the security team figures out what happened, Mason will be safely inside planting explosives."

DeSantos stared into nothingness. He didn't move any of his limbs, and his facial expression remained unchanged.

It was more difficult than usual to gauge his reaction. His poker face was astounding, and he was doing a great job of making sure he kept his feelings locked tightly.

"How do *you* feel about this plan?" He eventually turned to Cap and pointed at him with his bulbous finger.

"The plan is solid, provided Falcone can get each of these devices built and tested before the summer season hits." Cap cupped his face in thought.

"Why do I feel a *but* coming on?" DeSantos raised an eyebrow and turned his head slightly.

"But," Cap replied, "I don't think we should be doing this at all."

"What do you mean?"

"We have bigger things to worry about than infiltrating the Noor right now. The Creatures are gearing up for something...I can feel it."

"Never mind that." DeSantos's face relaxed. "Creatures will always be a nuisance, like a squirrel—cute, but you know they'll bite you if threatened. But the Noor...they need to be stopped. They are a virus that destroys thousands and thousands of lives worldwide—all in the name of a non-entity who mandates they prey on the poor and weak. They use resource after resource and expect the rest of the world to live off their scraps.

"Now is the time for someone to strike a blow to one of their biggest communities. They have stolen the spirits of more of my ancestors and brethren than I can count, and I *do* believe they are the largest threat the world faces."

"No." DeSantos stood and paced around the room, hands clenched behind his back. "No matter the cost, we must show the Noor they can no longer take advantage of us."

He looked to Falcone.

"You can get this done?" DeSantos studied the blueprints for each of the three devices Falcone was planning to engineer.

"Not a problem." He nodded to DeSantos.

"All right. Let's get this show on the road." He clapped twice. "Williams, you will report back to me with weekly status updates from each of your team members. From now until Mason gets back, this mission is your top priority. Consider your patrol duties taken care of, and nightly dinners a suggestion for the hungry."

"Yes, sir!" Williams saluted.

"Good work." DeSantos walked out of the conference room.

I breathed a sigh of relief. Phase one of Operation Phantom had gone smoothly. Cap's frankness was meant to be a distraction for DeSantos, something extreme to make the rest of our plan sound better. It was an insurance policy in case he was headed toward a "no," and it had worked perfectly.

"That went well." I broke the silence in the room.

"Yeah." Cap squinted. "It did."

"Almost *too* well." Falcone scratched the back of his head.

"Don't be so dramatic." Williams turned to Falcone. "Let's not worry about that. For now, we have a lot of work to do before the summer season hits. Mason, help Falcone with Phantom in any way you can. Let's see if a century's worth of knowledge can actually be good for something." He stood. "In the meantime, Cap and I will continue thinking about Horizon to keep DeSantos satisfied."

Williams spoke in a hushed tone and talked with a downward

inflection. I guessed that leading a double life was dragging him down a road of depression and anxiety, not to mention the exhaustion he was undoubtedly feeling from giving so much blood. He was trying his best to keep pace with everything, but it seemed there was clearly a part of him in need of some rest. However, he wouldn't rest any time before Phantom started. None of us would.

Chapter Ten

Though we didn't have any other responsibilities, there was an extensive amount of work to be done. I was somewhat familiar with engineering practices, but only enough to take and follow orders.

Falcone's job was the most demanding. He was going to develop cloaking devices, EMP emitters, and a whole new kind of pyrotechnic delivery system, all of which needed to be tested.

Operation Phantom didn't need pyrotechnic grenades. After we got inside the Noor Village walls, the plan was to use diplomacy. We needed to *talk* to Harrington, and he had to be alive for that. However, Operation Horizon called for us to destroy twelve buildings, so Falcone was making a baker's dozen of grenades. Each one was to work as intended since DeSantos was going to test at least one of them.

I was in charge of building the grenades while Falcone designed each piece's blueprint. The first part I built was the delivery system. It looked like an M67 fragmentation grenade, only flat, and with an adhesive strip on the back. There were fifty-three pieces to screw together and a casing on the inside to hold the napalm, sulfur, and fabricated lavic acid cartridges.

Developing lavic acid was the most difficult part of the process; it combined volatile chemicals designed to duplicate acid drawn from volcanic lava. The materials were highly unstable and making enough for thirteen grenades meant precision work in a sterile environment for at least ten hours a day.

When the pin is pulled, the substances drain into a basin at the bottom of the casing. Once ignited, the combination of chemicals sends out a fireball, engulfing everything in a thousand-foot radius. Their destructive power would be devastating if used properly, so we built in a fail-safe to keep the cartridges inside the casing protected for when I was running.

Falcone was also going to develop a new stealth engine and a micro EMP emitter that would fit into the bottom of my shoes. Neither device was going to be easy to engineer, even theoretically. Stealth technology had advanced a lot since the twenty-first century, however, so had stealth *detection*.

He wanted us to be invisible. No one was able to totally mask a ship, and he wanted to be the first. It wasn't a grasp at his ego. We needed the ship to be invisible to get me close enough to Noor Village. Otherwise, we'd be shot immediately after leaving Sooth territory.

The electro-charge emitter was easier than the rest. The technology had been in existence for centuries, but the physical device had to be a lot smaller.

I didn't envy Falcone. He was the most technologically capable person on our side of the Sooth Semisphere. If anyone could accomplish the chemical and technical engineering to create three of the most advanced devices the world had ever seen, it was him.

I spent every night in the lab with Falcone.

Cap continued breathing down my neck. He and Dustin Vander were spending their time in flight simulators working on their stealth tactics. A lot of their plan also hinged on Falcone's success. In the meantime, they wanted to train to prepare for any outcome. When the stealth engine was theoretically sound, the plan was to add the software to the simulators and test it out.

When Cap wasn't in the simulator, he was in the lab, making sure I wasn't sabotaging anything. He was annoying me with his presence, and he refused to believe I was on his side completely. He kept a close watch on me from a stool in the corner of the room. Falcone didn't seem to let it bother him, but I wouldn't have been able to tell either way.

Dustin spent a lot of time with Cap. So I was enjoying getting to know him despite Cap's presence. He was interested in weapons manufacturing and engineering, and he watched and absorbed all of what Falcone and I were doing. He was a good kid, maybe the nicest person I'd met in Sooth City.

Dustin was eager to learn, and he absorbed everything like a soft towel. He instantly understood whatever I told him, even when I talked about the complications of lavic acid poisoning and why the extraction process was so dangerous.

I liked Dustin.

"Can you tell me a little more about the Creatures' evolutionary attributes?" He was hovering over my shoulder one night after dinner when we were working in the lab.

"Sure," I replied with an upward inflection. "Do you remember what I was telling you about their cerebral cortexes?"

"That they're increasing in size?"

"Correct. Well, yesterday I found the biggest one yet. This one was so large it could have developed speech if it wanted to. It would seem they are now more akin to a dumb adult rather than a toddler."

"Does it mean they'll eventually be able to communicate more effectively with us?"

"Normally, I would say yes." I screwed in another bolt. "However, these beasts are communicating like creatures in the wild. I see no way for them to develop speech patterns humans will be able to understand."

"Aren't they sentient now? Doesn't murdering them in droves seem unethical?"

"That is a whole different conversation," I answered. "Humans have started wars over far less than what the Creatures have done. Wouldn't you say so?"

He nodded.

"Then I would say it's equally ethical as killing anyone in wartime." I stopped what I was doing and turned in my chair until I was facing Dustin directly. "It may be crass, but that is what's happening. We are at war with the Noor *and* the Creatures, so whether we like it or not, both are too threatening to ignore. The cost of human life has to outweigh the ethics of harming Creatures. Humans were once mindless murder machines, and look where we are now."

Dustin put his right arm across his chest and rested his left elbow on it, bringing his hand to his chin. He furrowed his brow and pursed his lips. "That's interesting," he said after a few seconds.

"Ethics aside," I turned back to the table, "I would be surprised if they developed speech in our lifetime, so we don't really have to worry about it."

I wasn't exactly sure whether I was correct. Truth was, the Creatures might be able to develop some kind of speech pattern humans could understand, but it typically took thousands of years to manifest. Not even the Creatures were *that* fast.

I wanted to know more about Dustin, so I asked him to tell me his family history.

Lester and Gweneth Vander passed their love of the sciences on to their children. Both were firm believers in the altruistic power of family, community, and loyalty, and spent most of their time dealing with human relations issues and overall morale. They were beloved by citizens of Sooth City for their compassion and their positivity.

Dustin and Marina were both inundated into the Sooth City community the moment they were able to speak in full sentences.

"Okay, you can join," Lester said one evening when they were sitting around the dinner table.

"This isn't going to be a walk in the park," Gwen warned.

"We know," Marina and Dustin said simultaneously, as they often did.

"The both of you are going to train harder than you've ever trained before." Lester leaned his hands on the kitchen counter with his back to the sink.

"We've talked about it for months…and we know what it's going to take. We're younger than everyone else and so we have a lot more to prove." Dustin sat attentively at the table.

"But," Marina said as if to finish his thought, "we care more about this town than anyone else, and we deserve to be in the nightly watch.

"That's why we're letting you participate." Gwen handed a dish to Lester for him to dry. "You two are as capable as anyone I've seen in the nightly patrol, and if you do the work you'll deserve to be there."

The twins made it their personal duty to ensure Sooth City was safe from Creatures and Noor alike. When Dustin and Marina's parents let them enter the patrol, the twins were eager to prove they were taking it seriously, which was why Dustin was following Cap so closely.

At eighteen years old, they were the youngest to be accepted into the patrol—a position typically held for citizens twenty-one years or older. By that time, they were more skilled than anyone in their unit. They trained in hand-to-hand combat, weapons use, and guerilla warfare tactics, and were experts in all three.

When I met them, Dustin and Marina had been in the unit for close to a year. Like all twins, they were born with a psychic connection they used to communicate non-verbally, and they were perfect for covert operations, rarely having to speak a word to each other no matter how far away they were.

Few people developed *legitimate* psychic connections. Some siblings were proven psychically in sync, but fraternal twins were born with a much stronger mental capacity.

In 1924, Hans Berger discovered the human brain was capable of emitting waves of energy that could be recorded whether we're awake or asleep. Twenty years later, he unlocked the secret to viewing the rest of the five types of brain waves.

Human brains emit Gamma waves that were in control of higher processes and cognitive functions; Beta waves that establish alertness and waking consciousness; Alpha waves that are dominant during times of daydreaming and light meditation; Theta waves that are in charge of dreams and vivid imagery; and Delta waves that are given off during deep, dreamless sleep.

In the early twenty-second century, Dr. Richard Carmine, a brainwave research engineer, discovered the mental connection between people in close proximity to each other. He tested several groups of people of various pairings: fraternal twins, mixed pairs of male and female siblings, close friends, long-term lovers, and total strangers.

Of the five groups, twins and siblings showed the most promise; lovers and close friends showed some, and in a few cases, there were strangers able to establish a psychic connection.

The tests concluded that people physically and mentally close to each other were able to read each other's intersecting Gamma and Beta brain waves. The largest Gamma-Beta connection was held by twins, and Dustin and Marina controlled the strongest I could imagine.

Most twins needed to be relatively near each other—Dustin and Marina could be a mile away and hear each other's thoughts.

They used their power in a way that none of us could *truly* understand. One or the other would stop what they were doing, their eyes would go dead, then start darting back and forth like they were speed reading a book no one else could see. They would emerge from the fugue state with new information only the other could possibly have known.

It was quite the parlor trick to witness.

~ * ~

I was working in the lab one night when Dustin and Cap arrived, this time with Marina close behind. That night Falcone was at home designing the ship's stealth system. He'd finished the grenades. All that was left to do was build them.

"Well, what brings *you* to the lab today?" I asked Marina directly.

"Dustin has been telling me so much," she replied. "I wanted to see for myself what you guys are working on."

I glanced at Cap quickly then looked back to what I was doing.

"Don't worry." Cap peered at me. "She's promised not to disclose anything she sees here, under punishment of death."

"That seems extreme." I turned my body to Cap.

"It was the only way DeSantos would let her come."

"All right." I spun around until I was facing Marina. "I suppose that's fair. Can I assume you would never, in a million years, disclose anything anyway?"

"Damn right." She smiled.

"Good girl." I grinned back.

"So, what's everyone working on today?" She clapped her hands and rubbed them together.

"Falcone is checking the ship's engine, and I'm still putting together the delivery systems. Dustin is here to watch, and Cap, I assume, is here to make sure I'm doing my job correctly?"

"I *am*," he answered sharply.

He went to his usual corner of the room where his stool was waiting for him. He leaned against the wall and crossed his arms.

Dustin tapped me on the shoulder with the back of his hand. "Tell her about the delivery method."

"It's pretty simple." I picked up a device from the table and held it up for Marina to see. "See this? Falcone developed this device that injects each of the liquids into this container simultaneously. The cup drains into this batch of sulfur, igniting the trigger. The ball explodes outward as soon as it drops."

"That's fascinating." Marina pulled out a chair and sat next to me. "How confident are you that there won't be any malfunctions?"

"At this point," I put the device back down, "I am fully confident Falcone's designs are going to work perfectly."

"And you're equally confident in *your* manufacturing skills?"

"I'm taking my time with every screw, and I'm carefully soldering each wire." I pointed to the wires on the table.

"Wondrous." Her eyes widened.

They were interrogating me. There was a chance they were doing so at the behest of DeSantos, but I wasn't entirely convinced.

"Has Falcone solved the cartridge issue?" Dustin asked.

"It seems he has, but we won't know for sure until the time comes."

"Enough," Cap yelled from the corner. "Let the man do his work. We can't lose any more time."

"Of course," the twins replied simultaneously. "Pardon us."

"Goodnight, kids," I said, using my grandfatherly tone.

The twins left the facility, and Cap remained behind.

"They could have stayed to watch." I kept my gaze focused on the soldering I was doing.

"Not tonight." He stood up and moved closer to me. "Tonight, you need to focus on the grenades."

He was insufferable. His constant staring over my shoulder was becoming a hindrance. The Vander twins didn't have to leave.

Unfortunately, Cap was too much of a bully to let me have any fun for even a second.

"Don't get too close to those kids." He lowered his face and his brow furrowed. "If anything happens to them, I'm coming for you."

~ * ~

The next night when I awoke, there was a commotion outside.

I put on a pair of pants and my shoes, then went to investigate. I stuck two fingers into my mouth and whistled for Scraps, but he wasn't there.

I remained on the porch for a moment to take in the scene. People everywhere were headed in the same direction, toward the center of town.

"Hey!" I yelled at a middle-aged man. "What's going on?"

"You didn't hear?" he asked from the sidewalk. "The twins caught a Creature!"

I closed the door, then stepped off the porch heading west to the center of town. Scraps was already there when I arrived. I took my place next to him, scratched his head, and looked up at the twins. They were standing on a podium with a Creature hanging from a makeshift-gallow, on display like they'd caught a shark.

Dustin and Marina were posing for pictures, proud of their kill, gladly accepting praise from the townspeople.

I saw across the crowd that Williams and Cap were standing together, expressionless, and talking into each other's ears.

Scraps and I circled the crowd and met with Cap and Williams, both of whom nodded a salutation to me.

"What happened?" I asked.

"The twins were patrolling last night after they left the lab." Williams leaned over to me. "And they caught one of those giant fuckers trying to claw through the inner gate."

"Are you sure it wasn't a distraction?" I asked.

"Nothing else is out of order." Cap kept his gaze forward. "Everyone in the town is accounted for, and there have been no reports from DeSantos regarding any other facility."

"Hmm," I mumbled. "What the fuck was it doing so far away from its group?"

Cap and Williams took me aside where no one was within earshot.

Williams looked around carefully. "Cap was testing for Phantom. The twins were able to catch the Creature because we purposely set it loose."

"Are you shitting me?" I whispered loudly, glancing around to make sure no one heard.

"Shh!" Williams matched my volume. "We had to do it this way to perform the test properly."

"Why did it have to be so dangerous?" I scratched my head.

"Look," he replied. "For Horizon, DeSantos has us testing a new blood formula that weakens Creatures and lowers their cognitive functions."

"It was the first opportunity we came across," Cap chimed in. "Which is why Marina and Dustin were with me in the first place. We used our injection system and pumped the Creature full of TB-457. When it was lethargic enough, the twins swooped in and captured him. It actually *wasn't* too dangerous. The new formula works pretty well."

"Fine." I relaxed a little. "It still doesn't explain what a Creature was doing here by itself."

"Does it *have* to?" Cap asked.

"I guess not." I stumbled to think of a reason why. "This new blood formula...who developed it for DeSantos?"

"His chemical technicians have been working on it for years," Williams replied.

"Fuck *me*," I said, exasperated. "Years?"

"Something like that." Williams spoke at full volume.

I stopped to think for a few seconds.

My thoughts were racing with questions. Why has DeSantos been working on this blood formula for so long? Had he somehow known of the Creatures's capabilities before I was able to dissect one? No. That was impossible. How did the new test blood work so effectively? Did it have the same effect as TB-456? I hoped not. What was the Creature doing alone? Why would it stray so far from the pack? They never traveled by themselves.

"So what if I wanted to taste test this new blood formula?" I asked.

"Are you kidding?" Williams's eyes bulged, and he pursed his lips. "That's out of the question."

A roar bellowed from the crowd, and the three of us stopped to see why everyone was applauding. The twins had cut the Creature from the gallows, and a few soldiers were dragging it off to an unknown location.

I looked back to Cap and Williams who'd taken the opportunity to walk away. I could have caught up to them, but there was no reason; there was nothing else they could tell me.

My confidence was waning with each passing second that our team could keep the twins and DeSantos at bay until Phantom was complete.

There was a much better reason the Creature that Williams and Cap drugged got so close to the compound in the first place. There was more to TB-457 than a simple drugging of Creatures. There was something off about the way the twins had caught the beast, but I couldn't put my finger on it. It wasn't sitting right with me.

I was under too close a watch to investigate the way I would have liked. Cap was around every corner, keeping an eye on me—all the while draining more of his blood than anyone else to make sure I was sated enough to stay conscious.

Scraps nudged me in the back of the leg with his snout. He was holding a ball in his mouth. I bent over to pick it up and throw it when I noticed it wasn't a toy.

The dark red bauble was the size of a golf ball. There were curved lines on the surface that looked similar to brain matter swirling underneath glass. It smelled like a rotten egg that had been sitting in a vat of sun tea for a year, then dropped into a jar of pickle juice.

I didn't want anyone to see what Scraps found, especially Cap and Williams.

"What have you got there?" Dustin asked from behind me.

"I'm not sure," I said.

Chapter Eleven

By the time Horizon and Phantom were set to launch, I was no closer to determining what the mysterious Creature-ball was. I wanted to dissect it, but none of the tools were strong enough to break off even a sliver. I put it under a microscope, but whatever the coating was made of reflected almost no light. It was impossible to see through.

I didn't really have time to dissect the ball anyhow. It was getting down to the wire, and Falcone needed my help working on the stealth engine at the same time the rest of the lab techs were building the EMP.

I finished the grenades, and they were ready for DeSantos to try. Kill switches were put in place in case I couldn't convince Harrington to give us permission to plant them.

The simulator test of the stealth engine showed it working with a ninety-percent success rate. It took Cap and Dustin a couple of weeks to get a handle on it, but by the time it was ready to fly into Noor territory, I was positive they would be able to get the ship precisely where it needed to be.

I reviewed several of the simulations. I was impressed with the way Dustin and Cap worked so seamlessly together. It felt like Dustin was using his psychic abilities with Cap, but I knew better.

In the weeks following the TB-457 test, there were no more encounters with Creatures trying to break into the compound or any building in the facility. Cap and Williams were able to test the plan only one time, so we were unsure whether it would work when the time came for us to hunt the Creature.

Nothing in the plan changed, and I was confident we might be able to accomplish Phantom without arousing any suspicions from

DeSantos or the twins.

There *was* one issue, however. We needed to convince Harrington to destroy a dozen buildings after I told him the Creatures possessed brains and eyes. Otherwise, it would not appear that Horizon was successful.

~ * ~

On the night of the grenade test, Falcone, Cap, Williams, and I said almost nothing to each other. We knew the grenades would work more than enough to satisfy DeSantos. If he discovered the kill switch, he would not be as keen to let us continue. None of us thought he would find it, not without opening the grenade, which, if done improperly, would have blown us and half of Sooth City to kingdom come.

Five of us were outside, waiting for DeSantos to arrive at the shooting range where we'd set up the test: Falcone, Williams, Cap, Dustin, and me.

It was a warm spring night, and there was a slight breeze in the air which shook the trees enough to rustle. Otherwise, it was a quiet evening.

The sun dipped below the horizon, and it was dark when DeSantos arrived.

He greeted us with his usual, "gentlemen."

"Sir." Williams saluted.

DeSantos got immediately to the point. "Show me what you've been working on all these weeks."

"This way." Falcone pointed to the table with the grenades on it.

Lifting one of the grenades, DeSantos inspected it. He stared at it intently, turning it around in his hand.

"Please be careful, sir." Falcone reached out a little bit. "Those are extremely volatile."

At the ominous warning, DeSantos gave Falcone a stern look.

"What you have here," he started again, "is a D78 proximity mine. It's a lightweight alternative to a hand grenade that can be thrown, remotely detonated, or stuck to any surface. When you pull the pin at the top, you have a thirteen-second clock to launch the fucker as far as you possibly can. If you use the proximity setting, anyone who gets within ten feet will be blown to bits. There is also a remote detonation option that will work from up to a hundred feet away. You can use the remote to direct the propulsion system with accuracy of five feet. Which is far more than enough to annihilate your target."

DeSantos pulled the pin on the grenade he was holding and launched it across the field. A spark shot out the back of the projectile, propelling it over a thousand yards into the air.

"Fire in the hole!" Cap yelled, ducking behind the plexiglass barrier.

A massive column of flame expelled from the ground, illuminating the night sky. When the blaze settled, the shed was gone, the field on fire in a circular pattern that extended a hundred feet in each direction.

"Holy fuck!" DeSantos yelled jubilantly.

The fire raged on in the foreground, showing no signs of dying. Falcone's grenades worked perfectly.

Most importantly, DeSantos hadn't inspected the unit thoroughly enough to find the kill switch.

"Good work, gentlemen." He looked at Falcone and me.

Neither of us gave more than a nod in appreciation. I'd learned that less was more with DeSantos, unless you were Williams, who was free to speak as he pleased.

"Thank you, sir." He smiled the tiniest bit.

"How goes the rest of the mission?" DeSantos put his hand on Williams's back.

"The stealth engine is in its final days of simulation testing." He spun around to face DeSantos. "So far, Cap and Vander have exceeded expectations. They've been able to land the ship outside of Noor Village without setting off any of the test's alarms. The EMP is in the works. We're going to start the testing phase soon. Falcone says he's overcome the size issue, and the first prototype shouldn't have any problems."

"Fantastic!" DeSantos replied. "Keep it up. We're all counting on you."

He strode from the firing range bearing a confident smile. He left without saying anything else.

"That went well." Cap looked over at the fire that was still going strong.

"Did it?" I turned to him.

"Why? What did *you* see, Mason?" Williams asked.

"Nothing in particular, but...did it seem a little *too* easy to anyone else? He barely talked, and he definitely didn't say his usual *goodbye*."

DeSantos was typically a much more difficult person to deal with, and it struck me that the test went so well. There were no questions on how the grenades worked or what the combination of chemicals was.

"You're paranoid." Cap continued looking at the fire.

"Maybe," I replied. "It didn't seem strange to any of you that he didn't ask to try the other detonation methods?"

"He knows we have a finite amount of them." Falcone scratched the back of his head.

"Yeah, but there are twelve grenades left on the table. He could have tried the other methods, but he didn't want to? That's out of character for DeSantos."

"Good point." Williams took a deep breath through his nose then exhaled. "Fuck...we can't worry about it right now. Let's assume the test went well enough, and he wants us to continue with our work."

The five of us left the firing range.

Dustin and Cap went to continue running simulations. Williams had another meeting with DeSantos. Falcone and I returned to the manufacturing wing to work on affixing the stealth engine to the ship.

The whole thing was the size of half a shipping crate, and it weighed more than a thousand pounds. It was oval shaped with six triangular power cells attached to either side of the exterior. The cells powered the engine, which sent a signal to the beacons. The beacons then bent the light around themselves, effectively making the ship invisible to the human eye. You could see a blur through the ship's matter, but it was so fast no one watching would be able to focus and notice what was happening.

We also attached a specially designed geometric plate made of carbonized steel and coated with Polymer-Xeta onto the bottom of the ship to deflect radar signals.

Both items were difficult to fabricate and had taken weeks to build and attach to the ship.

Falcone and I were working on the ship when he spoke. "You've *actually* been alive since the 1600s?"

"That's as far back as I can remember," I replied. "It's possible I had a life before that—a mother, father, brothers, and sisters—only I have no recollection of them."

"Are there more of you?"

"None have made their existence known to me. I've never passed this onto anyone else, and if more of me do exist, I haven't seen any evidence of them. And trust me when I say I have been *everywhere*."

"How is *that* possible?" He raised an eyebrow.

"Over a thousand years, even a paraplegic can cover the entire planet." I kept working while I talked. "I've been to places of which humans cannot even conceive. I've been to the ocean's depths; I've seen the core of the earth; I've witnessed the birth of every piece of technology from electricity to Polymer-Xeta to the stealth engine we've created. I can tell you from experience, humanity will go the way of the dinosaur soon if we don't push the Creatures back into hiding."

"Jesus Christ." Falcone looked down. "That's intense."

"You asked." I kept my gaze to the cell I was working on.

"This entire time, you've been surviving solely on human blood?"

"Save for the times I drank DeSantos's test blood, it's the only thing I can ever remember ingesting for sustenance."

"And without it, you black out and indiscriminately eat whoever is in the vicinity."

"Correct." I finished the box of screws I was using, so I stood up and walked over to the table where there was a refill waiting for me. "It's happened a few times and, before the Creatures, I had no idea what it meant to go two nights without eating."

"So, your life has been pretty cushy up until now, huh?"

"I guess you could say that." I knelt under the ship and continued screwing on reflective plates. "I used to be at the top of the food chain. There was nothing and no one to tell me what I could and couldn't eat. The idea of going to bed hungry was something I never would have considered."

"Then you truly *do* need us."

"I do." I stopped what I was doing. "Otherwise, nothing will survive other than the Creatures, until they run out of food, then who knows what will happen."

Falcone was right on the money. He already knew I was there for a specific reason. I think he needed to hear my story to know for certain I was serious about saving the human race. A part of me knew Falcone, Cap, and Williams would never completely trust me, but at least they were smart enough to fear me less than the Creatures.

It took more time and effort than we planned to spend, but we finished the stealth ship, and the lab technicians completed the ground-sensor emitter. Over the weeks, Falcone didn't ask any other questions. He was apparently content to continue our work under the assumption I was doing what I could for the greater good of humanity.

The last thing to do was get the final go-ahead from DeSantos, and it was *all systems go* for Phantom.

Chapter Twelve

Everyone was quieter than usual on the night of the drop-off.

Cap and Dustin were perfect in simulations every time with the ship, and the necessary equipment was theoretically sound. In field tests, the engine and the ground-sensor pulse emitter worked exactly as intended.

Cap, Falcone, Dustin, and I were waiting for Williams to arrive. He was to perform his final checks and send us off with his blessing.

"Don't be nervous," I told Dustin, who was staring at the ground.

"I'll be okay," he replied.

"Look," I grabbed his shoulder, "You've gone through this a million times, and this is going to be the last. If you treat it like the simulation, the real thing will be just as easy. You'll be in and out. No one will ever see you."

"What about *you?*" he asked.

"Me?" I raised both eyebrows. "I'll be fine. You worry about getting me there, and I'll worry about what happens after you do."

Williams was approaching from the distance, and I noticed Dustin was putting on his game face.

"Let's get a move on," Cap said when Williams was in earshot.

Cap finished loading the Creature Dustin and Marina caught. "Go ahead in." Cap nodded to Dustin. "I want to have a chat with Dr. Mason for a quick second."

"What can I do for you?" I asked after Dustin was aboard the ship.

"This is it." Cap used a more calming tone than I would have expected. "Your moment of truth. Are you ready?"

"As ready as I can be."

"All bullshit aside, you know this is about the human race and not your need to drink blood, right? We can't afford for you to go loco in there."

"I do, and I won't."

"All right." He patted me on the back a little harder than was necessary. "Let's get this fucker out of here."

He entered the ship, and a few minutes later, the engines were humming. He walked the ramp and came back into the hangar. The four of us waited in a line so Williams could deliver his goodbye speech.

"We've been working tirelessly for weeks," he addressed the group, "and now is the time to put our money where our mouths are. Each of you has been an integral part of this plan, and for that, I thank you. There have been no hiccups from DeSantos, which I think none of us were expecting, and our tech is the best the world has ever seen.

"Getting Mason to the compound should be easy." Williams paced down the four-man line with his hands clasped behind his back. "Cap and Dustin have performed perfectly through the last ninety-nine simulations, and they won't have any issues. We've tested the engine and the ground-sensor emission system repeatedly, and nothing is out of place.

"I know you're all nervous." He stopped in front of Dustin who was standing in the middle. "Use it. Harness those nerves to inform your gut decisions, to give you an edge in battle, and to focus yourselves on the mission.

"The fate of humanity depends on what happens the rest of this night. Tonight is the difference between whether or not we'll go down in history as an outfit that thought it could change the world. Make no mistake, we *will* go down in history for this.

"Well done. Success or failure, you have a lot to be proud of." His eyes widened. "Good luck, gentlemen." He left the hangar, heading back to mission control to monitor our comms.

I took my bag of grenades and walked up the ramp and into the ship's cargo area where I was to wait until we got into Noor territory.

The ship was able to travel up to three-hundred miles in an hour when it wasn't hovering, so the trip to Noor Village wouldn't take much time. Once the ship got in range, Cap and Dustin would drop me close to the ground. My mission was to book it to the outer limits of the town carrying a Creature's head and a bag of explosives.

We lifted off the ground and hovered our way out of the hangar.

We were on our way.

Half an hour later, the ship was getting close to Noor territory, and I was ready to go.

"This is it," Cap said from the captain's chair.

The ship stopped moving forward and descended.

So far, so good.

Twenty feet from the ground, the cargo bay door opened, and I jumped from the ship. I landed on the ground, stopping for a second to make sure the sensors didn't go off.

There were no sounds or sirens in the distance.

Dustin threw the Creature's head, and I caught it, placing it gently on the ground between my feet.

The ship hovered. There was an extra second to make sure the ship got away safely, so I stayed there and watched.

What would happen when I got back to Sooth City? Would they be waiting for me with a parade? Probably not, though it was a nice thought.

Cap was going to have a lot of questions for me that I wanted to answer. It would be a spirited debate and discussion about the history of vampires and whether I *was* actually what one would call a "vampire."

There were sounds of mechanical whirring, and before I could rush toward it, a loud explosion blasted in the direction of the ship.

The laser blast brushed past, and the ship went from a hover to a looser flow. Cap and Dustin started evasive maneuvers.

I wanted to leave my post to go find the source, but I couldn't risk exposing myself to the Noor, so I had to trust Cap and Dustin to outrun it.

Another cannon blast shot, this one also off target.

"They'll be out of range in two seconds," I said under my breath.

After the time was through, I breathed a sigh of relief. The ship was fast, save for when it was lifting off. I was glad to know that the simulations worked in preparing them for what to do when under attack in hover mode.

Another cannon blast fired. I wasn't worried when the blast went into the air—Cap and Dustin could easily outmaneuver it.

This time, the laser cannon didn't miss. It hit its target directly. In an instant, the ship went from a barely-visible blur to an amorphous orange ball. Debris fell to the ground. Before I understood what was happening, the sound of tin crumbling filled my ears—the waves from the explosion finally reached me.

"Nooooooo!" I yelled at the top of my lungs.

I wanted to run toward the ship and determine if there were any survivors, but there was a voice telling me to keep on with the mission at hand.

It was Cap's voice in my head. He was telling me not to abort.

He couldn't have survived. In any case, I listened to his message and headed toward Noor Village.

I could hear Dustin and Cap screaming in pain until I got out of range. Then, nothing. They were gone.

I wanted to take a moment to stop and grieve the lives of two men I'd come to respect. It was pointless. They were gone.

Though I didn't let it slow me, the grenades and the Creature head were heavier than I figured they would be. I ran toward the Noor Village gates, using all my energy to maintain my pace. I'd eaten before I left, so I had plenty of energy to get me there without having to stop.

I stopped when I was a hundred feet away from the entrance.

The exterior of Noor Village was exquisite. The wall was made of a gold and Polymer-Xeta blend that, when in the moonlight, reflected a glowing green color, lighting the area around the city. The purple and pink lights of the buildings peaking over the wall illuminated the black marble like bioluminescent fish at the bottom of the sea.

I was hit in the back of the neck with a bolt of lightning that shot through my body in an instantaneous blaze of heat and sharpness. Everything went black.

~ * ~

I awoke handcuffed to a chair in an empty room out of a bad cop show. There was one table with a light hovering above it, three chairs, and a mirror on the wall, undoubtedly with someone on the other side watching intently. I didn't know how much time had passed since I was in the forest. I was hungry, so I estimated it must have been several hours, maybe even a day.

There was no one in the room with me, but there were two faint voices behind the door discussing their next plan of action. When they agreed to question me, they came inside.

Two men sat on the chairs across the table from me. The first one, on my left, had light brown hair with the same color eyes, a short beard, and a short face with deeply set features. His nametag said "Parker."

The second man was in the corner behind the first, so it was difficult to determine his facial features when I was under the light. His nametag read, "Stevens," which was all I could really see.

"Who the fuck are you, and what the fuck are you doing here?" Parker asked bluntly.

"My name is Dr. Trevor Mason," I answered eventually. "I've been sent here by Juan Carlos DeSantos of Sooth City to destroy several buildings with the bag of grenades you no doubt confiscated from me when you brought me in."

"You've got to be shitting me." Stevens snorted. "Shoot this prick right now."

Parker did nothing to indicate he was going to shoot me. Instead, he continued his line of questioning, "How did you get a Creature here without being eaten alive?"

"I used a test blood sample called TB-457. It can knock one of those fuckers on their asses if you use it right. However, that's not why I'm really here."

"Why are you *really* here?" he asked with an attitude.

"I have an important message to get to Raymond Harrington regarding the Creatures."

"What would the message be?"

My tone grew dark. "I'm afraid I can't tell you."

"Why the fuck not?"

"I'm afraid I can't tell you *that* either. I'm allowed to talk to Raymond Harrington and no one else."

"Bullshit." Stevens snorted. "What about all those bombs you were carrying?"

"I never intended to use them without your consent. As of right now, they are useless paperweights unless you give them back to me and I arm them."

"Then why bring them?" He made a motion with his head for whomever was behind the glass to check the grenades and make sure I was telling the truth.

"Because DeSantos thinks I *am* going to use them." I leaned back and crossed my legs. "He thinks I'm sneaking from building to building, making sure these bombs are active. Getting caught was all part of the plan to get to Harrington."

"Get the fuck out of here." Stevens laughed. "You're trying to cover your ass. You came here to blow us up, and now that we caught you, you're feeding us a bullshit story about needing to get a message to our boss."

I said nothing.

"So, let me see if I have this straight," Parker said after a moment of silence. "You're here because you want to warn Harrington about the Creatures, but you can't tell us what the warning is. DeSantos sent you with several explosives great enough to destroy this entire compound, but you were never planning on using them. You realize how insane that sounds, right?"

"I do." I uncrossed my legs and sat forward. "However, it *is* the truth. I have something important to tell Harrington. I'm not exaggerating when I say the fate of the human race is delicately resting in your hands right now, gentlemen."

Parker got up and left the room, followed by Stevens. I hoped I'd convinced them that I was there to help. I wasn't sure it worked.

After what felt like an hour, the door opened again. This time, Ray Harrington was in front leading Parker and Stevens.

Chapter Thirteen

Prince Raymond William Harrington the First was eighteen when he took over Noor Village. His parents, King John XXIV and Queen Elizabeth XXXV, ruled their territory as true oligarchs, treating captured Sooth like medieval peons, forcing them to work in their poppy fields harvesting and producing opium. After the opium was processed, it was distributed to the ruling class who used it for medicinal and spiritual purposes. What was left was sold to other Noor communities who practiced the same form of mysticism. Most of the community smoked opium laced cigarettes all times of the day. Since opium was more or less plentiful and relatively cheap, no one considered opium addiction a problem.

The king and queen were assassinated during Raymond's eighteenth birthday celebration, poisoned by a Sooth who put Polymer-Xeta in their wine. At first the wine tasted like any other: sweet, fruity, and crisp. After a few seconds Raymond's parents were gasping for air. He rushed to them, kneeled, put his mouth over his mother's lips, and blew air into her lungs.

As he put his lips to his mother's for the final time, he felt a tingling sensation in and around his mouth and a copper taste on his tongue.

It was too late. The poison was already coursing through their systems, making the four-minute journey to the heart and the brain. Raymond was one of a hundred people who witnessed the king's and queen's deaths, and he was never the same after that.

The guards chased the assassin through the city for two hours before they found him scaling the wall beyond the inner city's gates.

When he was finally caught, the perpetrator took a capsule from his pocket, jammed it into his mouth, and bit on it. Ten seconds later he was foaming at the mouth and convulsing like he was having a seizure. The guards performed CPR, but they couldn't revive the fallen Sooth spy.

After the death of his parents, Ray took to smoking more opium than was generally recommended by Noor physicians. He would never grant forgiveness for the Sooth's role in the assassination of his parents, so he took it out on every Sooth he could by giving orders to invade their territories until he found who hired the culprit.

Using a fleet of soldiers and a crew of mech tank squadrons, Harrington laid siege to several well-known Sooth townships including North Sooth Town and Sooth Village. When he was unable to find the party responsible, he withdrew some of his forces and kept the territories occupied, sometimes having them advance into the next town.

He effectively restarted the war with the Sooth, and Sooth City was the next closest target.

Harrington focused his efforts on getting revenge on DeSantos and Sooth City for the death of his parents. He sent a majority of his forces to the edge of Noor territory to wait in compounds and periodically attack Sooth City whenever he felt like having them do so.

Raymond Harrington I, king of Noor Village, stood a stocky six-feet tall, barely missing the light hanging from the interrogation room's ceiling. He was mostly bald, and the stubble on the sides let me know he shaved them and the back to match the top. On his face was a neatly trimmed goatee that ended at the corner of his mouth. He wore a gray, pinstripe, three-piece suit with a pink rose in the lapel like a mobster at a wedding.

"Well," he said after a moment, "you wanted to speak with me?"

I hadn't expected to see him so soon, however, I was glad they hadn't kept Harrington from me any longer, or else my hunger would have grown uncomfortable.

"Yes," I replied. "But it can't be in this room or in front of those two."

"Get the fuck out of here." Stevens chortled. "I told you we should've shot this prick in the face when he arrived."

"No," Parker replied.

"Fine." Stevens sharpened his glare. "But we're not going anywhere."

"Enough." Harrington turned his head slightly but didn't break my gaze. "Leave us."

"Shit." Stevens and Parker begrudgingly left the room.

"You can tell me whatever you want, but we're *not* going

anywhere." Harrington planted his pointer finger on the table.

"I'm afraid I have to insist we do this in a more secure office." I smirked.

"And why exactly is that?" he asked.

"I have something important to tell you about DeSantos and the Creatures, why you're going to help me, and why you're going to make it look like we blew up twelve of your own buildings."

"That's funny," he said. "Do you legitimately think I'm going to do *any* of those things?"

"I do." I leaned back in my chair.

"Give me one good reason why I should let you go?"

"Because I can show you how to get to DeSantos."

It was the only thing I could think of to prey on Harrington's fears and get him to take us somewhere more private.

He nodded.

He led me from the interrogation room to another one marked "conference" in the same building. It was a far nicer space than any I'd been in for months. There were brand new marble surfaces, and in the middle there was a large square glass table with clear half-egg shaped chairs surrounding it.

I'd asked Harrington to make sure the Creature head I brought with me was in there when we arrived. It was sitting there waiting for us, along with a laser scalpel and the hard drive they'd confiscated from me.

"Go ahead." He motioned for me to begin.

Without saying anything, I took the hard drive, plugged it into the import slot, and a holographic Creature hovered over the table.

I gave Harrington the same presentation I gave to Falcone, Cap, and Williams back in Sooth City. I told him about the Creature's attack on Sooth City and how they could disable our communications so effectively. I told him about the Creature's cerebral cortexes and how they were becoming smarter, more calculating, and more dangerous. I told him they've developed sight.

After the presentation, he stared at me like I told him I hated his mother.

"You expect me to believe all this?" he asked.

"Not without a demonstration," I answered.

I took the laser scalpel, turned it on, then cut away at the Creature's head from the base of its skull to its ears, across the forehead and back down.

As expected, it had developed several new features I was yet to uncover. For instance, it was forming a second eye, which meant soon they would have the ability to perceive depth.

"What the hell am I looking at?" Harrington asked.

I pointed to the Creature. "This is what we're up against," I replied. "The Creatures are getting smarter and more organized, and the longer we allow them to come out of the woodwork, the more of our friends and family will be lost to these blood-sucking fuckers."

"So, what do you want from *me*? Clearly, this isn't how I'm going to rid the world of DeSantos and the Sooth."

"I want you to give up your war with DeSantos and help the human race defend itself from the Creatures. If Sooth City falls, Noor Village is next. Both places are filled with good, hardworking people who don't want to see their families lost to Creature attacks every night."

I clicked a button on the console, and another holographic image came up. The green and white map marked the Creatures's migration patterns through Sooth territories.

"Hmm," he mumbled. "What you're saying is that, if we don't help the Sooth, we'll become extinct?"

"More or less." I tilted my head a couple of times to either side.

"Why don't I just let the Creatures and the Sooth have it out?" He laughed a little.

"Because without the Sooth to hold them off, Noor territories are the next logical target. And we both know you can't hold the Creatures off forever."

"Who the fuck *are* you?" he asked.

"Dr. Trevor Mason." I extended a hand for him to shake. "And I am the man who is going to save all of you."

Harrington got up and came over to where I was standing. He didn't accept my handshake. Instead, he inspected the map with laser focus.

"Shit." He put a finger to his temple and scratched. "It looks like we have a deal...for now."

"We do?" I asked.

"For the moment, it seems we have a mutual enemy, so yes...we do."

I couldn't believe Harrington took so little convincing. There was a chance he was doing it to get closer to DeSantos. I'd have to keep an eye on him and make sure it didn't happen. At the same time though, I needed Harrington to go along with it until I could get him to truly understand why the human race needed to be saved, himself included.

I rubbed my hands together. "This part may be difficult to hear...I need you to take the explosives I brought with me and use them on twelve buildings of your choice."

"Fuck no." He laughed. "Why the hell would I do that?"

"Because DeSantos can't know anything about this meeting. He has to think the plan went off without a hitch, otherwise he'll be all over this place, and neither of us can afford that right now. You'll have your chance to rebuild, but for now, you need to evacuate the buildings and get everyone to a safe distance."

"Christ," he said. "You're serious?"

"I am."

"What will you be doing while I'm destroying my town?"

"While you're doing that, I'll be on my way back to Sooth City to explain to DeSantos why we lost two of our best men."

"I don't follow."

I stared at him. "Outside Noor Village, your men shot down the Sooth ship that was transporting me here. Piloting the ship were two high ranking members of Sooth City's government."

Harrington raised his left eyebrow, and his lips turned slightly downward. "How can that be?" he asked. "You arrived at almost the exact same time. That incident was miles away. No one could get to the city that fast."

"Never mind for now," I replied. "My men were supposed to come back alive, and I am going to have to explain why they didn't, and I did. DeSantos can't know we are working together. He needs to think this plan was a success."

"What else?" Harrington asked after a few minutes contemplating.

"That's all," I said. "If you do exactly what I've asked of you, your people will be fine, and we can work together to rid the world of the Creatures and get back to what matters."

"What matters to a man like you?"

"Everything, Mr. Harrington. Everything matters to a man like me."

Moments later, Harrington, Parker, and Stevens escorted me to Noor Village's outer gate. The sun had set, so I didn't have to tell them not to put me in the sun. Harrington agreed to place the explosives on a few buildings of his choosing and let me go to DeSantos as if everything proceeded according to plan.

I wondered why Harrington took the lack of convincing he did, however, I decided the best course was to ensure I safely returned to Sooth City without any run-ins with the Creatures. Since there was no transportation back and I needed to get some blood, I would have to stop at least one Noor encampment on the way. Harrington would not be happy about it when he found out, but I had to ensure I wouldn't kill anyone when I got back to Sooth City. It was also a good way to solidify our alliance. If he thought it was a Creature, then he might see the necessity in a mutually beneficial relationship. It would be easy enough to make it look like a Creature attack.

"We're putting a lot of trust in you, asshole," Stevens said. "If you're fucking with us, we will completely destroy your city. The war will be nothing compared to the hellfire we'll rain upon you if even a single one of our people is hurt because of you."

"Fair enough," I said, barely paying attention to the ramblings of what I suspected was an opium-soaked soul.

"Hey." He grabbed me by the arm. "I'm serious. Not one wrong move."

When Stevens touched me, a tinge emanated from the spot throughout my body, and the pain in my stomach was making it worse. It may have been the hunger, but at the moment it was getting difficult to remember why I needed so many humans alive.

Harrington, Stevens, and Parker let me leave the compound without saying anything else, an act of mercy, for which I was thankful. Otherwise, I may have eaten the three of them for fun.

The gates closed behind me. The forest around me was silent and uninviting. I walked ahead regardless.

~ * ~

Even without the Creature's head or the grenades, I was moving at a diminished pace. I estimated it was thirty hours since I'd eaten, and the running I did to get to Noor Village had depleted me. Hunger was going to strike soon if I didn't find a human within the next few hours.

After running for the better part of forty-five minutes, a Noor camp appeared in the distance.

Before I left Noor Village, I asked Harrington to warn the camps en route that I was coming and to be sure and give me safe passage. This meant they were expecting me, and I wouldn't have to sneak in.

I carefully approached the camp.

There was one person on guard that night. I could smell the blood cycling through his veins and heart.

The guard saw me and lifted his microphone to his face. "Target has arrived."

"Let him through," said the female voice on the other end.

"Affirmative." The man waved a hand at me to come through.

I was close. I lunged for the guard, his neck in my sights like a falcon to a mouse. I got to him before he had a chance to process what was going on. I took his head and sank my teeth deep into his jugular vein, covering his mouth with my right hand to muffle his screams.

His blood ran down my throat, and energy returned

simultaneously to every one of my limbs and muscles. I let the red juice engulf my spirit with nourishment while the man struggled to remain conscious.

When I finished, I dragged the body behind the fence and hid it in the foliage. I stopped for a moment to listen and make sure no Creatures were coming.

There were no sounds.

Confident I was unseen, I left the lifeless body and headed South toward Sooth City.

Chapter Fourteen

It was close to dawn when I got back to Sooth City, and I was thankful to see the gates. The moment they separated, Scraps came running to meet me, his ears perked, and his tail wagged with excitement.

"You missed me, huh, boy?" I patted him on the head.

There was supposed to be a debriefing. The sun was rising, and I hoped Williams would make an excuse for me to rest before I was expected to meet with DeSantos.

Going the short way through the city, I got back to my house with Scraps by my side. Since the sun was only a third of the way up, it did no more than give me a headache.

When I reached the bedroom, I found a communications drive stuck to the door. I examined the rectangular, black and red box with the Sooth seal embossed in silver.

After putting my finger on the seal and applying pressure, a holographic periodical popped up in front of my face.

"In a sweeping win for Sooth City," a computerized voice said, "our brave covert operatives were able to successfully infiltrate and destroy several buildings in Noor Village using a new incendiary device created by Captain John Falcone and Dr. Trevor Mason. Both men will be given medals of honor at the next family dinner. Opportunities for pictures will follow.

"However, this amazing victory comes at a price. Captain Nathan Caper and Private Dustin Vander did not return. They were captured piloting their ship into Noor Village territory and were subsequently tortured, then killed. Dustin's sister Marina is holding a service for her brother after the next family dinner. All are required to attend, whether or not they knew him."

They weren't captured or tortured, though they may as well be the case. To live with the knowledge I was responsible for Dustin's death was something I wasn't sure I would be able to deal with properly.

The periodical had more to say on both topics, but I was too tired to listen. Knowing that Harrington decided to detonate his town was enough for me.

He trusted me enough to destroy twelve of his own buildings, and I was relieved to have Horizon and Phantom off my plate for the time being. Everything else would gladly take a backseat until the next evening when I would be able to process more thoroughly what happened and the potential repercussions.

In the bedroom, I haphazardly threw my clothes to the floor and slumped onto the bed like it was the first time I'd ever experienced comfort.

I drifted off into nothingness.

~ * ~

The next night, I awoke with Scraps licking my face. It took me a second to recognize that someone was knocking at the door. I grabbed a pair of pajama pants from the dresser and put them on as the knocking continued.

"I'm coming!" My voice was hoarse.

Williams standing on the other side of the door.

"It's time." He brushed his way past me into the foyer.

He wore an air of business-as-usual while he went directly into my bedroom without saying a word and returned with a suit for me to wear. The suit was black with red pinstripes and a shiny red Sooth insignia sewn onto the pocket. At the bottom of the red tie, another insignia was embroidered, and one more on the red pocket square.

"Here," he said. "Put this on. We have a long night ahead of us."

I went into the bedroom and put on the suit. When I finished, I admired the fit and look. Normally I didn't care about my appearance, however, the red and black suit was the nicest outfit I had worn in some time, and there was stillness in my heart.

I went back into the living room where Williams and Scraps were waiting for me. Thankfully, Scraps stayed back so I wouldn't get dog hair on my new threads and wagged his tail.

"Hmm." Williams's eyes drooped. "All right, let's get out of here."

The three of us left my house and made our way toward the center of town for family dinner.

"Okay." Williams looked straight ahead. "Tell me…What

happened out there?"

I proceeded to tell him what occurred—that Harrington hadn't been a tough sell, that he'd agreed the Creatures were the first priority and decided to go through with blowing up his own buildings. I told him Cap and Dustin did their absolute best, and there was nothing they could have done differently. In the interest of transparency, I also told him I drained a man at a Noor camp outside of town.

By the time we got to the tent, Williams was filled in completely.

"Are you sure that's everything?" he asked.

"Everything I can remember," I replied.

"Okay, good. I haven't talked to DeSantos since you've been back, and I want to make sure I have all of my ducks in a row."

"Ready to aim at and fire upon," I said.

Williams and I went into the tent.

An uproar of cheers exploded from the people like they were waiting for us.

Falcone was already at the front of the room.

I made my way to the table with citizens congratulating me and extending their hands for handshakes. The people stood and cheered for us while Williams and I waved at them.

DeSantos stood behind the table, and everyone got quiet.

"Tonight," he said, "we honor great men. Men who risked everything to make sure Harrington and Noor Village got what was coming to them. They understood what the greater good is, and they knew that only through blood, sweat, and tears could they band together to become those which history will undoubtedly see as heroes. For our safety this evening, for this meal we are going to consume, for the metal used to make these medals of honor, we owe these men a great deal of gratitude. We owe them everything.

"Tonight, we honor these five brave souls, and what they've done will echo throughout eternity. And while two of them did not come back, their sacrifice will never be forgotten. Their stories will be written on the annals of our souls, our nation, and our lives."

Everyone in the room was clapping.

I admitted that DeSantos's speech was more elegant than I would have expected. Typically, when he spoke, it was with the grace of an elephant, but there was something different about *this* one.

There were five boxes on the head table that night.

DeSantos picked up one of the boxes and opened it. "To Dr. Trevor Mason, I bestow upon you the Black and Red Heart for valor in community."

DeSantos went down the line to Williams and Falcone

respectively, and as he spoke our names, he pinned the medal to our lapels.

"Nathan Caper and Dustin Vander," he said when he finished, "will also be receiving Black and Red Hearts for valor in community at their respective memorial services."

It was difficult to feel a sense of community pride, knowing the entire thing was a farce falsified by DeSantos to improve morale. It was also strange that I didn't actually do any of the things I was being touted for.

Everyone in the tent chanted "speech, speech, speech!" at the top of their lungs.

"I'm afraid we don't have time for speeches tonight." DeSantos looked around the crowd from his podium. "But please stay after family dinner for some warm words from Marina Vander about her brother. And don't forget tomorrow night we will have a similar service for Captain Nathan Caper."

I hunted for Marina but couldn't locate her through the crowd with everything going on. I forgot to think about how she might be feeling. I was so focused on myself and making sure Phantom went according to plan that she slipped through the cracks.

A few minutes later, the tent's scene was back to what I expected to see—the hustle and bustle of the evening transformed into hungry mouths and crying babies.

When everything settled and everyone finished with their meals, it was time for Dustin's memorial service.

I took a seat with Falcone and Williams at a table in the center of the room.

Marina came into the tent, walked to the front, then sat at the head table. She was wearing a black and red dress uniform with black shoes and a black hat.

Her face was extremely plain, her eyes were focused straight ahead, and her expressionless mouth was flat and unwavering. It was an expression I'd seen many times—true despair and anger coming through a furrowed brow was unmistakable. She definitely wanted revenge. It was written on her like a bad poem.

She went up to the microphone DeSantos's servants put in front of the memorial statue they'd wheeled in.

"My brother," she began, "was the world to me. Our connection was stronger than any human alive, and when he died, it was as though I were right there with him. I absorbed every moment, every scream, every inch of pain so I could help my brother live his final moments free of suffering. I can die a happy woman knowing I took in as much of his pain as I could.

"Dustin was strong." She gripped the podium, and her jaw tightened. "And he used his strength whenever he could. He never squandered one ounce of his determination, and he would have been one of the best leaders this community has seen." She released her grip on the wood platform in front of her.

"Not only was I robbed of a twin brother whose face I will see within the reflections I gaze into for the rest of my life, but this community and this world was robbed of a shining light that illuminated all that it touched.

"I remember the time he found a group of abandoned German Shepherds." Her face softened a bit. "We played patrol near one of the fences with some of the other kids when Dustin heard the high-pitched barks of a pack of newborn dogs." She smiled while a tear rolled down her right cheek. "We told him to leave them and let the mom come back and take care of them, but he somehow knew, beyond the fence, the mother's carrion lay still—she wasn't coming back.

"He put each one of the puppies in his shirt and brought them back to our home where he nursed them back to health. He even made sure they had homes. When he couldn't find a home for the mangiest one, he trained it to be an outdoor dog. Today, that dog is named Scraps; he's the most independent and capable dog I've ever met, even if he has recently gotten a little fat."

Scraps barked, and all of the citizens laughed. It was admittedly nice to put an end to the mystery. I looked at the dog fondly with a slight smile and scratched him behind the ears.

Marina's tone went from gentle remembrance to villainous melancholy.

"It is my vow," she continued, her face darkening, "that Dustin's death will not be in vain. My brother's life will be avenged at all costs. If I have to scour the planet to find the means to capture and destroy Raymond Harrington, then I will honor my dear brother with my last dying breath. He *will* pay for what he's taken from me, and the price will be his head on a pike. I don't expect any of you to come with me, but I do expect you to stand behind me and support me as I take the hunt for Harrington to his doorstep.

"Thank you."

Marina walked off the stage, her words lingering in the room like a thick mist on the moors.

I got up from the table, straightened myself, then left the tent with a heaviness in my chest. Though it was nice to hear heartwarming stories about the deceased, it didn't change the fact that Dustin *was* dead.

He was a good kid and didn't deserve to be killed for the delusions of madmen.

~ * ~

The next night's service for Cap was similar, though longer because of his age and military history.

Cap was slightly less endearing than Dustin, so there weren't as many words about happy moments or sentimentality as there was the previous night. He would have loved it.

Nevertheless, I had some form of fondness for Cap. His gruff, holier-than-thou attitude and his roving-street-gang air of masculinity had grown on me at some point. I wasn't sure *when* it happened, but I didn't want the guy dead.

My feelings for humanity were expanding beyond what I would have felt for a simple meal.

People were no longer mere cattle to me.

Of course, I still needed their blood to survive, though I was becoming more discerning when it came to who I might eat and when I was free to do so without being caught. I also knew eventually I would become complacent with the amount of blood Williams and Falcone would ration to me. It was enough to keep me alive, and no more.

Truth be told, I was fine with the idea of not hunting. I was even fine with people knowing I was a vampire. I just wanted to stay away from the interrogation rooms and lab tables.

When I got home from Cap's memorial, I remembered that for the first time in weeks, I didn't have anything to do.

My brain went to the red ball Scraps brought after Dustin and Marina's display in the center of town. I'd been so distracted by Phantom that I'd completely forgotten. I couldn't dissect it, and I didn't know what it was other than related to the Creatures. I had some downtime, and it was the perfect opportunity to try and learn more about what the red ball might be.

Chapter Fifteen

A week into my research on the red ball passed and I was getting nowhere. I tried dissecting it again and even the most powerful laser scalpel I could find made nothing more than a scratch on the surface. I tried dissolving it in acid, but that didn't work either.

I needed to examine one of the Creatures more closely.

I told DeSantos I wanted to run a TB-457 sample and perform an autopsy on a freshly dead Creature. He was happy to oblige. If I could determine where in Creature anatomy the ball lived, I could determine its use.

"This is Dr. Trevor Mason, Sooth City Medical Unit," I said into a recording device attached to my collar. "The time is zero five hundred hours, and I am beginning my autopsy of test subject number two four eight dash five three zero."

"There are no surface abnormalities," I continued, "so I am going ahead with the autopsy. Cause of death is blood loss from a cut to the throat. Time of death is somewhere in between zero one hundred and zero two hundred hours. Subject is eight feet, five inches tall, and weighs two hundred and ninety-five pounds. Subject color is light gray and tan, normal for full-grown male Creatures."

I sprayed the body from head to toe with a specially formulated reagent designed to illuminate any fluids which may have covered the body.

"There are no traces of urine, feces, semen, or saline anywhere on the Creature's dermis. I am now placing a body block."

I took the body block from the table behind me, lifted the Creature's body, and slid it underneath to expose its chest more easily.

"Beginning incision."

When I finished cutting through the tissue, I peeled the two chest flaps to the sides then placed the top one over the Creature's face.

"Removing ribs."

Taking out the ribs exposed the organs. I made cuts to detach the larynx, esophagus, arteries, ligaments, and a few nerve systems unique to Creatures, making way for the cuts needed to detach the organs from the spinal cord.

"Removing organs."

I recorded each organ's size, weight, and color, then took tissue samples from them. I noticed the heart was inflamed, but there were no signs of red spheres or anything which might evolve into a red ball.

I picked up the larynx and put it on a separate lab table. I took the scalpel and made a vertical incision that split it in half. Unfortunately, there was no strange red ball anywhere in there. I repeated the process with the rest of the Creature's organs and found nothing.

Then I removed the stomach sack and didn't notice anything that immediately jumped out at me.

"Subject's stomach contents include human blood combined with the test blood sample used to slow the Creature and scraps of human remains. Will examine more closely."

I cut a slit in the intestines, drained the blood into an IV bag then set it off to the side to examine later. Perhaps examining TB-457 post-mortem might yield some results.

The last step was to examine the Creature's brain.

I made an incision from under the ear canal, to the forehead, and back behind the other ear canal, the incision connecting behind the neck and back to the first ear. I pried open the skullcap, cut the Creature's dura then took out the bone, exposing the brain. As I removed the brain from the skull to look at it more closely, I noticed that it was rather heavy.

"Brain weighs approximately ten pounds. Once again, I see nothing out of the ordinary. Beginning brain dissection."

I found nothing other than a jumble of brain tissue and blood.

There was no trace of a red ball anywhere within the Creature's anatomy.

I was scratching my head, trying to think of what the ball might be. I'd run every test I could think of.

According to my research, it was organic in nature, but it was so strong, no other organic matter on-hand was able to cut through it. I thought that maybe it was made by the Creatures. I'd underestimated them before. Perhaps they found a way to build whatever the ball was. If so, what was it used for? What was inside? I doubted the Creatures possessed the capacity or manufacturing skills to make an unbreakable ball and couldn't think of a reason they would want to.

~ * ~

On the three-week anniversary of studying the ball, Scraps and I sat in my dining room staring at it. Unfortunately, the one other person who knew of the ball's existence had been Dustin. He was dead, and I didn't want to tell anyone else about it until I had more information on what *it* was.

Had the ball actually come from the Creature? I was starting to doubt it. After all, I hadn't seen it fall from one. I knew Scraps brought it to me at the same time the Creature was on display in the town square. It was covered in Creature blood, so I assumed that was where it came from.

During the time I was on earth, I'd never come across a material stronger than the red ball. Even the most stubborn material on the planet was susceptible to a laser scalpel.

"I don't know, boy," I said to Scraps. "What the fuck is this thing?"

Why I was expecting an answer from the dog was unclear, but I was.

There was a clicking sound.

It was the unmistakable clicking of a Creature, and it was right behind me. I was clueless as to how it got into my home without my noticing. There it was, standing no more than five feet behind me and getting closer.

Before I had the chance to get up, a scaly, leathery claw wrapped around my face.

The next thing I knew, I was in a bear hug struggling. I freed myself from the Creature's grip for half a second. Another Creature grabbed me with its scaly arm.

It was no use fighting any longer. The Creatures were far stronger than I was.

A Creature lifted me off my feet, clutching me like a baby in its two middle arms. It took me to the back of the house, where there was a hole in the kitchen wall waiting for us—no doubt their entrance method.

They led me through another hole outside the wall, into the backyard. It was big enough to fit a full-sized Creature carrying a full-sized person.

The tunnel was tight, and when my shoulders scraped the sides, I got dirt on my face and in my mouth.

By the time I was able to see the light at the end of the tunnel, I stopped resisting. The Creatures had captured me and were bringing me to a second location. If they'd intended to eat me, it would have been far easier to do so in my home where the advantage was theirs.

At the end of the tunnel, a large opening led to a wide cave adorned with bioluminescent matter which lit the entire area.

The Creatures had built an elaborate base of operations underneath Sooth City, which was how they were so adept at getting through the walls. This meant my theories were accurate. The Creatures were smart enough to coordinate, they understood the concept of depth, and they even created a way to illuminate their surroundings, undoubtedly because their eye system required light to function properly.

On the vast cavern walls there were a series of holes I assumed led to different vantage points, including my home and the rest of Sooth City.

I was beyond impressed. The Creatures had gone from mindless killing machines to intelligent workers and soldiers in the span of no more than a decade.

"Where the fuck are you taking me?" I asked after a few minutes.

There was no answer. I wasn't entirely sure why I thought the Creature's form of communication would be in any discernible language. I wanted them to hear the confusion in my voice and not the actual words I was using—much like when speaking to a pet.

Scraps was right behind us with the ball in his mouth, following the group as if told to do so. The monsters paid no attention to the fact I was being accompanied; it made me think their intention was to keep me alive.

If they didn't want to kill me, then what *did* they want?

They brought me to an alcove off to the side, ten stories above the cave floor. The opening was big enough to fit a single person. The Creature who'd grabbed me lifted his arm and motioned for me to enter. I bent at the knees and lowered my head into the opening.

When I emerged on the other side, I was in front of a fire.

Surrounding the fire was a group of six Creatures, staring directly at me with full sets of eyes. It looked like they were waiting for me to talk. I wasn't sure what, but it was clear they wanted something specific from me.

I sat cross-legged in front of the fire, staring back at the crew of Creatures gazing at me.

"What the hell *is* all this?" I waved my hand around to show them what I was talking about.

Scraps took the ball with his mouth, went around to one of the Creatures, and dropped it at their feet. The Creature lifted it with its massive claw.

"This is our home." The Creature didn't move his mouth.

My jaw dropped. I could hear the sound it was making, but it was entirely in my head. The Creature was speaking directly to me, and suddenly I had an idea of what the red ball was.

"How are you talking to me right now?" I asked.

The Creature handed the ball to his left, and the next one spoke.

"With this," answered a female voice. The Creature held the red ball and presented it to me. "With this ball, we can communicate with any creature on this planet in whatever tongue they speak and understand."

"So, it's a communications device?" I smiled with the left half of my mouth.

"That's correct."

"And the Creature that brought it...he wasn't a distraction, was he?" I asked. "He was bringing this to Sooth City to try and speak with us."

"Yes, the *Creature* as you call us." She squinted one of her giant eyes.

"What *should* I call you?" I raised my eyebrow.

"You may call me Teresa, and this is Thomas, Darren, Wilma, Normand, and Johnathan. Our species don't have a word for what we are, but you can call us 'Dwellers' if you are searching for a term."

"So, the Dweller...?" I paused.

"Christopher," Teresa said.

"Christopher," I nodded, "was attempting to make contact with us? That must have been disappointing."

"Indeed, it was." She lowered her gaze. "He was the messenger as well as the creator of the device. He made only one prototype before he was killed."

"How does it work?"

"It's made using substances found underground." She looked up. "A specialized steel is used to enhance the brainwaves of the person holding it. The outside coating is made of Cabondanium, a kind of amber-carbon material developed by Christopher." She tapped her finger on the ball. "The device uses the holder's gamma brain waves, which intersect with those in close proximity. This results in our ability to understand the language of whomever is holding it."

"And we never gave him a chance." I pursed my lips and looked at the ground.

"You did not," she whispered in my head.

"Then, what am I doing here? Why didn't you kill me?" I tilted my head and frowned.

"You're here because you're different." She pointed at me. "You're the only one of your kind on this planet, and since you discovered us in the Adirondacks, we've been keeping a close eye on you."

My mouth dropped a little. "How is that possible?"

"The first of us were born at the same time, yes." She straightened her back. "However, the six of us were born with genetic deformities, the brain and ocular systems you've discovered, and as a result we were able to break beyond the bounds of our original evolution" She put a finger to her head. "With these powers over our brethren, we made sure to keep a close watch on anything that might possibly hinder our evolution. You, Trevor Mason, are the one thing on this planet with whom we have to share our rung on the food chain."

"It still doesn't explain what I'm doing here."

"But it does." Teresa handed the ball to Thomas.

"You're here," he peered at me, "because we need you to speak with the humans on our behalf."

"Impossible." I closed my eyelids at the absurd request, then opened them after a couple seconds.

"Is it?" he asked, handing the ball back to Teresa, who passed it on to Darren.

"It is." I snorted.

"Those who know your true identity have accepted you," Darren said. "Why should we believe they won't feel the same way if they hear *us* speak?"

"They only like me because I'm not a mindless killing machine." I placed my hand on my chest to emphasize my point.

"Oh, but you *are* a mindless killing machine." Darren extended his arm then his finger. "We've seen what happens when you don't have blood in your system, and you become no better than what you perceive of us. Do you not agree?"

I hated to admit it, but I did agree. I *was* no better than the Dwellers, and when I explained myself, those I told *did* seem to accept me with open arms.

This was different though. Falcone and Williams only trusted me because they knew I was one of the beings in existence who had the capability to deal with the Dwellers. They did so because I was the lesser of two evils.

There was also a distinct chance that hearing the Dwellers speak might help alter opinions. The Sooth were somewhat progressive, and with the right amount of convincing, it was possible they'd change their minds on the topic of blindly killing Creatures.

I was giving people too much credit, DeSantos and Harrington included. I told Williams, Falcone, and Cap because I had no choice.

"I suppose I do agree." I relaxed my shoulders and back and slumped over a little. "But people are not easily swayed. They've hated you and your kind for such a long time I can't see them forgetting or forgiving what your species has done."

"Perhaps." Wilma received the ball. "Though are we beyond redemption?" She frowned.

"Of course not." I rolled my eyes slightly. "But it's not me you have to convince."

"*That* is why we need you. You are the only person alive who can convince the humans we deserve redemption."

"How the hell am I supposed to do that?"

"That's up to you, Dr. Mason. Tell them what you like. Tell them nothing at all. You know our position. Can you go on destroying us, our homes, and our families, now that you know what we truly are?"

"The bottom line is," I replied, "you need human blood to survive, and there is no way people are going to sacrifice themselves."

"Some of us have evolved beyond the need to consume human blood. Any blood will do for many of our clan."

"And those of you who do?"

"We are the result of survival of the fittest, Trevor Mason." She handed the ball back to Teresa.

"We can control the characteristics of our children." Teresa didn't take her eyes off me. "Whenever we need to, we adapt our physiology through birth, passing on new traits of our choosing. If we want our children to avoid the genetic disposition to disease, then we can do so. We can bring to the surface any dominant attributes using our blood-memory. We may take any human characteristic and give it to our offspring."

"Which is how you were able to develop some of your species to be capable of complex thought." I cupped my chin with my left hand.

"That's correct. We needed to develop our offspring's brains to give them the intelligence needed to follow our orders."

"Then why did you attack Sooth City and destroy their communications?" I wondered.

"We were hunting for weaknesses in your security system, and we didn't want it getting out that we were able to coordinate a well-planned attack."

"Jesus." I rubbed a hand over my eyes. "You guys have thought of everything, huh?"

"We've had much time to plan this, Dr. Mason. Our era of hiding in the shadows is over, and now that we have a way to communicate with the surface world, we finally have the means to tell our side of the story."

"Which is?" I asked curiously.

"We were scared children who knew no better. All we knew was to eat. We needed blood. We needed human blood, and now that we will soon be totally free of our dependence, it's in everyone's best interest to coexist with a modicum of peace. We are devising a way to make sure the humans are never able to harm each other, and only then can we all use this planet to live in harmony."

"You are?" I jerked my neck up a little.

No one said anything.

They made a few good arguments. Before that point, the only thing they had to base their decisions on was instinct, and I couldn't blame an animal for trying to survive.

"I'll do my best." I rubbed the back of my neck. "But it's not going to be easy. My friends barely trust me as it is. I will *always* need human blood to survive. To make this whole thing palatable, I have to convince them first that I'm not dangerous to them anymore—a task in itself that will not be easy to accomplish without ending up on the operating table."

"Now you know how we feel." Norm handed the ball to John.

"This is what we've dealt with since our brethren clawed their way to the surface and saw the light for the first time." He motioned up. "Only, before today, you have been able to talk your way off the dissection table, we have not."

He was right. The major difference between them and me was my ability to blend in as a human. The Dwellers did not have the same luxury.

It occurred to me that they were developing humanistic traits in an effort to *appear* more human. It was a good idea. Humans would be more sympathetic if they knew the Dwellers were like them underneath it all.

"Okay, fine." I straightened my spine.

"Then, you'll help us?" asked Thomas.

"I didn't say that." I raised both hands and flattened my palms. "But what I will do is think about what you're proposing."

"Good." Darren nodded a little.

"Good?" I asked, unsure of what made the situation a positive.

"We weren't even sure we would get you this far. That you are willing to consider our request is our best-case scenario."

Darren handed the ball to Wilma.

"You may now return to your domicile if you wish." She pointed to the entrance to the alcove. "You may remain here as long as you like, or you may choose not to revisit Sooth City at all. The decision is entirely up to you."

"Thank you all." I tipped my head to the group. "This has been an illuminating experience."

"You are welcome," Wilma said while the group nodded.

"I'll need an escort back to the tunnel leading to my home."

Darren took me from the alcove back to the opening they'd dragged me through. He led me through the cave's massive town square. There were Dwellers everywhere, all going about their business as if they had somewhere to be. I continued staring at what the Dwellers were able to accomplish without watching where I was going.

When we were at the final tunnel leading to my house, I gave Darren a nod. Whether he understood it or not, I didn't know, but the Dwellers had enough of a grasp on the human condition it was worth trying.

Before he turned around, he handed me the red ball. He left without returning my goodbye. It was easy to feel they were mindless.

In my backyard I covered the hole I'd come through. I didn't want to fill it entirely in case I needed to use it again.

I went back inside and sat on the dinette chair from which the Dweller had abducted me.

"Fuck me." I slumped down and let my arms fall.

All I could do was think.

The Dwellers were capable of thought, and they were also capable of communication using a complex device one of their scientists created. I couldn't even believe they had scientists to begin with.

They wanted me, of all people, to explain that they were breaking away from their original genetic makeup and were no longer dependent on human blood to survive. Perhaps they never were. If they were capable of thought and communication with people, it stood to reason they were capable of lying.

No. They weren't lying.

How I knew they were telling the truth, I wasn't sure, but they definitely were. Dweller attacks had come to a halt after the killing of their lead scientist. They'd been deescalating for months, and now they needed someone to speak on their behalf.

Recruiting me was a smart idea on their part.

Could I go on killing creatures of such intelligence?

No. I couldn't go on helping the Sooth perform tests on them, and I wouldn't continue helping the Sooth make weapons capable of destroying the Dwellers more effectively.

I stared intently at the red ball the Dwellers left in my possession. Now, it made a lot more sense. Christopher was trying to get a message to the Sooth, or maybe to me.

They weren't helpless creatures by a longshot; they did deserve the voice they'd found for themselves. Sentience bestowed upon a being, for whatever reason, was enough to get me to change my tune on any species, whatever they looked like, whatever was written in their past.

If I was capable of redemption, surely, they were too.

I was fascinated by their ability to morph their evolution to traits held in the blood they consumed.

If they were able to feed off animals like any other person, there was no longer any reason to fight the Dwellers. When they were a threat to my food supply, my goal was clear: get as many humans as possible to destroy as many Dwellers as possible. With the knowledge that my food supply was no longer in jeopardy, the one decision I had to make was to help them where I could.

At least I had something to do now.

Chapter Sixteen

The next couple of weeks went by in a blur of confusion and doubt. I wanted to tell Williams and Falcone about the Dwellers and the red ball, but I wasn't sure they were going to take it well. They'd accepted me in the months since my arrival to Sooth City, and even more so after seeing how I handled Phantom.

There was a part of me that wanted to continue as normal, keeping my secrets to ensure my survival. There was an equal sized part of me that wanted to tell everyone the threat wasn't real anymore.

The patrol became a kind of game for me to guess how many times we could continue the watch without any attacks. In the time since the Dwellers had abducted me, the most we saw of them was an occasional passerby not close enough to the compound to warrant any fired shots. I surmised that they were waiting to see what I was going to do.

TB-457 testing stopped completely because I hadn't put in any requests for new Dweller bodies. It would be a short time before they were able to evolve past the need for human blood. They would continue feeling the effects of TB-457, there was nothing on the planet capable of metabolizing it, so nothing had the blood memory to help them evolve through the side effects. I surmised that the Dwellers could've used it as a drug if they wanted to.

"What's been going on with you the past few weeks?" Falcone asked one night when he was dropping off my meal.

"I don't follow," I said, even though I absolutely did.

"You've been pretty despondent lately, bordering on melancholy. The Trevor Mason I've come to know doesn't typically care enough to be so down. So…what's going on?"

"It's not easy to explain, and I'm pretty sure you wouldn't believe me if I told you."

"Try me." He sat on the couch in the living room.

I hadn't finished sorting it out myself. I wasn't quite ready to tell Falcone what happened, so I lied. "It's nothing. I think I'm still upset about Cap and Dustin."

"You're right." Falcone laughed. "That *is* hard to believe."

"I know." I smiled. "There's something sticking in the back of my skull though. They yelled for me in their final moments, and I didn't do anything to help them."

"True, but you did something more important than that. You executed the plan flawlessly, and look, Creature attacks have been on the decline for weeks now. We have you and Harrington to thank for that." He leaned back and crossed his legs.

"Good point." I chuckled.

"I've known Cap for a long time and Dustin since he was born…I am positive they would both be proud of you." He made direct eye contact with me.

It was going to be difficult to tell Falcone the truth about the Dwellers. He posed the biggest threat to their existence, and if he knew they were done drinking blood, I was confident he would eventually agree with me. I needed to find a way to prove to Falcone and Williams I *was* telling the truth.

"Are you sure that's all?" Falcone asked after a few seconds of silence.

"I'm sure," I replied.

"You know we're friends now, Mason, right? You can talk to me or Williams if you need to."

"I know. And trust me, as far as I can remember, this is more open than I've been with any human."

"Is that a fact?" He smiled, and his eyes widened. "I'm honored." He went silent for a second and stared at the floor, his face growing dark. "I've been thinking," he said. "Maybe you can have a talk with Marina. She knows what you're going through right now, and it might be good for you two to hear from each other. Her thirst for vengeance has given me some cause for concern."

"What do you mean?"

"She's become isolated and obsessed. All she does is sit in her room at home and plot her revenge against the Noor. She's asking for pyrotechnic grenades so she can go in and bomb Harrington. She keeps saying, 'if Mason can do it, so can I.' She won't consider the consequences, and she's getting upset that I won't make them for her without DeSantos's permission. She hasn't taken the time to properly grieve her loss, and I'm afraid her actions are consistent with someone going off the deep end."

"That *is* cause for concern." I heightened the octave of my voice in an effort to sound more sympathetic. "But I can't talk with Marina."

"Why the hell not?"

"I won't tell her she can't go into Noor territory without telling her I'm a vampire. I can't tell her I didn't try and save her brother, and there is no way I'm going to tell her about Operation Phantom."

"I thought you might say something like that." Falcone looked down. "I was hoping you would surprise me. I guess not."

"You have to understand. No one can know about me. It's too important to keep my identity hidden from the town. I know Marina is hurting. I can't help her either."

"I know you can't." He sounded disappointed.

He scratched the dog behind the ears then left.

I went to the basement to try and think of a way to prove to Falcone and Williams the Dwellers weren't interested in human blood. There was no way they would believe me without evidence.

The Dwellers left the communications device with me, so I did have the option to show it to those I trusted. But with no Dweller to demonstrate what the ball was for, the chances were slim anyone would listen to me.

Sitting there staring at the red ball, knowing nothing about how it worked, I realized it was the one object capable of healing the world in a time of incipient danger.

Scraps was pawing at me and whimpering at my feet.

"What can I do for you, boy?" I got up from the chair, then kneeled to pet him.

An idea popped into my head.

Placing the ball next to Scraps's paw, I asked him again. "What can I do for you, boy?"

Scraps put his paw on the ball. "Keep petting me."

Holy fuck.

My eyes widened.

The dog was speaking to me, though it was less like speaking and more like thinking.

"Can I have a treat?" Scraps asked with a cocked head, paw on the ball.

With a gaping jaw, I reached in my pocket, pulled out a piece of beef jerky, and gave it to him. I wondered what else Scraps was capable of saying.

"Sit," I said.

"Okay," Scraps replied, complying with my order.

I gave him a treat.

"Play dead."

"Oh, noooo!" He rolled onto his side.

I laughed and gave him another treat.

"Scraps." I pointed to the ceiling. "Up."

Once again, the dog complied.

"Do you like playing dead?" I asked.

"Treat," he replied.

"No. Do you *like* playing dead?" I asked again.

"Treat."

I finally realized what Scraps meant. What he "liked" was treats. This meant that no, he probably didn't like playing dead but knew that doing so would earn him a treat.

I knew exactly what I needed to do.

~ * ~

In the days after discovering I could actually communicate with Scraps, I ran several more tests on the ball to determine its capabilities.

In the same way brain waves intersect with each other in twins and siblings, what I was calling a "Chris Ball" was a miniature brain designed to absorb and redistribute the waves of whomever was touching it.

The device was nothing short of brilliant. Christopher must have been an incredible genius to invent something as complex as the Chris Ball. He needed to have extensive knowledge of neuroscience, and he also needed to have a comprehensive understanding of human anatomy. Then to have built it using completely organic matter showed a knowledge of the planet's materials I simply didn't have.

How the Dwellers were able to learn the complexities of either topic in such a short amount of time was beyond me. However, the proof was in my hands, letting me talk to Scraps like he was an old buddy.

I ran more tests to see how much he and I could talk and what level of cerebral activity he was capable of. I created a harness to affix the Chris Ball to Scraps's collar so I would be able to hear everything he was thinking.

The results were more or less what I expected. I hypothesized that any animal could speak what they wanted with a series of gestures. Without vocal cords, they would never have a way to vocalize what they desired.

In the dog's brain, it was more like a series of impulses. People couldn't conceive of non-linguistic speech with animals, so when you added the filter of a human brain, dog brain waves came through in short bursts of language.

For example, when Scraps wanted to go out, he would scratch at the door and say "out." When he wanted a treat, he would simply say "treat." When he wanted to be petted, he would stick his snout in my hand or crotch and say "pet me."

It was simple yet effective. The whole process relied on a deep sense of interaction. I doubted I would have as much success with a wild animal that hadn't spent much time around the human population. A wild animal wouldn't have a baseline in which to translate their brain waves. They wouldn't know words like "pet," "treat," or "out"—those kinds of concepts needed to be learned through a training process.

My tests concluded that whatever animal I was trying to talk with would have to be somewhat intelligent. However, any animal who could be taught a trick could learn to speak.

Knowing what was inside the ball made it a lot easier to study. It didn't matter as much what it was made *of*. What was more important was what it was made *for*: communicating with humans. I decided to use it for the same thing.

~ * ~

It was a brisk autumn night when I invited Falcone and Williams to my home to show them what I was working on. A gentle breeze wafted through the open windows and into the house, cooling it enough for both men to be wearing long sleeves.

"Good evening, gentlemen." I nodded.

"Good evening." Williams and Falcone both nodded back.

Williams got to the point. "Why have you called us here this lovely evening?"

"I have some…news," I replied.

"Uh oh." Falcone raised his eyebrow while he took a seat on the couch. "Good or bad?"

"A little of both, depending on how you react." I pointed at the couch for Williams to sit down as well.

"Well, then, let's get on with it." He sat and rubbed his hands against his thighs.

"Scraps." I turned my head while keeping my gaze on Falcone and Williams. "C'mere, boy."

Scraps came running into the room and stood attentively at my feet, waiting for instruction.

"What can I do for you, boy?" I asked the dog.

"Pet me," Scraps said.

141

I scratched him behind the ear.

"Whoa." Falcone glanced around the room. "What the hell was that?"

"Scraps, sit."

"Okay." Scraps complied. "Treat?"

"Here you go, bud." I gave Scraps the treat. "Will you play dead?"

"Treat?"

"Of course."

Scraps played dead, and I gave him a treat.

I glanced at Williams and Falcone, who were both staring back at me with lifted eyebrows like they were seeing a dinosaur in real life.

"What the fuck did I just see?" Williams asked.

"This," I held the ball up, "is what I am calling a 'Chris Ball.'"

"And what the hell is a Chris Ball?" Williams scratched his temple.

"A device that lets two different species communicate with each other using intersecting brain waves. Turns out Scraps is pretty smart when you get to know him."

"Impossible," Falcone almost slurred. "There's no way you were able to create a device that lets humans and animals speak to one another."

"I didn't say that." I turned to him.

"Then, what *are* you saying?"

"I'm saying the *Dwellers* created a device that lets humans and animals speak to one another."

"Wait a second," Williams interjected. "Did you say 'Dwellers?' What the fuck is a Dweller?"

"How on Earth were they able to do that?" Falcone didn't give me a chance to answer Williams's question.

"I'm not entirely sure. I *do* know this device can be used to talk with any moderately intelligent animal, including Dwellers."

"What makes you say that?" Falcone perked up his back and shoulders and tilted his head to the side.

"As you well know, everything with a brain emits waves of energy. If we get this ball close enough to anything with a brain, we should be able to communicate with them, in theory. That brings me to the real reason I brought you guys here. Scraps dropped this in front of me when the twins were having their display in the center of town, and I'd been completely unable to figure out what it was."

I handed the ball to Falcone.

"Since then, I've performed every possible test I could think of.

A few weeks ago, I was abducted by Creatures, who, as it turns out, prefer the term 'Dwellers.'"

"You were what!" Williams hollered. "How the fuck are you still here? What do you mean they 'prefer the term?' That's insane. What the hell are you talking about?"

"Please." I turned my palms down and slowly waved to indicate they needed to slow down. "I'll explain everything in the next two minutes."

"My God…" Falcone leaned back in his seat.

"As I was saying, I was abducted by Dwellers a few weeks ago," I repeated, ignoring Falcone. "They took me through a system of tunnels they'd dug underneath Sooth City and brought me to their lair a mile beneath the surface." I paced the room like I was giving a lecture. "There, I met what I'm calling their Council of Six, who informed me they've been trying to get in contact with us, but we literally shot the messenger who, coincidentally, was also the creator of the ball you're holding.

"In the time I've been here." I stopped. "The Dwellers have evolved more quickly than any species this planet has ever seen. It typically takes millions of years to accomplish what they have in a mere decade. Their brains have grown ten times their original size, and they informed me they are evolving past the need for human blood, which is what they were trying to communicate with us.

"Below us now is a fully functioning Dweller society, complete with citizens that'll soon be free of their dependence on human blood. They want the same things we want: an end to the bloodshed, an end to the hiding, an end to the fear." I locked my hands behind my back. "They asked me personally to try and reach out or help with their cause. Until today, I wasn't sure what I was going to do."

"You realize how ridiculous this sounds?" Williams asked.

"Of course I do," I replied. "This is a lot for me also."

"They've taken so many lives." Falcone sat forward and put his elbows on his thighs, interlocking his fingers. "Even if they apologize and refuse to eat another human being, it won't make up for the destruction they've caused."

"I know. I have been thinking about little else. You two have been good to me, better than I would have ever expected a human to treat a monster like me. I hoped telling you would be the right segue. Be proud. You're a credit to your species."

"I don't think 'proud' is the right word." Williams made air quotes with his fingers.

"It's not," Falcone agreed. "What you're asking of us can't be done. There's no way the three of us can convince the entirety of humanity that the Creatures are actually decent enough to be left alone."

"I know." I put up my hands. "If this experiment is any indication of what the rest of the world will be like, we have some real work to do."

Though begrudgingly, Falcone and Williams were acting like I knew they would—apprehensive, yet curious. All that was left to do was to keep talking.

"Look…" I sat down in the chair across from the couch and leaned forward. "This is our chance for peace…it's our *only* chance for peace. There has to be a way for us to pull this off. Otherwise, there will be no end to the violence of perpetual war."

"Who's to say things won't be the same with the Creatures living among us?" Falcone asked. "Who's to say *they* won't be the ones to overthrow *us*? Who's to say this isn't a tactic to lull us into a state of comfort? Without more testing, we can't know if your 'Chris Ball' isn't some kind of playback device with scripted answers."

"I suppose those are risks we're going to have to take if we want to try and change things as they are," I said. "DeSantos and Harrington are far too similar to give up their quest to destroy the other. Harrington hasn't been in contact with me since I left, and I'm starting to get nervous that he's planning a double-cross. If so, he'll be here soon. Maybe not today, probably not tomorrow, but he will definitely be at our gates once he's amassed an army large enough to get through our defenses.

"As far as the ball goes, we should take some time to figure it out as well. Maybe with the help of you and Williams, I can finally crack it open and see what is going on inside."

"All right." Williams stood. "I've heard enough. I want to meet these Dwellers for myself."

"I thought you'd never ask." I grinned. "Follow me."

I guided Falcone and Williams to the hole in the backyard.

"Jesus." Williams rubbed the back of his neck. "This is where they took you?"

"This is nothing," I answered.

Chapter Seventeen

When we finally made it through the tunnel, Falcone and Williams were devoid of entry-level questions to ask. We'd entered the realm in which the Dwellers could provide answers better than myself. They asked about the Dwellers's society, their diaspora, their history, and the origins of the Chris Ball. I didn't have any answers.

It was cooler in the tunnels than the previous times I'd been in them, and I noticed a strong breeze hitting me in the face. The smell of dirt and clay filled my nostrils—a combination they used to strengthen the walls. It was surprisingly effective. A force directly in the center of their cave-cities could take them down, and they placed breaking points strategically in case they needed to close access or cave-in one of the tunnels. They were good architects. I couldn't tell where the weak spots were, but I had a feeling they existed somewhere.

The light at the end of the tunnel was dimmer than before. I guessed they must be asleep, and the lights were turned down to help with their circadian rhythms.

In the town's main area, there were almost no Dwellers, where previously there were Dwellers in every conceivable direction.

"What the fuck is this?" Williams asked with an open jaw.

"This is the society the Dwellers created under our noses while we needlessly fought each other," I said. "Yes, they were once terribly mindless killing machines, but who among us can say our ancestors are without sin? I don't even know who my ancestors were. If I were a betting man, I would place my life savings on them being invested in one sin or another."

"Fair enough," Falcone said.

Between Falcone and Williams, the former was the hardest to gauge. Williams was typically a pragmatic person, and in this instance, he was showing his true inner altruist. He was reserving judgment.

I didn't blame him. The evidence in front of him was hearsay at best. I wasn't even sure myself whether the Dwellers were on the level. For all I knew, Falcone was correct, and the Chris Ball *was* a device capable of reading an AI script to formulate responses. Passing the ball around may have been the way for them to answer, each Dweller programmed to provide a response to different kinds of questions.

No. They weren't lying.

I continually reminded myself to give the Dwellers the benefit of the doubt before assuming they were being dishonest. I believed they were capable of such because of the amount of humanity they must have studied to create the Chris Ball in the first place. Scripted answers or otherwise, they were right. I was definitely inserting my own bias into the situation and needed to remember the Dwellers had as much to lose as any person I knew. They had friends, families, jobs, children— everything to live for that humans did.

To that end, they were no different.

By the time we reached the entrance to the cave wherein sat the Council, there was no activity in the town. No one was patrolling, no one was working on anything.

My feet were wet.

I looked down. There were red streaks of liquid dripping down the wedge to the entranceway at our feet.

I ducked and entered the alcove as I'd done before. This time, however, there was no fire burning.

When I stepped in, something pooled around my boots. I produced a flashlight from my pocket and turned it on.

In the circle of light, there was a mangled mass of flesh, bone, and blood.

The Council sat there cold and lifeless with stakes propping up their soon-to-be-rotting bodies.

One of the council members, Teresa, took a deep, struggling breath, like a deer with liquid in its lungs, or a cow with pneumonia.

"Holy fuck!" Williams exclaimed.

"My God..." Falcone was slack-jawed.

"Shit." I ran to her, jammed the Chris Ball in her hand, and closed her fingers tightly around it. "What happened?" I held Teresa's hand. "Who did this to you?"

"Raymond Harrington," she managed to say through deep breaths.

"How did he find you?" Williams came around and knelt near us.

"We don't know," she replied. "We think he may have been following you."

"Damn it." I stood. "He must have put eyes on me after I drained the guard in that town."

"I *still* can't believe you did that." Falcone's face tightened and turned red.

"I had no other choice!" I snapped. "It was either that or kill everyone in the outpost. Which would you have preferred?"

"No." Williams got up and put a hand on Falcone's chest. "We don't have time for this."

"If this is true and Harrington did this," I let go of Teresa's hand and turned to Falcone and Williams, "then we need to get back to Sooth City on the double. I'll go ahead of you and try to stop the Noor before they get there."

"Wait." She breathed heavily. "Some of us were able to escape. There is a cave of Dweller soldiers on the other side of the forest. If you follow the tunnel to your left, you'll find them. They are ready to help you hold off the Noor. It should take you no more than a few minutes to get there if you travel alone."

"Okay." I got up and stepped toward the alcove entrance. "I'll get there as fast as I can."

"Hold on." Williams put a hand on my shoulder and stopped me. "How the hell are the two of us supposed to get back to the city before the Noor?"

"You *may* not." I was halfway out of the cave.

"Fine, let's get going," Williams said in a low tone.

Falcone and Williams headed in the direction of the tunnels.

I aimed myself toward the tunnel Teresa pointed out, and ran, leaping off rocks to get to the entrance. Stopping at the threshold, I listened for anything on the other end that sounded off, some rocks falling, screaming, anything that might tell me I was headed into danger.

I heard nothing other than the lingering static of silence encased the tunnel.

I went in.

This particular tunnel was one-way between the city and camp Teresa was sending me to. I didn't bother slowing at any of the curves to inspect them. Instead, I continued without slowing down, racing through turns and ducking through entrances.

When I arrived at the opening, there was nothing that appeared to be a camp in which the Dwellers would live. It wasn't nearly as extravagant as the first Dweller city I'd visited.

The air was unmoving in the cavern.

"Hello," I said to an empty room. "Is there anyone here? I was sent by Teresa of the Council of Six."

One Dweller came out from behind a rock.

I moved forward, but the Dweller was apprehensive—he or she seemed frightened of me and had probably never heard a human voice it could understand before.

I took the ball from my pocket and walked carefully toward the middle of the space between the Dweller and the opening of the cave.

"I'm not here to hurt you." I inched forward. "I'm here to help you. I need your assistance in defeating Raymond Harrington, the man who drove you into hiding."

I placed the ball on the ground a few feet from the Dweller and stepped back.

It came forward and took the ball. "You must be Trevor Mason." She extended her hand and I accepted it.

"I must *be*." I wanted to be almost anyone else.

"I am known as Charlotte. The Council told us you might be coming."

"Where is everyone? I was told there was a town here."

Charlotte made a noise I couldn't decipher, and several hundred Dwellers decloaked themselves. They were everywhere.

Never had I seen a Dweller hide so naturally in its environment. Each one took on the precise color of whatever they were touching, so they blended in perfectly with their surroundings.

"How are you able to do that?" I asked.

She motioned to the room full of Dwellers behind her with her arm. "For the past few months we've been altering our biochemistry with animals adept at camouflage, particularly chameleons. We've been breeding them and drinking their blood to help us relieve our dependency on humans."

So, the Council *was* telling the truth. They were now able to take the blood memory of any animal they ate and use it to alter their evolutionary characteristics.

"Incredible." I looked around at the Dwellers.

"If you're here," she looked down with her surprisingly human-like face, "then the Council is gone, and you need our help defending your city."

"Right." I locked my fingers behind my back.

A dweller came up from behind Charlotte and took the ball from her hand.

"How do we know we can trust you?" he asked.

"Look," I replied, "I know humans are not the best thing the planet's ever produced, but we both need them to survive. For me, like yourselves, I have been aware that humans could be more than food for no more than a short time. In that time, the ones I have come to trust have been worthy of such."

I couldn't believe what I was saying. If someone told me a century prior that I would be appealing to giant creatures about the pros of putting an end to war, I would have sunk my teeth into them for the sheer irony.

"You want an end to the needless hunting and killing?" I asked. "This is your chance to prove you are more than your original programming. If the Sooth know you are helping them to defeat a common enemy, they will be far more willing to listen to you when it's over. Rally around them, and they will show you they can be warm and goodhearted. Of course, not all of them are good, but the ones that *are* make the bad ones seem insignificant.

"Right now, there is a city up there exactly like yours which can't defend itself from the massive storm barreling upon them. If we move now, we can stop the Noor soldiers before they reach Sooth City gates."

Charlotte and the other Dweller conferred with each other.

After a second, Charlotte took the ball. "What's the plan?"

The truth was, there was no plan. I hadn't prepared any contingency for Harrington performing a full-frontal assault on Sooth City. Trusting him was a bad idea. I didn't think he would be audacious enough to storm the front gates after such a short amount of time. That Harrington couldn't have been fully prepared with enough equipment and tactical discussion was our best potential advantage.

"Follow me." I waved to the Dwellers.

I took the platoon of fifty Dwellers back through the main city tunnel, then to one leading to the outskirts of Sooth City.

When we got to the surface, it was surprisingly quiet. The night was windy, and it was difficult to hear.

Either Harrington hadn't arrived, or he'd come and gone, I couldn't tell which. I instructed Charlotte and the rest of the Dwellers to hide in several tunnel exits along different vantage points throughout the forest. When Harrington's army *did* pass, we would be ready to surprise them.

After a few minutes, I heard the clamoring of footsteps beating a war drum on the forest floor. I felt them in the roots beneath my feet.

I leaped up through the treetops to try and get a better view of their position.

Harrington led the pack from atop a slow-moving ATV. Behind him were thousands of ground troops armed to the teeth. They were accompanied by a squadron of mech tanks and ten armored trucks carrying additional soldiers.

There'd be no reasoning with him. We were going to have to fight.

Chapter Eighteen

From my position in the tree, I would be able to see when Harrington was outside the ballistic range of Sooth City.

The troops were getting closer.

I hadn't talked to Falcone or Williams since leaving the cave, and I hoped they were prepared to witness the Dwellers and me fighting alongside one another. In my gut, I knew seeing the Dwellers vulnerable and in need of help convinced Falcone and Williams they were capable of redemption.

Or, at least, I hoped it had.

What I wasn't sure of was how they planned to hold off Harrington, if at all. There was a distinct possibility that Falcone and Williams sold us out to DeSantos and decided to let us duke it out amongst ourselves before deciding whether or not to get involved.

There was a lot of uncertainty, but none of it mattered. If the Noor got through my team of Dwellers, Sooth City was fucked either way.

Harrington and the Noor drew closer.

I had no weapons, so I relied on whatever strength was in my reserves to get me close enough to Harrington to drain him or rip his lying throat out.

This would be the first time I would enter a battle I wasn't sure I could win. I would win in a fistfight, having been in many, yet I wasn't sure I could lead an army.

I stared at the Chris Ball in my hand.

It was the one tool I owned which might help direct the Dwellers and give them orders. I hoped they would hear me, but again, I wasn't sure what the range of the ball truly was.

I was ready to end Harrington right then and there. I wanted him dead. There was a twitch in the back of my neck that wasn't going anywhere, and I wanted to make sure Harrington got what was coming to him.

"Now!" I yelled when Harrington was close enough for me to see his balding head. I jumped at him with tremendous force.

He grinned a crooked smile at me. "Attack!"

A swarm of serpent-like Dwellers emerged like a flock of birds. They were jumping everywhere, landing on soldiers, and ripping their heads off when they ran through them.

Terrified screams bellowed from every direction as Dwellers tore soldiers open like they were ragdolls. The Dwellers were doing their jobs perfectly.

I took the soldier closest to me, moving fast enough he didn't notice me until it was much too late. I gripped his head and shoulder, spreading them to expose his neck. I sank my fangs into his jugular. His blood poured into my mouth and down my chin. I swallowed, then moved on to the next.

A soldier charged at me with a knife. I spun around and swept his legs with my own. I jammed the side of my hand into his throat when he hit the ground. The soldier choked on his larynx and spit blood onto his chest. He gurgled, then his muscles relaxed, and he fell to the side.

Harrington was off in the distance staring at me like I was the only thing he could see.

I leaped high in his direction and landed fifty feet in front of him. He revved his ATV and charged in my direction.

When he got into second gear, he hopped off the vehicle and let it shoot at me like a missile. I jumped and cleared the ATV, starting my run at Harrington the second I landed. I went for him with my fangs exposed.

"What the fuck are you?" he screamed.

When I got close, he caught me, one hand on my chest, the other at my belt. Bending, he hoisted me over his shoulders then threw me to the dirt.

I hopped off my back and lunged at him, this time going low for his feet. He flipped in the air and landed hard on his back. I jumped at him, intending to land on top and sink my teeth into his neck or the side of his head. Harrington rolled out of the way, and I landed with one knee on the earth, hands clenched in fists.

"You can't stop this!" He threw his hands up.

I ran toward him full speed, picked him up then slammed him to the ground. All of the air left his lungs, and he gasped. After he breathed in, he let out a cough that startled me.

I pounded my fist onto the side of his skull again and again.

Harrington kicked his knees and wrapped his ankles around my neck.

The roles reversed, and now he was jamming his fists on the side of *my* head.

"What are you trying to accomplish here, boy?" he screamed. "What do you want from us?"

Though I wasn't completely drained, I was losing energy every time he landed a blow.

"I want peace." I groaned.

"Bullshit! I saw what you did to those soldiers. Now that I know what you are, everything makes sense. You and those abominations want nothing more than food. You never wanted to help us destroy the Creatures!"

"You're wrong," I said.

What if he was right? Were Falcone, Cap, Williams, and Dustin truly enough to get me to change my mind on the entire species?

Probably not. I truly believed, if nothing else, the end would justify my means.

"I don't think I am." Harrington hammered my face and temples.

I couldn't speak. Fist after fist filled my field of vision.

The next thing I knew, a Dweller tackled him.

A Noor soldier shot the Dweller off Harrington before it tore into him.

I heard yelling behind me. The battle was interrupted by a new platoon coming from the direction of Sooth City. I couldn't tell through the commotion and head trauma, but I hoped it was Falcone and Williams coming to save my ass.

The second wave of soldiers was more than the Noor could handle. The Sooth soldiers surged forward, and the Noor fell back. Dwellers flew past me, overwhelming Noor forces as they continued to scream and fruitlessly fire their weapons.

"Retreat!" Harrington turned around and waved for his men to follow him.

A cheer roared from the Sooth City soldiers as the Noor retreated.

The world spun around me, and after a second, I couldn't hold myself steady. My eyes grew dim, and my body buckled under its own weight.

I stared at the sky. It was getting brighter as the sun made its way above the horizon line. The world went black.

~ * ~

I awoke to Scraps licking my face. I was at home, in my bed, with Scraps keeping guard over me.

"Finally," a voice said.

Williams and Falcone were sitting on the chairs in the reading nook of my room. There were IVs attached to both of their arms, and the tubes coming from the other ends led to me.

"What the fuck?" I asked no one in particular. "How am I...?"

"Good evening." Williams gave me a slight smile.

"What the hell happened? How am I not dead right now?"

"You don't remember?"

I tilted my head down and looked back and forth. "I remember something ripped Harrington off me, and the Noor were retreating."

"That was me." Charlotte stepped out from behind me.

"Holy shit!" I spun around.

I hadn't seen her in the room, and I was shocked she was there.

"Sorry," I relaxed. "It's been a long night. How did you survive, Charlotte?"

"After I tackled Harrington," she stepped forward, "we tumbled around before another soldier was able to shoot me off him. Captain Falcone here, shot the soldier, and I made my escape during the retreat."

I raised an eyebrow at Falcone.

"It's true." He returned the gesture.

"Does that mean—"

"For now." He crossed his arms.

"And Harrington?"

"We think he got away," Williams answered. "No one was able to find his body in the wreckage. However, there is some good news."

"Harrington didn't get close enough to the gates to do any damage," Falcone said, "and he hasn't been heard from since the battle. There's been no attempt to make contact with anyone in Sooth City."

"How is DeSantos taking the news?" I wondered aloud.

"Exactly how you'd expect," Williams said. "But we have bigger things to worry about when it comes to DeSantos."

"Of course, we do." I leaned my back against the headboard.

"DeSantos will be here any minute now to discuss the whole situation."

"That doesn't seem so bad."

"Well...he's seen what you can do now, and he has a lot of questions the three of us weren't exactly able to answer."

"Such as?"

154

"Such as, why you sank your teeth into that soldier's neck, and how you are so fucking strong and fast."

"I see."

Luckily, there was an answer to all of those questions, and they were all the same.

Chapter Nineteen

As promised, DeSantos arrived a moment later. He came into my room without knocking or announcing himself, the same hardened expression on his face as the first time I'd seen him.

He instructed Falcone, Williams, and Charlotte to stay close in case he needed any of them. Falcone and Williams unhooked themselves from the IV tubes and left the room.

In the time I was asleep, DeSantos had come to some positive conclusion regarding the Dwellers. It gave me a good feeling that I might be able to get to the other end of the conversation without running for my life.

There was nowhere for me to run. There were no supplies left within a close enough radius to survive without human interaction, and there was a big part of me that didn't care to continue fighting simply to survive. Essentially, I was at the end of my rope.

DeSantos picked up one of the chairs and placed it next to the nightstand on the right side of the bed. He sat down, put his elbows on his knees and took a deep breath. He then interlocked his fingers and rested his chin on the knuckles atop the pyramid.

"The past twenty-four hours have been quite informative," he finally said.

"I know," I pleaded. "But—"

DeSantos put a finger up to indicate I was to be quiet and listen.

"In the time you've been here," he stood and paced around the room, "we've had Creature attacks, mysterious deaths, not-so-mysterious deaths, and a slew of additional issues. Even the things I *knew* went according to plan, went according to someone *else's* plan. Falcone and Williams were nice enough to let me know about Operation Phantom. How did you get Harrington to agree to destroy his own buildings like that? You'll have to teach me your skills as an orator." He stopped pacing and looked directly at me.

"I have seen some fucked up shit in my day." He leaned over slightly. "But, never have I seen a man sink fangs into another human being, move as fast as you did, or toss around a grown adult like a rag doll. So, tell me…what are you really?"

"You wouldn't believe me if I told you," I replied.

"Try me." He started pacing again.

I got up. "Have you ever seen *Nos Feratu*?"

"Let's pretend I haven't."

"In that case…I am what *you* might call a vampire."

"Bullshit," he snapped. "You're telling me vampires exist?"

"No." My face tightened and grew a little warm. "But I am saying I'm likely what humans would call a vampire. The plural implies there are more vampires at large, and as far as I know, there are no other creatures in the world, other than the Dwellers, that are anyway similar."

"Saying for a moment I believe you." He returned to his seat. "How long have you been a vampire?"

"For longer than you would imagine." I leaned forward and met his gaze.

"If there are no vampires other than yourself, how did you get to be one?"

"I have no idea." I shrugged. "I can start from the beginning if you'd like."

"I would." He straightened his back in the chair.

"One night, I woke up buried in the ground, struggling to breathe. I pulled my way from the dirt, and when I emerged, there was a group of men standing over me. I didn't recognize the way they were dressed. I had no idea who they were or how I got there, and I possessed no memory.

"It's possible I had a family, friends, a life…I was in a full grown adult male body, so I assume at some point I must have been born. It's also extremely possible that I am a demon summoned to this realm by heretics looking to play a cruel joke on the world. I don't know which is the full truth. I never got the elders to tell me."

DeSantos sat back in his chair. He didn't take his eyes off me. His blank, expressionless face made it hard to tell what he was thinking at the time.

"When I first awoke, I was among the Native Americans. I lived with them for nearly a hundred and fifty years in peace. I was there to make sure their territory stayed safe from harm. They summoned me after an attack on their hunting group left them lacking protection. In exchange for blood, I was the one who patrolled the territory." I turned my body so I was sitting on the edge of the bed, locking my elbows while I held up my torso with my hands.

"Legends grew around the monster protecting the tribe." I heaved a troubled sigh. "They kept me fed with a daily sacrifice. Much like Cap, Falcone, and Williams, they rotated citizens who made sure I was satisfied. I was a God to them. Or at least they treated me as such. I wanted for nothing, and I needed nothing.

"Then, when the English took the new world, my tribe was overrun. They came at us with technology I'd never seen before. One end of their weapon flashed, and in the blink of an eye, whatever was on the other end had a hole in it. It was like magic at the time.

"Not even I could stop the onslaught of soldiers with their new weapons." I lowered my shoulders. "Eventually, I was left on the battlefield alone, standing in rivers of blood up to my knees—men, women, and children slaughtered at my feet."

DeSantos went all the way down in his chair and rested his forearms on the arm rests. He looked down, no longer making eye contact with me. I thought maybe he was starting to feel sorry for me.

I had never told the story out loud before and thinking about everything that had been sacrificed was making my heart heavy, and my palms started to sweat a little.

"After the carnage, I exiled myself from humanity, never to be seen again by anyone who wasn't going to die. I'm not entirely sure what year it was when I was reborn, but I can tell you I have lived for hundreds of years. I'm afraid I lost count quite some time ago."

DeSantos's face slumped a little. "You were around for the American Revolution? I find that hard to swallow. How the hell do you look so young?"

"To that," I answered, "I have no reply. I haven't investigated my own anatomy past what will harm me, and even then, I'm not positive I've discovered everything."

"And what would harm you?" he asked slowly.

"For sure the sun. A lack of human blood will send me into a psychopathic rage and possibly kill me after a few days. Silver burns my skin. I've never jammed a wooden stake through my heart. I can't eat human food without becoming ill, including garlic. Other than that, your guess is as good as mine. I stopped my research after realizing the less I knew about how I *could* die, the better."

"I see why you were reluctant to tell me this." He scooted back in his chair and furrowed his brow.

"I know, but think about it this way. The Dwellers exist and have the same characteristics as me, save that they were incapable of controlling what they ate until recently. If they can exist on this planet under our noses for so long, who's to say werewolves aren't real, or magic. For all we really know, ghosts are literally haunting us right now."

"I guess that's a good point." His face relaxed. "What else can you tell me about the creatures you are now calling 'Dwellers?' And what can you tell me about the red ball we found on you after the attack."

"I was the first to discover the Dwellers, and since then, they have evolved unlike anything I've ever seen. They can manipulate their own traits to match that of anything they want. If it's in their 'blood memory,' as they call it, they can develop eyes, hands, feet, or any evolutionary feature they wish. In the last year, they were able to create a device capable of letting two species talk to each other. No doubt you've met my dog Scraps? Well, we've had some surprising conversations talking about play and food."

"So, you're able to communicate with them?" His ears wiggled a little, and his back straightened.

"I *am*." I pointed at him. "You are too. Anyone can communicate with any Dweller they want using the red ball. The potential uses are endless."

DeSantos got up and ran his hand over his head. It was clear he was starting to believe me, which was good because I wasn't prepared for such a thorough interrogation. He went over to the window and stared into it for a moment, peering at the darkness. It took me a second to realize he was staring at his own reflection.

After a while, he sat back down.

I adjusted my position on the bed so I was resting against the backboard.

"What does this mean for us?" DeSantos asked eventually.

"It depends on who you mean when you say 'us.' Are you referring to humanity, the Sooth, or Sooth City?" I asked.

"All of the above. If everything you say is true, we are all at the complete mercy of you and the Dwellers. We can offer redemption to the Dwellers, but will the Dwellers let us redeem ourselves? Are they willing to do that? Are you?"

"Look, we all want the same thing. The Dwellers want you to stop hunting them, and in return, the Dwellers will stop hunting people. They want peaceful coexistence."

"I'm not even sure we're capable." DeSantos stared at his hands.

"Neither am I," I said. "But there is only one way to find out. If we *can* try, don't we owe it to ourselves to do so? I've met some humans recently I know for sure are willing to give it a shot. Sure, some won't understand at first, but they will eventually."

"You're old enough." DeSantos peered at me. "I assume you see what happens when people perceived as different are introduced. We tend not to remain calm in situations where we think they're in danger. The KKK, the National Socialist Party, and the rise of Communism in the late twenty-third century, were all people who were scared to death of what they did not understand. You and I know better, but we will have to deal with a lot of the same hate speech disenfranchised groups hear. The difference this time, is the Dwellers are guilty of the crimes of which they are accused."

"Don't you see?" I snapped. "That's exactly the problem. Half of the Dweller population alive right now have never tasted a drop of homosapien blood. Should the actions of their ancestors condemn them to a life of hiding in fear of what *you* might do? You of all people should understand. Your grandfather was one of the most bloodthirsty men I've ever witnessed. Would you want the Dwellers to hold you to the same standard? All the good you've done, blown into oblivion because of actions over which you had no control?"

"I suppose not." He looked down, silent for a moment before speaking again. "For the first time in my life, I have no idea what to say to the townspeople."

"Leave it to me," I said. "Give me one week, and I'll tell everyone at family dinner."

"Are you sure you want to do that?" He put a finger up to his temple and rested his head on it.

"No, not really, but there's going to have to be a time where I tell everyone, and it might as well be now."

"Deal." He grabbed my hand and shook it. "In that case…what do we do next?"

"I'm not sure."

~ * ~

After meeting with DeSantos, Williams and Falcone came back into my room.

"How did it go?" Williams asked.

"Exactly as well as you'd expect," I replied.

"So," Falcone said, "what now?"

I scratched my head behind my ears. "I told DeSantos I would explain everything to the townspeople at family dinner next week, but that doesn't help us with Harrington and Noor Village. They're going to hit us again, and this time we have to be more prepared."

"What if we don't wait for Harrington at all?" Williams asked.

"What are you proposing?" Falcone looked at him.

"I'm proposing we take the fight to Harrington ourselves. We have a full army of Dwellers at our disposal. You two saw what they were able to do to those soldiers. If we plan a coordinated attack, we might have a chance to damage Noor Village enough to get them to stop."

"That's not possible." I got up from the edge of the bed and moved to the chair.

"Why not?" Williams asked.

"If we do that," I turned to Williams, "then we're in the exact same spot we have been. The way to get rid of Harrington using violence would be to kill everyone in Noor Village and any other Noor who decided they wanted revenge for their fallen comrades. No, we can't outright attack them."

"We know he doesn't respond to diplomacy, which doesn't leave us with many options." Falcone took a seat on the bed.

"I know it doesn't," I said. "But a full frontal assault on Noor Village will further ignite war."

I needed some time to myself to determine what to do next. If neither violence nor diplomacy would work with Harrington, what would? In general, the one thing truly capable of changing a human's mind is to see the outcome applied to them or a loved one. Harrington was a monster. It was clear no amount of planning could prepare us for whatever it was he had in store for Sooth City, especially after a failed attack. His pride was sure to be bruised.

I needed to think of a way to use the Dwellers to our advantage without throwing them to the lions.

"If anyone has any ideas, now would be the time." I looked at Williams and Falcone.

They stared at each other without speaking.

"What happened to Charlotte?" I glanced over to see if she was outside the open door.

"She went to her people to debrief them and see how they feel," Falcone said.

"And DeSantos, he let her leave?" I frowned a little.

"Correct." Williams sat next to Falcone.

"What did she say to him? I can't believe they talked. Someone should mark the day."

"Don't worry." Falcone laughed a little. "Someone will. As for the conversation DeSantos and Charlotte had, you'll have to ask one of them about it. Neither of us thought it appropriate to sit in."

"Hmm." I grunted. "Yeah, that was probably a good call. What time is it?"

"Sunup is in twenty minutes," Williams replied.

"Shit. Okay, there's nothing I can do about this until tonight."

"Haven't you slept enough?"

"I'm not going to be sleeping," I said.

Chapter Twenty

I got up from the bed, my limbs and muscles no longer aching. I went to the vanity mirror to see how I was healing. My wounds were mostly closed.

There weren't many Dwellers left in the underground city. I would be able to get to Charlotte's alcove from there. I could have made it through the tunnel entrance outside of town, but there were any number of Noor soldiers waiting in the forest for me, not to mention it would be impossible to avoid the sunlight.

At my behest Williams and Falcone were helping me come up with a palatable way to tell the rest of the Sooth that fearing the Dwellers was pointless. They obliged. After all, they were the only people in the world who knew what it was like to digest my story, and they were in a unique position to explain the way they would have preferred hearing it.

They agreed not to reveal anything regarding my vampirism, because I *did* still need blood, and the people in the town were likely to take that bit of news poorly. I didn't want to be a martyr until I was done helping them. After the war was over, I would accept whatever fate the Sooth had in store for me. I'd lived long enough. I'd seen everything there was to see in the world. If they wanted me hanged, so be it. If they wanted to put me up on a pedestal, I would let them. If they wanted to make me a martyr and chase me for the rest of their lives, then I would run as long as I could.

There was a whole world of possibilities, so many ways they could take it all. Based on what I knew of their history, the cold feeling which started in my brain and went into my stomach told me they would let their nature get in the way of pragmatism.

I was right to be afraid. Humans were as savage as the Dwellers had been in their past, and their capacity to act violent was staggering.

Ducking into the tunnel in my backyard, I made my way toward the Dweller town beneath Sooth City. The air inside was moist and dank like always. This time it was almost welcomed, pleasant even. I listened for any sounds coming from the other end, and there was nothing other than static.

When I got to the end of the road, I was still expecting to see a bustling community, but the Dweller's home was no longer active. Instead, there were massive machines throughout the cave laying still, motionless and deadlocked in their positions. Harrington was building something in the town. There was a hundred-foot communications tower in the middle of the cave responsible for the static I was hearing. There were guards manning several outposts placed in the corners of the new city.

There were voices off in the distance coming toward me. I bent my knees and ducked my head behind the cave entrance. The static sound made it difficult to discern, but the voices belonged to Raymond Harrington and a female. The woman's voice was familiar, but I couldn't put my finger on it for some reason. Maybe I didn't want to.

As they drew closer, I jumped to the nearest platform, hiding behind a large rock.

"This whole place is going to need serious restructuring if we're going to use it as a new base of operations," Harrington said to the woman he was with.

I could only see them from behind, but the woman had dark hair and was close to six feet tall. It was Marina Vander.

The pair stopped and turned to each other.

His face was bruised, and he walked with a bit of a limp. He otherwise remained unharmed.

"Affirmative," she said with a straight face. "We've begun construction on the steel beams needed to reinforce the structures, and the team has already started expansion to get the rest of our equipment down here."

"Perfect." He started walking again. "Have you determined what happened to the Creatures that inhabited this place?"

"As far as we can tell, those not destroyed in the altercation outside Sooth City have all relocated to parts unknown. We have recon teams searching the tunnel system to see where they might have gone, but our efforts have turned up nothing."

"Find them." His face grew dark underneath his brow. "I don't care what you have to do."

"Affirmative."

"And what of the vampire?"

What little there was of a heart skipped a beat in my chest. Harrington had put the clues together and determined my true nature.

I wondered why he hadn't acted yet. It seemed like the perfect opportunity to throw me under the bus to DeSantos and the rest of the humans. Instead, Harrington was planning his expansion into the underworld.

I shifted my position, and a few pebbles fell to the ground. Though the rocks were small, the sound echoed off the walls like they were boulders. I hid myself as best I could, praying they see me.

"What was that?" Marina glanced around cautiously.

He snapped for her attention. "Just a rat, I'm sure. Now, tell me about the vampire."

"He's recovering in Sooth City." Her face dropped.

"Shit." He tugged on his ear a little. "I was hoping we got him."

This was terrible. They knew who I was and what I was doing. Seeing Marina working with Harrington was a bad sign for me and for Sooth City. I wanted to jump down and drain both of them right then and there, but there were guards everywhere, and I couldn't risk being captured.

"The vampire was close to death, but he acquired the blood he needed to survive, and he is now resting comfortably."

I needed to leave the vicinity, but I couldn't find an escape route. I was directly above Harrington and Marina, and any movement was sure to cause them to notice.

"All right." He patted her on the shoulder. "Keep up the good work. Let me know if anything else develops."

"Yes, sir."

She broke off and headed in the direction of the tunnels.

"I can hear you up there." He turned his head up at me when she was no longer in earshot.

I leaped off the platform and landed ten feet in front of him.

"How long?" I asked.

"Since the death of her brother," he frowned. "She never forgave you for leading him on a suicide mission."

"I haven't forgiven myself." I peered down at my feet.

Harrington chuckled.

"How did you find out about me?" I looked back up to meet his gaze.

"I suspected something was amiss when you came to Noor Village, but Marina confirmed it for me when you returned from your little mission. No one can travel that fast, and I knew no Creature could have infiltrated one of my camps so easily." He started walking toward me. I stepped back in case he was going to try and capture me, but instead he walked past me. I followed him.

"The cover up was far too clean for a Creature attack. You were sloppy in your haste to get back to Sooth City and explain away why you lost two of their best men for a nothing mission. Then, when I saw you rip your fangs into my men, I knew exactly what you were."

He was right. I was sloppy on my way back to Sooth City because I assumed I would be safe once I got there. During the battle, I used my fangs and didn't care whether Harrington saw them. I didn't count on Marina Vander's grief to manifest itself to the point she would betray her family. At the same time, I understood she no longer had a family. Her brother was gone. Her parents became isolated and reclusive, and more or less disappeared into their work. DeSantos, Falcone, Williams, and I were equally responsible for Dustin's death, and we were easy to blame for the misery she was feeling. She had no one left.

This was all my fault. If I'd reached out to her when she was grieving, I might have been able to stop this.

It was no wonder she sought refuge in the one place she knew her malicious intent would be nurtured.

Her rage would have been a welcome surprise for Harrington, who sought to keep the flames of hatred fanned for those who wanted to see the Sooth in embers.

I didn't have time to continue thinking, and I certainly didn't have time to let him pontificate.

"What now?" I asked, brandishing my fangs in expectation of a fight.

"Now," he said, "you get the fuck away from here."

"You're not going to try and have me killed?"

"No, I'm not. You're a large part of my plan. If we fight now, you wouldn't be around for the finale, and we definitely want you nice and healthy to witness it."

I backed away from him before he changed his mind. I wasn't sure I had enough energy to take him on right then and there.

I hurried back to my house. In my head, I could all but hear the screams of the townspeople as Noor troops tore upon the city, Harrington's men burning everything while people frantically ran back and forth.

It was too late.

Whatever he planned, there was nothing I could do to stop it.

Everything I'd done was leading to that moment. Every drop of blood I drank to keep myself alive meant nothing if I couldn't save the people of Sooth City from the harbinger of death, Raymond Harrington.

Finally getting to the entrance in my basement, I couldn't hear anything. I lifted myself from the hole and ran to the front door. I threw it open, expecting mayhem.

"Ow!" I yelled the moment the sun hit my skin.

Putting my arm up, I shielded my face from the sun's rays.

The city was operating like any other day. No Vikings were pillaging the village, nothing was out of the ordinary.

So why the fuck had Harrington let me go?

As the worst of my fears went unconfirmed, I exhaled a large breath.

I wasn't sure what to do next.

Did I run and tell DeSantos that Harrington was up to something? Did I say nothing and call his bluff? If he *was* bluffing, why did he let me go free? Was there any possible way I could predict what he was going to do next?

My brain couldn't figure it out. A simple attack didn't seem grandiose enough. Harrington's scheme must have been more violent than I could imagine. Whatever he had in store for the Sooth was big. Big enough I couldn't affect the outcome.

As I made my way back in the house, my eyes were heavy, then my stomach growled.

I went through the hallway, walked into my room, then disrobed, throwing my clothes haphazardly onto the floor. After making sure the curtains were extra tight, I got into bed.

~ * ~

I was awoken abruptly by Williams who was standing over me shaking my arm back and forth.

"We have a problem," he said.

"Of course, we do," I replied, my voice hoarse. "What's wrong now?"

"DeSantos jumped the gun and told the town who you are."

I hopped up from the bed. "Are you shitting me?" I yelled.

"Get ready." He stared hard at me. "You have some explaining to do."

I couldn't believe DeSantos. Why would he give me time then sweep the rug out from under me?

I put on the plainest clothes in my closet, hopefully, to humanize and humble myself. I thought quickly on what I would say.

"Marina is a traitor," I said nervously while I got ready.

"We know." Falcone was in the corner of the room, arms

crossed.

"How?"

"It's not a coincidence DeSantos told everyone," Williams said. "It's not his fault. Marina came in this afternoon and explained everything to DeSantos. She gave him an ultimatum...either tell everyone the truth about the vampire living among them, or Harrington would."

"Crap." I rubbed my temples with my fingers. "I guess I can't blame him. What's the temperature?"

"Nobody has a torch lit if that's what you're asking, but they *do* want answers." Falcone peered out the window.

"Okay," I replied.

I went to the door and inhaled a deep breath before taking the handle. The sun was almost down, so the pain to my eyes was minimal, barely enough to make me squint. I could hear the low murmur of people outside the house.

There was a crowd of two hundred people standing there, waiting for answers.

It went silent as I stood there. No one spoke a single word. You could've heard a pin drop a mile away if the wind wasn't blowing. "Look—"

"What the fuck is going on here?" a man's voice bellowed from the crowd.

A rumble destroyed the calm and silence. A few words here and there turned into a low rambling of indistinguishable phrases. It turned into a loud roar, as the yelling became screaming.

"Leave this place!"

"Stay away from our children, you monster!"

DeSantos pushed his way through, and the throng of people parted like the Red Sea. "Enough!" he yelled, his booming speech echoing over the din. "Let the man speak."

"Why the hell should we do that?" a woman's voice cut through the crowd.

"Listen," DeSantos said. "This man has done a lot for us. He's put his life on the line like the rest of you. I don't want you to like him, or agree with him, or accept what he is, but I'll be damned if you aren't going to listen to what he has to say first."

The crowd grew silent again.

I wasn't sure what I was going to say, but I needed to say something.

"I don't truly know what I am." I put my arms behind my back. "I've been around for a long time, and I'll be the first to admit humanity

168

has not always been my favorite.

"For ages, I've had no one. A year ago, I wouldn't have cared enough to come to you. I would never have been the kind of person who cared enough to consort with anyone other than myself. But then I found Sooth City.

"This isn't exactly how I wanted to show you who I am, but now it looks like I have no choice. I believe I am what you would call a vampire."

I showed them my fangs.

"What does that even mean?" the first man said a little more calmly than before.

"It means a lot of things." I retracted my fangs. "But…mostly it means I need blood to survive. The reason I came here in the first place was to save my own ass. Since then, I've learned that you are more than a simple meal for me to consume. I've learned that if I want to continue living with people, I have to show them who I truly am. Otherwise, there can be no peace for anyone. I've lived in the Dwellers's shadows for decades, and it's time for me to step into the light."

I looked over the crowd to see how they might be reacting. They all seemed to be waiting on bated breath. None of them were making any kind of face that would indicate they were upset or happy about what I was saying to them.

"I know now the Dwellers are no longer capable of using humans as food, which makes me the one real threat left on the planet. I would understand if you wanted me strung up by the heels and put into the sun. I won't try to stop you. But I want you all to know, right here and now, I am here for you. I need you to survive. Sooth City can be the kind of community that doesn't have to worry about the threat of violence from any source."

I paced around the porch.

"Right now, Raymond Harrington is planning something big. I'm not sure what it is, but he's working on a way to destroy this city and everyone inside, to prove a point. He's building a base of operations in the Dweller city beneath us, and you can bet he's going to use it.

"I don't want to be an enemy of the people. I am going to help you out of this. I will make sure the Raymond Harrington's of the world don't get the satisfaction of picking on those they perceive as weak."

I stopped. "You are all stronger than you know. There is a massive world out there and only one Ray Harrington. The Dwellers aren't a factor. If you can accept the Dwellers, I hope you can find it in your hearts to do the same for me."

I quit talking. I wasn't expecting a cheer, but I also wasn't expecting what happened next.

Starting with the man who first questioned me, the crowd dissipated without saying anything.

I wasn't sure what to make of it.

Had I done a good job of explaining I wanted to help them survive? Had I convinced them? I couldn't imagine it was going to be as easy as a few words, especially the few that'd come out of my mouth.

After the last person left, I went back into the house, not bothering to close the door. I sat at the kitchen table and stared at the surface.

Williams, Falcone, and DeSantos followed me inside.

"That went well." Williams closed the door.

"Did it?" I asked.

DeSantos took the chair across from me. "It may not seem like it now, but they'll come to understand. Right now, they need some time to process. I don't think any of them were expecting a vampire to be living in their midst.

"They know you. They've seen you fight for them. You've sunk your teeth into this community and taken responsibility for its safety. Pun intended."

"Have they though?" I leaned back and closed my eyes. "Or have they seen a man who was so desperate to survive he did the one thing he thought unthinkable? Do they know I want them to live, or was I simply caught?"

"I suppose we won't know *that* until later." Williams took the seat next to me.

Falcone was more than his usual quiet self that evening. He stood in the doorway behind me with his hands in his pockets. I wondered what was going on in his head.

"What do you make of it?" I turned around and asked him directly.

"I'm not sure." He didn't break his gaze. "You're both right. I think half of them looked terrified, and the other half didn't know what to do with themselves. There is a distinct possibility they will string you up in the sunlight, but if you want *my* opinion, we're good for now."

I couldn't help feeling like Falcone was omitting something. Some miniscule detail I didn't see yet. There was also the chance I was being paranoid and starting to suspect everyone the way I should have suspected Marina.

Marina.

I'd almost forgotten about her.

Her defection wasn't a surprise. That said, I wasn't upset with her so much as I was disappointed in myself for being blind enough to assume her brother's death impacted her to the point where she'd remain a non-factor. She'd vowed in her speech she would get revenge, but I never fathomed she would do something like joining Harrington and the Noor in their quest to destroy Sooth City.

"Never mind the vampire stuff." I looked DeSantos directly in the eyes. "What are you going to do about Harrington and Marina? If they are planning an attack, you can bet it'll be soon."

"Is there anything else we can do?" Williams replied. "We gear up and get ready for battle."

"That isn't going to work." Falcone moved to the corner of the room behind DeSantos.

"What other choice do we have?" DeSantos asked.

The room went silent.

"How about the Dwellers?" Williams put his hands on the table.

"No," I replied. "I won't see them become a weapon against the Noor. That makes us no better than Harrington."

"How do you reason with a man like him?" Williams's shoulders lifted.

"I'm not sure, but I know we have to plan something other than a counter-attack. Whatever we do has to be more clever. I understand lives will be lost no matter what, but we have to do what we can to minimize the loss to the best of our abilities."

"How does one defend themselves without retaliating?" Falcone turned to peer out the window.

There were a lot of good questions being thrown around and not a lot of answers.

The truth was, I didn't know what we were going to do about Harrington. I was sure he was planning something violent but meeting him with more violence was not the answer. I certainly didn't want history to keep repeating itself, and I definitely didn't want the Sooth to hurt any more than they already were.

"Were you able to get to Charlotte and the rest of the Dwellers?" DeSantos asked.

"I'm afraid not." I looked back down. "I got to the town before Harrington and Marina arrived. I was discovered, and I walked away. I raced back here as fast as I could."

"They must know something that can help us. I want the three of you to get in touch with the Dwellers right now. I don't care what it takes. Harrington won't get anywhere near us again!" DeSantos left the house, closing the door briskly behind him.

Scraps came up to me from his bed across the room and licked my hand.

"What now?" Falcone sat down in the newly empty chair.

Chapter Twenty-One

A few nights went by, and though we didn't have a plan yet for what to do about Harrington, we *did* have a plan for getting to the Dwellers through the forest.

Williams, Falcone, and I got our supplies together before we headed to the tunnels located in the forest outside of the city limits. We packed light, a few weapons and some ammo were all we were able to take with us. We briefly discussed using Falcone's stealth engine, but I vetoed the idea because of what happened the last time we used it for a mission.

This time was going to be different.

After the battle outside of the city, Harrington doubled soldier outposts in the forests between Sooth City and Noor Village. It was going to take some careful work to avoid the encampments, but my recon skills were unmatched, and now everyone knew I was a vampire, there was no reason to try and hide them.

Planning was a lot easier. Instead of working around DeSantos and his possible reactions, we were free to plan on using my skills to their fullest.

The townspeople appeared to be accepting of my being a vampire, or at the least, they weren't saying anything to my face. DeSantos must have said something to the town to get them to work with me for the time being.

From what I could tell, the people were trying their best to treat me like normal, yet there was something behind their faces telling me not to get my hopes up.

They blamed me for Marina Vander's defection. I knew it. Hell,

I blamed me for her defection.

It was definitely my fault.

I led her brother into a battle he had nothing to do with—one I should have known would fail.

"This shouldn't be too hard." Williams packed his bag. "We mapped out a good route thanks to Mason, so there should be no patrol units on the way."

"Correct." I looked over at Williams. "I checked it last night, and nothing has changed. There have been no additional troops deployed, and the ones that have, are starting to look apathetic. I saw them shooting the shit around a campfire."

"Good." He closed his bag. "That's exactly what we want from them. Hopefully, tonight isn't the night they decide to take their jobs seriously."

"They won't." Falcone zipped up his bag.

"Perfect." Williams put his bag on the floor. "Let's go over it again."

"Tonight, the encampments are here, here, and here." I pointed to a map on the table. "So, we're going to take route two point five starting here. To keep from bunching up, we'll stagger our entrance into the forest by two minutes each, starting with me, who will stay no more than one mile away from the next closest person, then Falcone, then Williams. Using this route, it should take the three of us no more than two hours to get to the tunnel located here."

"Sounds easy enough." Falcone cracked his knuckles.

"If there's nothing else..." Williams said, ignoring his comment.

I shook my head to acknowledge there was indeed nothing else from my end. It was my job to clear the way and make sure Falcone and Williams got to the Dweller tunnel unscathed—a job I planned to take with extreme seriousness. I would not lose another member of Sooth City on a mission. I couldn't afford another Marina Vander nipping at my heels.

"Then, let's get the fuck out of here." Williams turned then walked out the door.

The three of us left the lab and went in the direction of the forest line outside of the city.

The season was changing, so the night air was cool and breezy. Falcone and Williams wore black turtlenecks, hats, and balaclavas to blend in with the backdrop of the witching hour. Though the hike was going to be a lengthy one, I was certain I could clear the way for them to get there safely.

I needed to. Otherwise, I would never be able to show my face in Sooth City. There was no contingency plan. If I couldn't return to Sooth City, I'd have to start from scratch in a new place beyond Noor and Sooth's influence.

"Look…" I stopped before we entered. "If for some reason this is the last time I talk to either of you, I want you both to know you two are the best humans I've had the pleasure of spending time with."

Falcone and Williams stared at each other for a moment. I didn't think either was expecting me to say anything, let alone anything so sappy.

"We *would* say the same of you," Williams said, "but you aren't human, and we've never spent time with any other vampires. I think we can both say the pleasure has been all ours for better or worse. We make a pretty good team. Yes, we've had some casualties, but we're not going to let that stand in the way of protecting our friends and loved ones."

"Well put." Falcone smiled for the first time I'd seen in several weeks.

I ventured into the woods to make sure there was nothing in between us and the tunnel.

~ * ~

An hour into the journey, and everything was quiet. We'd done a thorough job of mapping the new outposts, and unless something had appeared in the twelve hours since I last checked, our route was clear.

I crept through the trees, watching carefully to ensure even the deer were in the right places.

I smelled something coming from the ground beneath. It was a foul stench that reminded me of mulch, but not as strong. I hopped from the branch and landed on the ground, sniffing the air like a dog would, searching for the odor's source. There was nothing.

The sound of a twig snapping from fifteen feet ahead caused me to do a double-take. There was a large ball of gray fur in front of me. A wolf the size of a horse was baring his teeth, tail erect, hind hairs standing on end. I froze in my position and brandished my fangs in kind. It must have been hiding and tracking me, waiting for me to do something.

The last thing I wanted to do was fight a pack of dire wolves. Of all the animals in the forest, I identified with them most of all. They were fiercely territorial and some of the most efficient hunters on the planet. Not to mention, a fight with a wolf pack was sure to cause unwanted attention.

I stared at the wolf, dead in its glowing red eyes, and when I tried to take a crouching step forward to frighten it away, the rest of its pack appeared.

The pack leader circled me, growling a warning I took to mean not to make a false move. I stayed at the center and rotated with him as he passed, and when he got behind me, he kept walking like I wasn't there.

The rest of the pack followed with less hesitation, and soon they were headed east in the direction of Sooth territory. They wanted nothing to do with me. Instead, they were going somewhere with purpose. They were either fleeing from something or running to something.

I didn't have time to ponder any longer. We didn't have much time to get to the tunnels, and we needed every second we could spare.

I would have warned Falcone and Williams there was a pack of wolves, but they were moving in a different direction.

Fifteen minutes later, I approached the area where the access tunnel was located. I climbed into a tree and waited for Falcone and Williams.

Falcone arrived ten minutes after me, and Williams ten minutes after, as per our arrangement. They each took cover behind shrubbery until we knew it was clear. When I determined it was safe to proceed, I went to the access point and gave the hand signal for Falcone and Williams to come inside.

None of us spoke a word the entire time we walked through. I was worried Harrington had found the Dwellers hiding in the caves, so we did our best to keep our wits about us.

I wanted to believe Charlotte and the other remaining Dwellers had found a way to keep themselves camouflaged. I checked my pockets for the hundredth time to make sure the Chris Ball was still with me. I couldn't lose it. I was paranoid the journey would have been for nothing if I'd dropped it on the way.

After half an hour we approached the entrance to the cave where I'd last seen the Dwellers who helped us during the attack.

It was quiet and dark. I wasn't exactly sure what to do next, so I held the Chris Ball out and said, "Charlotte?"

Nothing.

I listened for any sound, but there was nothing other than the dead silence of an empty cave.

"Shit." Williams's shoulders tensed, and he looked around. "What do we do now?"

"I'm not sure," I answered, "maybe they've…"

Before I understood it was happening, the Dwellers in the cave showed themselves one by one. When they changed positions, their camouflage changed colors with the background they were in front of.

Out of the crowd of Dwellers, Charlotte was coming toward us on her hind legs.

"Thank the maker, you're here." I offered her the ball.

She waved my hand off and presented a Chris Ball of her own. I was in awe. "How did you—"

"Christopher's son Walter was able to extract the plan from his blood memory. We're lucky Walter was born after the ball was originally developed."

Using her long, jagged index finger, she pointed to the ball I was holding. "You no longer need that. The Walter Ball lets anyone in the vicinity hear and understand each other, whether they are near it or not."

I slipped the obsolete Chris Ball into my pocket. It was a useful tool I wanted to study more closely.

"For what reason have you come here, Trevor Mason?" she asked.

"We came to warn you and plead for your help," I said.

"Warn us of what?" another Dweller asked.

"Raymond Harrington is plotting, and we're positive it includes you."

"In what way?" The Dweller raised his massive head.

"*That* we are unsure of. It may be another attack, it may be far worse, the details are unclear. Marina Vander, one of our former family members, has defected to the Noor, and we're worried they are trying to wipe us off the map."

"I don't know," Charlotte said.

"You don't know what?" Falcone peered at her.

"I don't think we can help."

"What the fuck do you mean, you don't think you can help?" Williams yelled.

"I mean," she looked directly at Williams, "we don't want to meddle in your affairs any longer. The less we have to do with you and your *causes*, the better. We've seen all the violence we'd like, and we can no longer willingly participate. The world will carry on as it has without any help from the Dwellers. Since communicating with you, we have been all but wiped off the planet, and the best thing we can do for our survival is to stay away from Sooth affairs."

"You've got to be shitting me," Falcone said under his breath.

I didn't want to admit it, but she made a good point. Since learning how to speak with humanity, the Dwellers had lost almost as many of their people. I didn't blame them for not having any faith. They were going to require far more convincing than I did.

I wasn't sure what to say next. If they didn't see the danger in letting Harrington continue, there was no way to change their minds. They believed their survival hinged on a lack of interaction, and I was inclined to agree with them.

"Shit." Williams ran both of his hands through his hair. "What the fuck are we going to do now?"

"I'm not sure," I said. "For now, we need to get back to Sooth City and regroup. We knew there was a chance they wouldn't help, but at least we warned them. That's the best we can do."

"Damn it." Falcone looked around at nothing in particular.

"We leave you with this." Charlotte pointed to Williams. "Harrington is but a symptom of a larger disease. The planet *can* be cured of him."

"Thanks." I rolled my eyes.

"You're welcome." Charlotte was either ignoring my sarcasm or not understanding it.

Chapter Twenty-Two

We returned to my basement. It was disappointing, but the Dwellers were right not to help us.

I kept trying to convince myself there was nothing else we could have done to persuade them, but it wasn't exactly working.

"Well, that was a bust." Williams broke the silence.

"Not entirely." Falcone raised his hand slightly to get our attention.

"How so?" Williams tilted his head.

"Well, if they aren't helping us, they aren't helping Harrington either."

"I suppose that's a silver lining."

I didn't have anything to say. I was wrong in assuming Charlotte and the Dwellers would see the injustice and choose the right side.

My blood boiled.

I'd grown soft.

We warned them. *That* was the best we could do?

There was no way to stop Harrington with anything other than violence, and I was willing to meet him on the battlefield to prove it. I was blinded by a newfound love of humanity when I was anything but human. I was a slave to my inner desires, and my inner desires were that of a cold-blooded killer, a bloodthirsty vampire.

Never in my life had I chosen to be anything other than what I truly was, and what I desperately needed was a dose of reality.

To make Harrington go away for good, I had to harness whatever of my old energy remained in my barely-present soul and beat him into submission.

I didn't care what humanity would think of me after the battle was over. If everyone wanted the vampire killed, they would have to do it themselves. If I wanted to survive and see Harrington drained of his blood, it was time to drop the hopeless act and return to the killer I'd always been.

I would work with Falcone and Williams to kill Harrington, but more as resources and less as friends. Our friendship was ostensibly complete.

I vowed after Harrington was killed, I would leave Sooth City behind me. I hoped it would be better off than it was at present, I was also sure it wouldn't be. At a certain point, my interference accomplished nothing other than failure. I was far more successful at surviving on my own, making plans that relied exclusively on myself and my stomach.

"Are you all right?" Williams asked me. "You're far more quiet than usual, and you look like you're about to pop."

"I'll be fine." I didn't want to seem *too* out of sorts. "I just need some rest."

"Are you sure?"

"Yeah. Come back here tomorrow at sundown, and we'll try and formulate a plan."

"If you say so."

Falcone and Williams left through the front door.

I wanted to hop back into the tunnel immediately, but I *did* need to rest. If I wanted to catch Harrington, I needed to be at full capacity, and at the time, I wasn't.

Every muscle in my face and all of my bones and joints were heavy and difficult to move. My stomach rumbled. I needed to eat.

My energy was draining faster and faster in the days since my arrival to Sooth City. At first, I didn't notice anything wrong, but whatever it was, was starting to build up in my system.

It was time to do some investigating.

Staying in the basement, I got to work after the front door closed.

I took one of the bags of blood Falcone had given me and stuck a syringe inside. I pulled back on the stopper and drew enough to use for a sample.

After I grabbed a slide from the box laying on my desk, I put a drop of blood on it then covered it with a plastic square. Picking up the specimen, I placed it under the microscope, adjusting it to one hundred times magnification.

"Off the bat," I said into a recording device, "there is nothing irregular regarding the cells in Williams's blood. Switching to one hundred thousand times magnification."

Something wasn't right about the blood.

I had a hunch on what it might be, even though I didn't want to believe it.

I moved my chair to the computer on the opposite end of the room. "Computer, run diagnostic check, and compare blood sample with that of TB-457 sample number one zero two four five. Display on microscope screen."

After I rolled back to the microscope, I peered in one more time. My fears were confirmed. Someone was slipping me TB samples. No wonder I was so lethargic. They were giving me enough TB-457 to keep me alive and complacent.

It was time to get some answers, and I was going to get them from Williams.

I got to Williams's kitchen window, opened it then crawled in. There were a couple hours of moonlight left, and I was prepared to use them to my advantage. I crept through the kitchen, down the dark hallway, and to the door of his bedroom. I took the handle lightly and rotated it. He was sleeping on his bed.

When I got close enough, I put my hand over his mouth.

He awoke instantly, letting out several muffled screams before he knew what was going on. He squirmed under my weight, trying to get free from my grasp.

I bared my fangs and hissed at him like I was in a movie. I couldn't think of any other way to scare him into stopping.

"Shut the fuck up!" I whispered loudly. "I have some questions for you, and I need the truth."

Williams quit fighting me and nodded.

I stepped back and lifted him by the shirt, his feet hovering in the air. I put him on a chair in the corner of the room.

"What the fuck is this?" he asked, confused.

"You've been slipping TB-457 into my meals," I responded.

"Whoa." His body tightened. "That is absolutely not true. I had no idea anyone was putting anything in your food."

"Bullshit!" I squeezed his arm. "If not you, how did your blood sample come back with traces of test blood in it?"

"I have no idea!"

"You're not convincing me." I peered at him.

"Maybe *I* can," a voice said from behind me.

It was Falcone. "I knew you were being given TB-457 samples."

"By whom?" I asked.

"By DeSantos." He kept a straight face.

"Why would you not say anything about it?"

"Because it was my idea. We started with a small amount in the blood we gave you. Then, each night, we gave you more and more while you built up a tolerance."

"I don't understand why you would do this." The blood in my face grew hot.

"Because we needed to know whose side you are truly on. We knew something was up with you the moment you got here. Your stories never totally added up. After we discovered you were a vampire, I went to DeSantos to help him think of a way to keep you down but useful."

"Even still? You've *seen* me grow and come to accept humanity as more than my food."

"That's just it! You haven't accepted humanity at all! You only see us as a resource. You're not here to help us survive, you're here to make sure *you* survive until your next meal. It's the only thing you care about."

He was right, even though I didn't like it.

"You bastard!" I yelled.

I made a step toward Falcone, then stopped.

No. I had to be the change I wanted to see. I couldn't drain him…however badly I want to.

Storming out of the room, I said nothing else.

Done being a nice guy, I was no longer willing to act like I cared. I was sick of humanity and acting like I gave a crap.

When I got back home, I had no choice other than to fall asleep until the following night. I wanted to bolt into tunnels. However, restraining myself was necessary. I was nervous that Falcone and Williams were going to try something during the day when I slept, so I instructed Scraps to keep a close eye on my bedroom and warn me immediately if either of them got anywhere near the house.

I got into my bed, closed my eyes, but didn't fall asleep.

Chapter Twenty-Three

I woke the next night alone, my chest pounding, drenched in sweat, and my eyes burning in the back of my head.

Getting up from bed, I stretched my limbs.

There was a part of me that wanted to leave Sooth City to Harrington and his cronies. There was an equal sized part of me that didn't. I would not yield to tyrants.

I was hungry, but hesitant to drink anymore tainted blood. However, it was the one thing available for me to eat, and I didn't have the time or energy to drain anyone.

The plan had been pretty good on the part of Falcone. Slowly feeding me TB-457 was the perfect way to make sure I stayed alive, but not energetic enough I was able to kill those who weren't willing.

I packed my gear bag with blood to eat. There wasn't much, only three bags. If I drank them fast, the effects of the TB-457 should have been nullified for long enough to keep me awake.

Skipping family dinner, I didn't say anything to Williams and Falcone about my plan. Neither held my trust, especially Falcone. I was done relying on humans to help me move forward. Each time I did so, they proved themselves untrusting and unworthy.

This time, all I needed was myself. My scheme was simple, precise, and, if executed correctly, would result in the death of Raymond Harrington and no one else.

Though I was losing my faith in humanity, I was also gaining a new hatred of Harrington. He'd destroyed the only chance I had to be something beyond myself. Thanks to him, there was no way humanity would ever accept me.

As soon as I was done packing, I went to my backyard. I went through the tunnel carefully in case there were any Noor working on restructuring.

It looked like they'd finished. It was a solid tunnel now. Previously, the passageway had been wide enough to fit two people side by side. Now, the tunnel was large enough to fit the width of a sedan, paved with concrete, and the walls were covered with a black asphalt-like material that hardened the dirt walls till they were rock. It smelled a lot like Polymer-Xeta, and I surmised it was embedded into the compound somehow.

The Noor had been working right under my nose. They could have killed me in my sleep if they'd wanted to. Lucky for me, they didn't. Unlucky for them.

The idea was to locate Harrington and strike when he was alone. There was no way I was going to get through a full platoon of his soldiers, and I didn't want to try.

I got to the end of the tunnel and hunched in case anyone happened to be at the entrances, all of which were now lit with LED bulbs.

There was a two-ton light bulb at the top of the cave illuminating the entire area, and each of the passageways was labeled with a series of colored lights in seemingly random order. The signs meant something, but it would take some time to figure it out, and I was too focused on my goal to try.

Instead of the alcoves where the Dwellers had lived, the Noor cleared the structures, the stalactites, and stalagmites, and replaced them with cubed buildings that had furniture inside.

The Noor had completely annihilated the thriving city once there and had done so in a surprisingly short period of time. Using their advanced knowledge and equipment, they were able to create a masterpiece of industrial construction.

It was sad but mourning the loss of Dweller culture would have to wait until later.

The tunnel appeared to be empty and lacking in security measures. Though they progressed quite a bit, the new Noor headquarters wasn't finished, and I guessed they hadn't put in the security systems or allocated the resources yet.

Picking a direction, I leaped on top of one of the buildings near an access tunnel. I chose a safe spot to study one of the LED signs above the entrance to determine what it was telling me. Each one was a nine-by-ten grid system with rows of red, blue, white, or green lights placed in no order I could discern.

Entering the tunnel, I hoped it led to the Dweller militia's cove.

The sign above was lit mostly by white lights, with colors alternating from green to red, to blue, every three rows, top to bottom.

As I stared at it for a time, the light burned into my eyes. I heard footsteps coming from behind me. It was two soldiers on patrol.

Ducking lower into my hiding place, I continued staring at the sign. The sign led to the Dwellers, but I couldn't determine how the Noor were using it to find their way around. I knew several different languages…it wasn't any of *them*.

I'd done some work on military symbology and the evolution thereafter, but there were no hidden messages in there. No, it was something everyone could learn without too much of a learning curve.

Recalling some of the military codes I'd studied, it was closest to the "Ecriture Nocturne" or the "Night Code." It was designed by Charles Barbier in the eighteen-hundreds as a way for soldiers to see messages on the battlefield at night. The symbols weren't quite the same, though.

I was stumped.

Was it some new kind of code?

Then it hit me.

Braille! I yelled internally.

The Night Code was the basis for braille, and though it was only used in the twenty-first century until cybertronic eyes were invented, there was some knowledge of braille within some of the opium communities. They cut the braille section from signs to denote the houses that were safe places to consume opium and those recently raided by the authorities. For instance, a sign to a woman's restroom meant the site was okay to visit. If it was from a men's bathroom, it meant police, or "the man" had eyes on the place. An elevator button told you how high the opium would "elevate" you, a ten or above was best. It was a safe bet that a house with a woman's washroom sign and an elevator button to the fourteenth floor meant the place would be crowded that day.

Finally deciphering the sign, I knew exactly where to go.

The green row spelled N-R-V-L-G.

The red row spelled E-A-S-T.

The blue row spelled R-L-R-T.

The blue row I didn't understand, but I did the first two. It was the tunnel leading to the east part of Noor Village.

This particular hole wasn't finished yet, and construction vehicles were blocking the entrance, so I climbed over a forklift and made my way in.

Halfway through the first stretch, where there previously was a curve that would have led me to the left, another LED sign with an arrow pointed me to the right.

The bottom row was directions. R-L-R meant right, left, right. I didn't know what the "T" stood for, I guessed it meant it was the entrance.

As I decided to take my chances the rest of the way, I felt a cold feeling in my stomach. East Noor Village was not an easy part of town to get through, but it *was* possible to get to Harrington before sunrise if I wasn't caught.

While I walked, I realized I was going on a suicide mission. I didn't care. One way or the other, this was the night everything would end.

The tunnel came to a dead-end, and I looked at the access point. Instead of a well-hidden hole in the ground, there was now a large metal hatch with a complicated opening mechanism. I pulled a lever, and a rush of air blew through the tunnel. The hatch opening sounded like a suction cup.

I peeked my head enough not to be seen.

When I was sure the coast was clear, I pulled myself from the hole and closed the hatch carefully, then jumped to the nearest rooftop.

Thankfully, I already knew where Harrington's compound was. What happened when I got inside was a different story. I didn't have directions to anywhere other than the torture room.

Leaping from rooftop to rooftop, I made my way to the center of town where Harrington's compound was located.

When I got as close as I could using the rooftops, I stopped to take in the scene.

Twelve armed guards were patrolling the main house. None of them were talking to one another, and none of them were breaking focus. Unlike the soldiers in the outer encampments, these guards definitely took their jobs seriously.

After staring at the guards for an hour, I had their routine memorized. Each one was guarding a section of the house, which they patrolled in a steady circle. There was a split second where I could get through the guards near the northern wall, but I needed a distraction. Something bigger than throwing a rock, yet not so big I would risk getting caught in the process.

I got exactly what I wanted.

From the west end, an explosion lit up the entire city like it was noon. In the same direction, there was another. Then another from behind me.

Then I understood what Harrington's plan was. He was going to destroy his entire city and relocate to what the sign said was called "New Noor Village."

He was in the city somewhere. I could smell him through the fire and brimstone like Satan waiting for his own demise.

Another building blew up behind me. This one was closer, and a few pieces of debris hit me in the back, causing me to stumble forward. I caught my balance before I fell off the roof.

The soldiers at the house scattered; I didn't see them anywhere. I took a step toward the gate, but I was too late. Harrington's house was next.

It was time to flee back to Sooth City, despite my lack of desire to do so. Whatever Harrington was planning was happening now, and it was imperative I arrive and warn the people first.

There was another explosion.

Shit, I need to get the fuck out of here.

Running back to the tunnel through which I entered the city, buildings were being destroyed around me. Rock and rubble landed all over the ground.

A massive slab of concrete fell from the sky. I stopped dead in my tracks as it hit the ground and smashed into a hundred pieces in front of me. I pivoted my angle and narrowly missed a sharp piece of rebar.

The hatch was off in the distance.

Buildings continued to blow up and the force threw me a hundred feet into the air. I landed directly on top of the hatch, chest first.

Picking myself up, I pulled the lever and the door opened. This time I couldn't hear the sound over the explosions. I picked up the hatch, jumped in the hole, and closed the lid in time to avoid a massive fireball.

Fuck me. Another failure.

Sitting back against the tunnel wall for a moment, I tried to regain my senses. The sounds of detonating buildings blared above me, debris falling to the ground. Dust fell onto my head as each building was blown into oblivion.

I hoped Harrington wouldn't sacrifice an entire town's worth of people. They weren't in the tunnels, so I surmised they were on their way to Sooth City to make their final attack.

Harrington was right to let me go. There was almost nothing I could do to prevent his plan from success one way or another. He was smart. Too smart. I never thought he would do something like destroy his own town.

It was time to change my plan. I was going to have to meet him on the battlefield after all.

I made my way through the tunnels back to New Noor Village.

The town was still empty but this time, there were more guards on duty than there'd been an hour before. There were no more stalactites for me to hang from, but there were plenty of new buildings for me to jump to and hide behind.

The guards either didn't notice me or were instructed to let me be.

When I was able to see the tunnel leading to Sooth City, there was a large wall blocking the entrance.

Shit.

I stopped on the highest rooftop somewhere in the middle of the town. I deciphered some of the braille signs to see where they led. There were hundreds of tunnel signs to read. The available tunnels led to various places within Noor territory. Each of the Sooth City tunnels now had walls in front of them, with guards stationed at each one. My only escape was further into Noor territory.

It was a part of Harrington's plan, to trap me in New Noor Village while they attacked Sooth City.

I scanned the area.

My best bet was to fight the guards at the Sooth City tunnel.

A falling rock hit me in the back of the head.

"Ow," I grumbled, quietly.

Another rock hit me in the head. I glanced around and saw nothing.

A third rock hit me in the back of the head. I looked again and saw a camouflaged Dweller was staring directly at me. I took the Chris Ball out of my pocket and handed it to them.

"This way," he whispered, extending his hand.

The Dweller's stubby, five-fingered hand was like touching a leather construction glove. He pulled me into the tunnel and wrapped me in the rest of his arms.

We were headed to the surface.

He made a right through the wall of the tunnel and burrowed. Dirt and soot shot into my mouth, so I closed my lips and breathed through my nose.

We were in an alcove surrounded by Dwellers, all moving in different directions—all doing so with purpose.

When I finished spitting dirt from my mouth, I asked, "What's going on here?"

Charlotte was coming through the crowd.

The Dweller handed me the Chris Ball, and I placed it in my cargo pocket. He scurried away and went to perform another task.

"We thought you might be in trouble." She made direct eye

contact with me. "So, one of our men hid in our old town and waited for you."

"I sure am glad to see you." I smiled.

I took one of the bags of blood out of my pocket and gulped it down. "Look, we need your help. I know you won't fight on behalf of us, but would you be willing to do a solid for a friend?"

"That depends," she said.

"Take me to the outskirts of Sooth City. I'll handle the rest."

Chapter Twenty-Four

Charlotte pulled me through a tunnel leading outside of Sooth City. She dropped me off and turned to leave.

"Are you sure I can't convince you to stay?" I asked.

"I'm afraid you can't." Her brow furrowed. "We have caused enough human suffering, and we can't willfully participate in any more destruction."

"Fair enough," I said. "I guess I'll have to make do."

I could feel Harrington and his army drawing closer and closer. Vibrations in the ground helped me put them at a mile away. They would be there any minute.

Behind me was DeSantos and the Sooth City army. They too, would be there any minute.

I leapt into the trees to wait for my chance to get Harrington. I wanted his to be the only life I took.

From my position, both armies were visible.

He was the biggest threat of all. The people of Noor Village would have to do their best to understand their leader was a rabid dog who needed to be put down. It seemed impossible that anything, save for more violence, would get him and DeSantos to lay down their arms, accept their differences, and move on.

The Noor and Sooth drew closer to each other. The vibrations in the trees grew heavier.

The Sooth were larger in number, and those who knew how to use them were equipped with X8s and a few of the weapons Falcone and I developed, including the pyrotechnic grenades. They were powerful. I wasn't sure it was enough to do the trick. The soldiers without X8 rifles had grenades strapped to their chest. The grenades could be used from a safe distance, so they *could* potentially have an effect if there were enough of them.

A ship flew overhead that I couldn't see. I assumed Falcone built another stealth engine behind my back. He would have barely had the time to make one, especially if he was busy making grenades. He must have been exhausted.

The Noor traveled with a caravan of massive war machines.

Armored tanks topped with X8 lasers left trees falling in their wake. Mech suits followed, stomping the land like mythical giants. Thousands of soldiers made their way through the forest; all were heavily armed. The entirety of Noor Village—man, woman, and child alike, walking into slaughter.

Though I couldn't see Harrington anywhere in his army, I was sure he was there somewhere.

I also hoped to see Marina in the crowd, though I couldn't find her either.

Elevating to a higher treetop to get a better view of what the Noor were doing, I still couldn't see Harrington.

He had to be here.

Peering inside the mech suit at the back of the cavalcade, I could see him inside. The suit was at least a hundred feet tall and was easily the biggest I'd ever seen. On one of the side panels, it read, "AX3-841T." There were two massive X8 cannons on each shoulder. The AX3-841T was twice the size of the rest of the mech suits at their disposal, like a giant shark baring its teeth on top of two legs.

Glancing back to see where the Sooth were, I saw Falcone and Williams leading the army with DeSantos.

A warning wouldn't help much, but it was the least I could do.

Taking a bag of blood from my pocket, I twisted the top open then dumped it into my gullet. I jumped from the trees, landed on the ground then ran toward the Sooth with all the energy I had.

A moment later, I was standing in front of Falcone, Williams, and DeSantos.

"Halt!" DeSantos put a hand up.

The entire army stopped on a dime. Every single soldier stared daggers through me.

"What are you doing here?" Williams asked. "I didn't think we'd see you after your disappearing act."

"I came to warn you," I addressed the crowd.

"No need." Falcone adjusted the strap on his rifle. "Our scouts know exactly what's ahead of us. We know about Harrington's war machines. We know there are women and children up there. We know they think they're defending their homes. We know Noor Village was destroyed. We know about New Noor Village."

I looked directly at DeSantos. "Then you know this is a suicide mission."

"Look, son…" He tapped me in the chest with his pointer finger. "You've been a human for a few months. All of *us* have been humans our entire lives. We know we're walking into certain death, but sometimes humans have to do what's best despite knowing it's going to harm them. What kind of leader would I be if I let Harrington take our city without a fight?"

"What about the people you are going to kill?" I asked. "Don't they deserve something?"

"No." DeSantos laughed. "They don't. There's no convincing those people we are worthy of redemption. Harrington blew up his town in the name of the Sooth. There's no coming back from that kind of anger."

He was right. I wanted to be a human for a short time, which was nothing compared to any human older than a baby. They didn't have a choice in their humanity; they were born humans and were immediately forced to deal with the turmoil that came with it. I was through trying to convince them they were worth saving. I kept focused on Harrington.

"Fine," I said.

"What's fine?" Williams's brow furrowed, and his mouth tightened.

"I know I can't convince you to back off, nor can I convince the Noor. I've made my decision to remove myself from humanity when this is over. So…fine. The past months have been the most productive, worthwhile months I've spent since being awakened, and I have you to thank for that. Unfortunately, I can't seem to get a grip on what makes you human. But I think I understand now. As my last act, as I planned on doing, I am going to throw myself at Harrington and rip his throat out."

"Fine." Williams frowned.

I expected more from him. Of all people, he possessed the most sympathy.

I drained my last bag of blood like it was a juice box then dashed back into the forest.

I leapt from treetop to treetop, making my way toward Harrington and the Noor. The blood I had to drink was becoming less and less potent by the moment, and I wondered whether it would have any effect soon. The more I drank, the less energy I had.

It didn't matter. Nothing mattered.

One way or the other, this was going to be my last parade. After all the preaching, pontificating, and lies, it was going to come to raw and primal violence, and I wasn't sure the strength was in me to survive the ordeal. At the least, I would never be the same again mentally or physically. TB was going to leave me a docile pet for whomever wanted to tie the leash.

The Noor were almost close enough to smell.

Both armies halted at the edge of a clearing. I needed to let the battle start so as not to draw attention to my true purpose. Trying to get ahead of the battle was going to result in my being shot long before I got a chance to get through the frontline.

Harrington's mech peeked its way above the horizon. He stopped, left his mech suit, then went toward the center of the soon-to-be battlefield.

DeSantos broke from the rest of the crowd and walked toward Harrington.

I was close enough to determine what they were saying.

"We don't have to do this!" DeSantos yelled. "We can turn around and go home and pretend like this never happened."

"You know we can't do that." Harrington smirked. "You've taken our homes from us, and now we have to go into hiding underground!"

A roar bellowed from the Noor side of the crowd. He put a hand up, and it went silent again.

"That's bullshit, and you know it!"

"Is it?" Harrington hollered back. "It doesn't matter who pulled the trigger. You and your Sooth are responsible for this."

"You son of a bitch!" DeSantos returned. "You orchestrated all of this. You are the reason you and your people are now going to become what the Dwellers were. They *can* be redeemed, *you* can be saved, and we can *all* just go home. Whether it be above or underground, we are willing to let you have your home and be at peace."

"How dare you address those monsters by anything other than their true name! The Creatures are far beyond redemption. For fuck's sake, DeSantos, you sent a vampire to manipulate us with its mind powers. Can you honestly say that he, too, is worthy of our sympathies? I think not. If not for him, Marina Vander would still be alive."

What the fuck was he talking about? Marina was dead? He had to be bluffing.

Harrington's people booed.

Time was up.

"I'm done with this." DeSantos was loud enough to be heard by a few other people and me. "I don't believe you. If Marina was dead, you would have some kind of proof!"

Harrington waved, and one of his men ran to him, holding something in a bag the size of a cabbage. Harrington took the bag and threw it to DeSantos' feet.

DeSantos bent over and picked up the bag. I couldn't see what was inside. However, I had a good idea. He closed his eyes and mouthed what appeared to be "you son of a bitch."

The back of my neck grew hot, and I had tunnel vision. The blood rushed to my face, heating it with every passing second.

The two men walked back to their respective armies, their inane chatter accomplishing nothing.

I was angry at Marina, but I didn't want her dead. In the end, her defection actually accomplished little more than the fates already planned.

Even though I was close enough to Harrington to smell him, I wasn't in striking distance. I desperately wanted to pounce. I needed to attack before he got back inside the AX3-841T, but I wasn't sure my body had enough energy.

There was a lot of uncertainty when it came to how much longer I'd be able to keep hold of my consciousness. I needed to drink something other than tainted blood, otherwise I wouldn't have enough energy to make it to Harrington.

I looked down and saw a few Noor soldiers standing on the outskirts of the crowd, all looking at the scene attentively.

Jumping from the trees, I used what little speed I had left to make my way closer to the men. My palms began to sweat a little. It had been a while since I had drained a human, and I needed to be sure I didn't fuck it up.

When I was within two feet of the first man I saw, I grabbed him. I covered his mouth with my hand, then pulled his head to the side. I could almost smell the blood pumping through his veins. I exposed my fangs and sank them deep into his neck. Blood dripped down my throat. My muscles loosened, my brain cleared up, then my stomach stopped rumbling.

"Hey!" one of the men yelled, before I was able to drain my victim fully.

I leaped back up into the trees.

Bullets flew by my head as I started my run toward Harrington. This time, I wasn't going to let anything stop me.

"Attack!" Harrington yelled.

The crowd roared.

The sound of weapons firing and screams from soldiers surrounded me. When I was twenty feet away from Harrington, I lunged toward him. Before I was able to get to him, he turned around and jammed his bear's paw of a fist directly into my face. The impact changed my inertia, and I fell, landing on my back.

"I was wondering when you'd show up." He cracked his neck.

When I leapt again, he tried to punch me with his left fist. I caught it with my right hand, pulled his weight toward my hip then jammed my knee into his gut. He staggered back and coughed, but it had little effect. He regained his bearings within seconds.

I threw a barrage of calculated fists in his direction. He dodged each of them with the ease of a pro boxer.

Harrington caught one of the blows and wrapped my fist up in his arms. He cocked his head back and slammed his forehead into the bridge of my nose, causing blood to spurt and flow down my face.

Dizzy, I staggered backward.

The stealth jet hovered above Harrington's abandoned mech. On the bottom of the ship, I noticed a version of our pyrotechnic grenade ten times the size of a normal one. The soldiers pushed it to the edge and stepped away. A third soldier with a remote activated the bomb and shot it toward the AX3-841T. A fireball engulfed the suit, killing dozens of men surrounding it.

When the flames died, the glowing of the shield's protective energy made sure no more than the hull of the ship was burnt.

The ship's cloak failed, revealing the vessel's entirety. A platoon of Noor mechs aimed their weapons on the ship.

When I regained my bearings, I got up and saw Harrington coming at me. I ducked a punch and came back with an uppercut that hit him directly in the jaw, causing his teeth to slam together.

I was growing weaker.

Leaping forward, I landed a kick to his chest. I felt his sternum crack, and he simultaneously lost his breath.

Harrington was coming again. His face was red as he darted toward me.

I jumped and flipped over him enough to avoid hitting his head with my own. When I landed behind him, I jabbed my fist into the small of his back. He fell forward onto his face.

A smile crossed my cheeks, then my abs vibrated with laughter. I finally had him. After everything he put me through, it was time to finish him once and for all. More so than the Dwellers, Harrington had truly put me through the wringer and I was happy to put an end to his miserable life.

I picked him up by the hair, then lifted him until he was off of his feet. I drew my fist back, then punched him in the nose several times.

He laughed.

"What the fuck is so funny?" I yelled at him at the top of my lungs.

"You think killing me is going to stop this war?" He chuckled. "You're even dumber than you look, vampire. You see those humans behind me? They will believe anything I tell them and trust me when I say they will never accept you, the pitiful Sooth, or the Creatures you've come to defend so willingly. Well? Where are they now? The Sooth are nearly destroyed, and your Creatures are nowhere to be found."

"I don't care about any of them! All I care about is making sure you're in a grave before the sun comes up."

"You care for yourself and not a damn thing else." He struggled through coughs of blood.

Once again, he was right. From my beginning, my summoners bred me to be a monster, not a protector. To call me anything other than a creature would have been a mistake.

Roaring, I pummeled Harrington with my fist. The will to live left his face— his haunting crimson smile, and everything else fell into nothingness.

I pulled my arm back for one last life-ending hit to his brain.

Something stopped me from moving my limbs.

My fist was suspended behind my head, and I was in a dream, unable to use my arms in any way.

Soldiers were frozen in place with their fists cocked back—their expressions locked in anger. Blood splatter hung in the air like a thin mist above the violence. I attempted to speak, but my vocal cords were halted in line with the rest of my body. I was able to breathe, control my eyes, and blink, that was all.

A gust of wind blew through the area, scattering dust and tree particles throughout the open field.

A two-hundred foot red ball floated above the tree line. It descended, and I recognized what it was.

The red-amber material reflected almost no light, and the brain matter material underneath the surface was visible. It was a Chris Ball the size of a moon.

The ball stopped and hovered thirty feet in the air. I strained my eyes trying to see it.

I couldn't believe what the Dwellers had accomplished. It must have taken all of their manpower to construct a vessel of that size in such a short amount of time.

"Enough!" a woman's voice boomed throughout the battlefield. "There will be no more bloodshed this day!"

A bright green light encased Harrington and me; we were both locked in place.

Jagged pain hit the bottom of my stomach and spots formed in front of my eyes. I was blacking out. I hoped whatever the Dwellers were planning, they did it soon. Otherwise, I wasn't sure the force field they were using to stop everyone from moving would be enough to keep me from terrorizing an already gruesome battle scene.

Harrington didn't seem bothered by what was happening because he continued to stare straight into my eyes. He knew he was going to survive, and his frozen smile was enough to let me know how happy he was.

The spots soon took everything, and darkness filled my field of vision.

Warmth took me over, and the blackness set in.

Chapter Twenty-Five

I was submerged in some kind of yellow liquid. I had hoses connected to a mask covering my mouth.

I wasn't hungry, and I had no memory of how I got into what I was now thinking was a human-sized tube. When my eyes finally focused, I saw five other containers with people inside—Williams, Falcone, DeSantos, Harrington, and someone who appeared to be Marina.

They were still asleep, suspended in the same yellow liquid.

I lost track of Falcone, Williams, and DeSantos during the battle, and for better or worse, I was glad to see they were there with me, seemingly unharmed. I was, however, enraged by the fact Harrington was in there. The Dwellers took the time to spare his life. For what reason? I couldn't fathom. It wasn't easy to think while I was floating in a container of liquid.

The viscous liquid started to drain. The floor of the vat was cool against my feet, and they gently landed on the grate when I lost buoyancy.

I was overwhelmed with a sense of calm, my limbs were light, and there was a warmth in my head giving me cause to believe everything would be all right. In fact, I was feeling a lot more like my former self. Better even.

The Dwellers must have cleared the test blood from my system.

The door opened after the liquid was gone, and I stepped out. My legs were weak, and I stumbled.

"Be careful." Charlotte caught me in her arms and helped me up by the elbow. "The effects of the Anton Tank will wear off in a few minutes, but until then, you may find your motor skills a bit shaky."

Charlotte and two other Dwellers were checking on the other subjects, pressing buttons on the screens in front of them, I assumed to make sure their vitals were nominal.

She walked to me and handed me a red piece of cloth that, when unfolded, appeared to be some kind of garment. I slipped the crimson cloth over my head and stuck my arms through the respective holes. Made of a cotton-like material, it was a one-piece garment that ended right above my ankle.

"Where are we?" I asked.

The inside of the giant ball was one large, spherical room with a see-through dome and a red marble floor.

The sun was clear. The ship must have contained an ultraviolet filter because I didn't feel sick.

I was on what appeared to be an examination platform off to the south end of the ship. Below the platform, there were hundreds, if not thousands of Dwellers scurrying in different directions.

"Welcome to the John Ball. We are hovering in the Mesosphere above Africa," Charlotte said from behind me. Her voice was audible like I was talking to any other human.

"What's going on?" I asked. "Why do I feel so different?"

"You feel different because you are healed."

"What do you mean 'healed?'" I clenched my jaw.

"Don't worry," she replied. "You are who you've always been. We couldn't heal you of your vampirism like we were able to do for ourselves, but you are now clear of any toxins in your body. We developed a substitute for you by isolating what makes your system crave blood, then reverse engineered nutrients in the red blood cells of human beings. You'll need to take one of these pills every twenty-four hours, and you should be free from your dependency on human blood."

I was cautious of taking any more experimental blood sources, yet I genuinely believed the Dwellers wanted me to stop feeding on humans, so I took the pill from her, popped it into my mouth then swallowed.

"And the rest of them?" I asked after the pill cleared my throat.

"They'll be out of their respective tanks in no more than a few days," answered Charlotte. "You heal far more quickly than any human we've tried the tank on so far, so you woke up well before your comrades."

"What happened to the rest of the Noor and Sooth? Where is everyone now?"

"They have all gone home. The Noor went to our old

underground city, and the Sooth went back to Sooth City."

"Nobody else died? I didn't kill anyone?"

I remembered Harrington was in one of those tanks.

"Wait a minute!" I yelled. "Why did you spare him?" I pointed to the tank with him inside.

"Why did we save Raymond Harrington?" she replied.

"Yes." My face tightened. "Why *him* of all people?"

"Because you were going to extinguish his life for no reason."

"No reason?" I barked.

"Just because you think you have a reason," she continued calmly, "doesn't mean it's a good one, or even one anybody other than you should expect to care about. All we see is violence, Trevor Mason, and we will tolerate it no more, regardless of justification."

"I don't get it."

"You don't need to understand our reasoning, just as we don't have to pretend to want yours. However, what you will learn is that we are going to stay right here, in the Mesosphere, to be a reminder that whenever humans get violent, we have the power to stop them at any moment."

"So, you're going to *live* up here?" I walked over to the edge of the platform.

"*We* are." Charlotte followed me. "Down there, we are monsters that will never be accepted by humanity. Up here, we can at least use our monstrosity to help those who can't help themselves."

Something told me she wasn't talking about the Dwellers, but it seemed like a good plan. A global catastrophe was the one thing capable of bringing humans together. So, they were going to act like an ever-looming threat, hovering above the world like a war moon, ready to pounce if anyone got out of line. Peace after previous attempts was fleeting at best. This was different.

"What are you planning to do with us?" I asked.

"You six aren't going anywhere," she replied.

"You're kidnapping us?" I turned to her.

"More like imprisonment. You'll be able to roam the ship freely, but none of you will be allowed to return to the planet's surface."

"Why the hell not?" I screamed.

"Of the Sooth and Noor, those five are the most dangerous. We've calculated the risks, and if we let any combination of them free, they will destroy themselves and everyone around them. Humanity will never be able to heal as long as they exist."

"What about Falcone and Williams? What about Marina? Surely, *they* deserve to have their lives back. They wouldn't've harmed a fly if not for Harrington and DeSantos. That doesn't make any sense."

"No. They do not deserve their lives back, Trevor Mason. As I mentioned before, our reasons are our own, and your misinterpretation of them makes no difference to us."

We were talking in circles. I wanted to know her reasons, but Charlotte didn't care whether I grasped it, she didn't even care enough to explain.

"Damn it," I said.

"We understand this may be difficult to hear—"

"*Difficult* to hear? *Difficult* to hear! You're telling me I'm trapped here for the rest of eternity!" I threw my hands up.

"Not quite." She raised a hand and put it on my shoulder.

"What does *that* mean?" I pulled her hand off.

"In a few generations," she answered, "everyone currently on this ship will be dead and gone, and they have been explicitly forbidden from speaking to their offspring about what brought the vampire aboard the ship. They will instruct them that you are to be left in charge and nothing more.

"Eventually, no Dweller alive will know anything about you other than you are a high-ranking member of our society. When that happens, this ship is yours."

"Mine?" My eyebrows raised, and my forehead tightened. "What the hell am I supposed to do with *this*?"

"Whatever you like." She waved a hand at the massive space. "If you want to crash the ship and kill every Dweller on board, you may. If you want to stay here and continue keeping the peace, that's your prerogative."

"Why would you do that?"

"There are many reasons." She turned around. "Most of which you won't be able to comprehend, but simply because you cannot die, you are the most qualified person to take control when the last of this generation expires. This place is completely self-sufficient and requires no maintenance. If you'd like, this ship will be capable of interplanetary travel in the next fifty years. By the time you find a habitable planet, you should be perfectly clear to lead.

"You don't need human blood if you don't want it, so you don't need to be on the surface. With our pill, you are more or less invulnerable, and if you stay up here, you can affect the kind of changes we know you want to make."

Shit. She was right. I had to stay on board. There was no one else on Earth able to do it, and if I left, humanity could expect this to be nothing more than another failed bureaucracy.

"Fortunately," she continued, "you have close to a hundred years to decide. Until that time, you are no different than any of the other humans aboard this ship."

It seemed like a lot of time, but in the grand scheme of things, a hundred years could go by like a normal human's decade for someone who had lived as long as myself. However, it was a good opportunity to get my mind straight and do some real thinking. I could detox and make sure it wasn't *simply* the test blood giving me an affinity for humanity.

I was having a difficult time trusting my feelings. I was upset by Harrington and his actions, and I wanted to make sure someone like him wouldn't exist again, but there was a renewed part of me that was sure I wanted to leave humanity behind like I planned before.

There was something wet and warm on my hand. Scraps was licking me.

"Holy shit, boy, how did you get here?"

"Hello, my friend," he said. "I started working with the Dwellers after I found the first Chris Ball."

I was dumbfounded at Scraps's diction. The Walter Ball attached to his neck gave him the ability to tell me what he wanted, and now he was able to communicate in a way that expressed more than his most basic instincts.

"They took me up in their ship before the battle," he continued. "I signaled them when it began. I told them about your plans to kill Harrington. I was the scout who told them everything Harrington was doing."

"Why?" I asked.

"Everything I do, I do for the greater good."

"The greater good?"

"Yes. You may not think me capable, but I can assure you, I agree with the Dwellers and their methods for achieving the greater good. There is a lot about their plan that neither of us can comprehend, but there will be peace."

"So I've heard," I said sarcastically…to a dog. I came to grips with the fact I wouldn't understand some of their reasons, but I was sick of hearing it.

~ * ~

A few days later and everyone was back to their normal selves. Marina and Harrington were separated from DeSantos, Williams, Falcone, and myself. Scraps was the only one allowed to communicate freely with any of the humans on the ship. The rest of the Dwellers were strictly forbidden from speaking with any of the five humans aboard. They *were* allowed to talk with me but were instructed to answer questions I might have, and they were required not to engage me for any other reason.

I didn't see any of the other humans aboard the ship after each of them were removed from their Anton Tanks. I was promised there would be a meeting with everyone once they were debriefed.

From what Charlotte told me, Williams, Falcone, Marina, Harrington, and DeSantos had differing opinions when it came to the Dwellers's plan to leave me in charge, but it would be discussed on the day of our meeting.

Each day I did my best to learn the ins and outs of Dweller society on board the ship.

Most of them held maintenance positions. The various ranks they filled didn't seem to matter if each of them was playing a role.

I learned there was no real power structure. For instance, Charlotte was never appointed to her position as the liaison between Dwellers and humanity. Instead, each assigned themselves their role, and if they were working for what they called "The Greater Good," each Dweller was satisfied with their station.

They were also able to use the pills to sustain themselves. Though the medicine was modified for their anatomy in terms of dosage, it was more or less the same formula as the pills they were giving me. Dwellers no longer needed to kill anything to eat.

The Dwellers were evolving at an astonishing rate, looking and sounding more human every single day. They were learning far faster than I what it was like to be human, and I admitted to some jealousy.

~ * ~

Tensions were high on the day of the meeting. None of us wanted to be there, see one another, or be the first to speak.

There were eight of us sitting at a large round table, including Scraps and Charlotte. We sat in silence, making awkward eye contact with each other as we glanced around the room.

I didn't blame any of us for being angry at one another. Everyone in the room, with the exception of Charlotte and Scraps, had reason to want to kill one another. The most surprising thing was Marina. After Harrington cut her head off, I didn't think she'd be comfortable sitting so close to him. She didn't expect to be alive, let alone be invited to the table.

Charlotte straightened her shoulders. "I'll speak first."

I'd hoped she would talk before anyone else. She alone understood the Dwellers's motives and was in a unique position to speak on their behalf.

"If none of you wants to say anything," she continued, "I am perfectly happy to let you live out the rest of your lives quarantined from one another. The six of you have caused more destruction than any other humans on the planet. If you think we aren't happy to keep you confined to yourselves, you have sorely misunderstood your position."

"Then what are we here for?" Williams asked.

"To negotiate the terms of your imprisonment. If you humans can determine a way to live together freely on the ship, we are prepared to let you do so. If not, as I mentioned, you are perfectly free to remain in your cells."

"This is pointless." Marina stood to leave the room.

"Wait." I got up and put my hands on the table. "Don't leave yet. We have a lot of time on this ship with each other, and this is our chance to make sure you can live the rest of your lives in relative peace."

"What if I don't want to live in peace with you monsters?" She put her hands on her hips.

"Then, you may return to your cell and remain there for the duration of your sentence." Charlotte waved at the door.

Marina sat back down and slumped in her seat, crossing her arms as she did so.

Harrington and DeSantos were surprisingly quiet. I assumed they'd be at each other's throats on sight, but both said nothing.

"What are you proposing?" Falcone scratched his chin.

"At the least," I turned to look at him, "I'm saying that the five of you come to some kind of agreement. Divvy up the ship into quadrants, make friends, or don't. I don't care what you do, but one way or the other, you're going to come up with an arrangement right now. And *that* is going to last the rest of your lives."

"Look who's stepping into some new shoes," Harrington said under his breath.

"Haven't you heard?" DeSantos gave a sarcastic chuckle. "Dr. Mason here is going to be running things for all of eternity."

It was clear Harrington and DeSantos weren't happy. If they had their way, both men would have preferred to have me strung up in the sunlight.

I'd hoped after the battle, DeSantos would have changed his mind about me. I did my best to be the kind of person he would want on his side, but in the end, my base instincts kept me from being trustworthy in his eyes.

"That's right." I sat back down. "I'm in charge now, and there is nothing to be done about it. In a hundred years, when you are dead and gone, no one will care about that fact, but I'll be here, looking at the ancestors you left behind, determining their fates. You're lucky anyone cares about what happens to you *now*. Your deaths will mean nothing to anyone. You're here because you're too dangerous to remain on Earth any longer.

"I'm still not entirely sure what 'The Greater Good' is, but *I* have plenty of time to learn, *you* don't, and I can assure you it isn't dependent on you being alive. If you can't determine a way to live together right here, right now, I am going to come up with something for you, and you likely won't be happy with it."

"I concur." Falcone rested his elbows on the table and folded his hands. "There's nothing left for us on Earth. All we have now is the short amount of time remaining on this ship. It's pointless for any of us to stay alive, and if we don't want to spend the next seventy years stuck in one room, I suggest we hash this out."

"Falcone is right." Williams nodded.

Harrington and DeSantos agreed as well.

"All right then," I said. "Let's get to work."

"Where do we start?" Marina scratched her head.

"We start by dividing up the ship into Noor and Sooth." Harrington straightened in his seat.

"No!" DeSantos snapped. "We're done with this Noor and Sooth bullshit. Those of us who can't get along should be left in their rooms to die in peace."

"You *would* say that." Harrington sneered.

"Things are different now." DeSantos shrugged. "There is no point in continuing the charade that the Noor and Sooth are anything but false constructs."

"How different are things, really?" Marina sat forward and put her elbows on her knees. "I hate all of you for what you did to my brother. I *let* Harrington take my life, but I will never forgive you for taking Dustin from me. I genuinely don't think I can live in peace with any of you at any point in the next fifteen, twenty, eighty years, it doesn't matter how long.

"That said, I'm with Harrington, we should split the place up. If not, I have no issue staying in my cell, apart from you assholes."

"You may want to reconsider." Falcone turned in his chair until he was facing her. "People change, situations change. If you choose to stay isolated, you will never have the chance to see another human being."

"I don't give a shit!" she barked. "The only other human being I want to see is Dustin, and the Dwellers inform me he is too far decomposed for their stupid tanks!"

"What if we don't speak to one another?" Williams asked.

"Fine with me." Falcone crossed his arms.

"I think we all know that isn't going to happen," I said. "I give you a month before you're at each other's throats."

"We have to be better than that," DeSantos said solemnly. "We have an obligation to humanity to try and live in some kind of relative harmony."

"No, we don't." Harrington shook his head. "For all intents and purposes, we are the last humans left. None of us are going to see another day on the planet's surface, so there is no point in pretending we owe anything for the sake of humanity. No. The best thing we can do is divide up the ship."

"Fine," Charlotte agreed. "If you can figure out how to do that without seeing each other, the Dwellers can be amenable. However, keep in mind we have one mess hall and one human washroom for you to use, so you will have to contact each other at some point."

"That doesn't leave us with a ton of options." Falcone stared blankly at the table.

"That is not our concern," she replied.

The meeting continued for several hours before a reasonable compromise was reached through a vote on each policy.

They abolished the notion of Noor and Sooth, an idea Harrington didn't care for. They were able to agree that division among class lines didn't hold any value in a place where there was no wealth to hoard. Williams, DeSantos, and Falcone were content to stay with each other, and Marina and Harrington did the same. It was the sole remaining essence of the Noor and Sooth.

They decided they would eat their meals in shifts. Marina and Harrington were allowed to eat first, then Williams, DeSantos, and Falcone. It was the same with the washroom.

They also made provisions for when each person died. For instance, DeSantos and Harrington were quite a bit older than Williams and Falcone, and both were older still than Marina, so when the first to die off had done so, it was only fair the humans be able to readdress the terms of the agreement.

Upon each person's death, there would be a chance to renew their deal. Charlotte was less than happy with the concession, but I convinced her a compromise was best, and they would probably feel the same way when each age group died off.

They would eventually renegotiate the terms of their agreement, but not until Harrington and DeSantos were dead, and Marina was truly alone in her hate for the two remaining Sooth.

I hoped they could use their compromises to live the rest of their lives in relative peace, but I wasn't particularly optimistic. Marina was angry and traumatized from her own death and the loss of her brother. She was the most deserving of her hate. She was lucky she would be the last to live, and she would eventually be the one person in the group who would get some peace; the one who would get to live a portion of her life without any of the men responsible for her misery.

My position was non-negotiable as far as the Dwellers were concerned, and I was ready to accept my role as the new gatekeeper to Earth.

Epilogue

A lot changes in eight decades. A lot stays the same.

With the John Ball hanging above the planet, there was no more than a small amount of turmoil every ten years or so, when groups of humans figured they could lure the Dwellers to the surface and take them out. The Dwellers never fell for it, and unfortunately for humankind, the John Ball was far too powerful, and updates were constantly being made to ensure human weapons had no effect on it.

With Falcone's help, the John Ball was leagues ahead of anything the Surface Humans could hope to invent. X8 lasers were nothing compared to the John Ball and its impenetrable shielding, and thanks to their evolutionary abilities, the Dwellers weren't affected by the weapons.

The John Ball ran like a well-oiled machine. Charlotte was right about the ship being completely self-sufficient. The maintenance crews knew their jobs perfectly and passed their knowledge through their blood memory, so there was no reason to hold classes for new recruits.

Eventually, Charlotte's generation died, and I was the one left in charge. I changed close to nothing about Dweller culture. Their society wasn't perfect, but it was the closest thing to perfect humanity was going to get, and it was up to me to make sure humanity kept itself from imploding.

In any case, Earth had given me quite a bit for the millennia I was alive, and the best I could do was to stay put for the duration and leave it a better place than it was before I was summoned.

Aboard the ship, there was no more disease, so when each of the humans died, it was natural. Harrington and DeSantos were in their early hundreds when they died from brain failure. Williams and Falcone died twenty years later from the same. Marina Vander was the last human, and at ninety-eight years old, she was the second oldest thing remaining on the ship.

The humans were able to live in relative peace for the duration of their lives. There'd been a few skirmishes here and there, but nothing more. As predicted, Marina wasn't happy until Harrington and DeSantos were gone, at which time she was able to amicably renegotiate terms with Falcone and Williams.

She didn't talk to them much, or anyone for that matter, but she did make it possible for everyone to eat and use the washroom whenever they wished.

Falcone and Williams helped the Dwellers in their research efforts.

When it came to military tactics, Williams offered a lot. He taught the Dwellers how to use their camouflage to their advantage in stealth combat.

Falcone was one of the most brilliant engineers I'd ever met, so letting him work with the Dwellers on the ship was a pretty easy decision to make.

Throughout their lives, the humans did their best to tolerate my existence. Harrington and DeSantos never did come around. I hadn't expected they would end up changing their tune on me and what I brought to the table in the few years I would spend with them. Much like the Dwellers, Harrington and DeSantos were unable to forgive the lives I'd taken in the name of my own survival.

Williams and Falcone were a little different. By the time Harrington and DeSantos died, Williams and Falcone were far more willing to let me be the leader. Either they accepted their circumstances or were legitimately okay with them as they were. They never told me one way or the other.

For better or worse, I was leaving a positive mark on the world. If I couldn't be on the surface living my life as I'd done for centuries, being able to have my say aboard the ship was the best I was able to hope for.

I decided to never use the John Ball to leave the Mesosphere above the planet, even though I was fully briefed on the ship's intergalactic engines. I kept them maintained in case anything ever happened, but they were a contingency plan I never wanted to use.

Save for the Dwellers, I was back to being alone. Marina wasn't good company, as she continued to possess a deep-seated hatred of me and everything I'd done to screw up her life on Earth. Throughout her years, she never got over the fact she wasn't allowed to see any of her family members. On the planet's surface, she had everything she needed. Aboard the ship, all she had was hate. She never complained, at least not audibly. Like me, she accepted her fate aboard the ship and knew the Dwellers were correct in their decision.

It took me several years to truly come to grips with what the "Greater Good" was. It meant no matter what the circumstance, removing the most dangerous element from the equation was always the best option. For the Dwellers, the five humans they took aboard the ship were only a small portion of the danger awaiting the world. The true plan was to remove themselves from the equation.

The Dwellers were pragmatic in that way. They knew a significant number of humans would never accept them as a part of their society, and instead of fighting a pointless fight, they took their technology and everything they had to offer and simply found a new home in the sky.

It meant a lot of sacrifices, but leaving the planet was the best thing for human beings' overall plight. The Dwellers saw it way before anyone else was able to. They were truly the children of empathy— something Earth desperately needed. They saw the world for what it was and decided the best route was to ensure they couldn't be used as weapons, either for the humans or themselves.

Whether it was for the Greater Good or some other selfish purpose didn't actually matter anymore. I made my decision, and I had no choice other than to live with it until my own natural death.

When or if death would come, I would never know.

About the Author

A Chicago native, Jeremy Handel was a lover of writing even before he knew how to write real words. Creating squiggly lines of adventures for his favorite movie characters, he painstakingly filled notebook after notebook with stories no one but he could read at the age of 4.

Now that he does know how to write stories, Jeremy has become enamored with it. Graduating from University in 2010, he took a job as a copywriter and has since been honing his craft as a science fiction writer.

Whether it be in the form of movies, comics, or television, Jeremy is a lover of all science fiction, vampire, and creature feature stories and vows to ingest as many as possible, as often as he can.

Jeremy loves to hear from his readers. You can find and connect with him at the links below.

Twitter: https://twitter.com/AuthorHandel
Facebook: https://www.facebook.com/Jeremy-Handel-Author-104346464487638
Instagram: https://www.instagram.com/jeremyhandel_author/

~ * ~

Thank you for taking the time to read *Blood Habits Die Hard*. We hope you enjoyed this as much as we did. If you did, please tell your friends and leave a review. Reviews support authors and ensure they continue to bring readers books to love and enjoy.

Turn the page for a peek inside *Witchslayer's Scion*, a fantasy by L.T. Getty.

Some men fear becoming the monster they're sworn to fight. Others laugh at the abyss.

Koth's life was decided for him since before he was born, for his ability to heal wounds by touch is rare even among his people. When an attempted kidnapping turns to sacrificial murder, he embraces vengeance and the sword. As he journeys far from his small, isolated village in the north, he learns the truth as to why his bloodline is targeted by strange magic, in a world still rebuilding from a time when dark sorcerers didn't bother with secrecy.

Koth thinks his quest is straightforward enough: find the men responsible and kill them—and any who aid them. He will soon learn that those who have both privilege and power, there are few things they lack—and in the pursuit of godhood, their allies can prove even more sinister as mere mortals seek to advent empires and dynasties.

EXCERPT

Nisiris stopped loading the net and watched the Imperial warships docking near the partially constructed fortress. Several merchant vessels traveled the calm sea waters of their distant wake, likely to drop off more quarried stone, as well as their strange cows, pigs, and women folk. It wasn't enough to fly their flags, and defile their temples, but now the mainlanders were going to breed them out.

"Perhaps there are Honturian warships in the area, or pirates," Vared said as he finished loading the net into Kesir's slender boat.

Nisiris turned back to his friend and smiled. "We're the only pirates they need fear."

"Be quiet," Kesir said. The old man didn't dare look in the direction of the Imperial ships. "There are a dozen boats in the bay, each carrying a hundred soldiers."

"Think they'll draft soldiers again?" Lenson asked.

"Only if Hontue presses them, then they'll take only laborers. They'll get their fighters from the mainland," Vared said.

"My wife and I might sail for Keruban Island and get away from the Empire," Lenson said.

"Even if you were to escape these waters, there's nowhere the Empire's gaze won't spread. All the western islands will fall under their flag eventually. No island can stand on its own, and there isn't a chieftain who can unite the islands against them. If we all must bend a knee, it's better to bow to the Tenageen King than to the Honturian one."

Vared snorted. "Perhaps when they've conquered everything here, they'll sail farther south, to the jungle lands," he said, untying the mooring and casting off from the docks.

"Still your chatter," Lenson demanded. "Everyone knows those jungles are beyond the great sea witch's domain, and the siren drowns all who cross her waters without her favor."

"I suppose you think those storm clouds are proof of her wrath, too," Kesir said, laughing and pointing to the dark clouds in the distance. "With these winds, the storm will miss us entirely."

Vared took control of the wheel as the old boat caught the wind. There were plenty of fish where the warships docked. To go near them was to invite trouble, so they had to travel farther outward, away from the bay and its promised bounty. Nisiris would have preferred to steer the scow to take better stock of the merchant vessels but said nothing as they sailed toward open water.

The old scow was a nimble vessel that cut through the choppy waves effortlessly. "Nisiris, climb up and ensure there are no Imperial ships before us," Lenson said. "Even if that storm passes us by, I'd like to be home at a decent hour."

Nisiris scaled the old skiff's mast and held the spyglass to his left eye. "Ask the old one what he feels in his bones," he called down, scanning the horizon, wondering how long they'd have before the winds turned the waters hostile. "I can't see anything, save—"

A dense black mist hovered in the far distance. At first, he assumed it to be storm clouds, but the winds came from the north, whereas he could see something smoldering on the eastern horizon.

"I see smoke!" he shouted.

The two older men scrambled toward the ship's bow. "I see nothing!" Kesir shouted so Nisiris could hear.

"Nisiris's eyes are the best," Lenson said, before raising his voice for Nisiris. "Are you certain?"

"It's due east," Nisiris said.

"Give me the spyglass," Kesir ordered, before Vared turned the wheel.

"Are you daft?" Lenson demanded. "I have to fish to feed my family. It will do us no good to poke our noses where they do not belong."

"Your wife might thank us if we trim your nose somewhat." Vared snickered.

"If a ship's been set afire then all the plunder's been taken," Kesir said.

Nisiris dropped to their level. "I say we sail toward it. We may find a ship in distress, or booty worth a month's fishing."

Lenson could be content to do nothing but cut fish heads all day. Kesir should have been braver. He'd seen over fifty years, but he had a few good stories to tell on stormy nights.

While he himself proved no weakling, Vared often was among the tallest of the men on their island. In their youth, Nisiris had taught Vared to put his brute strength to proper use in learning hand-to-hand combat. Neither Kesir nor Lenson spoke as Vared steered the vessel away from the cove.

The ship was further away than Nisiris expected. He prided himself on his keen eyes, but as he tried to make out the smoke, he saw something bob atop the waves that seemed much closer than the dark clouds. Though Vared groused that Nisiris should make up his mind, he still veered as Nisiris bid him.

Vared stopped his grousing when the ship was no longer a distant blip. The frigate drifted along with the current. Nisiris tried to make out the ship's banner. He recognized the sigil of the Tenageen navy, but the other flags hanging beside it were too damaged and similar for him to discern. Not that it mattered to him which of the military houses the ship belonged.

"Do you see any movement?" Vared asked.

As Nisiris trimmed the sails on the scow he watched intently for movement. Burned and wind-torn sails flickered in the wind, and the damage to the hull seemed superficial. Segments of the mast seemed broken, likely the result of canon fire, one large piece threatened to fall over, held to the ship by the rigging. He scanned eastward, to the still far away smoke. The frigate was a Tenageen warship, but it didn't fly the same banner as they had seen back on Tredonia. Did the crew perish, or had the ship been abandoned? The latter was unlikely. Though no expert, he knew if the ship were to be destroyed it should have been sunk, not set adrift for scavengers to loot.

"I see no movement on the deck. Hello! Is anyone there?" Nisiris called. Only the sounds of flickering sails and waves crashing against the hull replied.

"It might be a ghost ship," Kesir warned.

"Shut up, old man," Vared snapped. "Look at the markers! This boat sailed with the Imperial navy. Even if the soldiers are ghosts, there must be enough swords to arm a hundred men!"

"You speak madness!" Lenson exclaimed. "To bear arms is to lose your hand, but to take that which belongs to the king…"

"That is not the Imperial Crest."

"I don't care whose flag they fly under!"

"Lenson, do you not remember what it was like to be able to hold steel?" Vared asked. "When the mainlanders came, did your family bear blade, or wear crowns of flowers?"

Nisiris did not recognize the tattered banner, though he was familiar with the Tenageen flag and the seal of the Royal Tenageen navy. Among the high born on the mainland, there were to many noble houses to keep track of with this prince or that noble with a personalized set of arms in addition to flying a family crest. He suggested they board and see for themselves.

"I'll not expect you to accompany us," Vared said to the cowards as he and Nisiris threw ropes to the deck. "Sail off, and we'll remember."

Though they were a simple fishing vessel and other a tall warship, Nisiris and Vared had no trouble boarding. Their lives were spent scaling hulls and rocks. Ropes and knots were their old friends. Both had a gift for making their way to places they shouldn't be. Nisiris found the way, while Vared tested it with his weight. They bid Kesir and Lenson to join them, but the two said they'd wait below on Lenson's boat.

Though the fine craftsmanship of the larger vessel did not disappoint either man, the deck smelled maggoty. "Where are the bodies?" Vared asked.

Nisiris scanned the deck. No birds traveled with the vessel, and most ships with any room for cargo likely held some manner of vermin. Bugs and rodents should have roamed the deck freely. He was not familiar with warships but knew they must have a hold. He followed the stench and found it.

"Down there," he called to Vared, gesturing.

Waterlogged bodies were piled upon one another unceremoniously, not yet stripped of their armor and weapons, and the odor of rot was only a few days old. Nisiris wondered why but reasoned the bodies should have been looted before turning them to the sea. Likely, most of the dead had been relieved of their armor and received a sea burial. There must have been survivors to drag the bodies to the hold. Perhaps those who gathered these bodies all perished in their cots below deck or were too weak to return his call.

Nisiris found a corpse that didn't look too badly rotted and helped himself to a sword before tossing another to Vared. "We'll come back for their armor," Nisiris said, trying to hide his grin. "If we can pilot this vessel, there's no need to move anything quite yet."

"You'll sail under Tenageen colors?" Vared asked, belting the blade. "The king's men in Donolys will see you approach leagues away, Nisiris. That sail will need to be replaced. We should take weapons, and other plunder, and return to our boat."

"There are places the king's men have grown careless," Nisiris said. "This ship will be a boon to the resistance."

"Resistance?" Vared gave him a familiar smirk. "Is that what we call ourselves now?"

"Get our women on board." Nisiris said with a grunt, climbing out of the makeshift morgue. "They can trade ghost stories, while they mend the main sail."

"Let's see if we can steer this ship with that broken mast. See those clouds in the distance? The old man was wrong."

Nisiris had been so intent on making it to the warship he'd not checked on the darkening sky behind them. "This vessel is not likely to be overturned by a storm."

"Our boat is. The rains will be upon us before sunset. We've no time to fish so let's make this worth our while, Nisiris. We can return to this ship tomorrow to try to claim it, if it is not seen by the Imperials first. Let's find the helm. If we can't take the ship, there must be something worth more than a day's catch of fish."

Nisiris followed his friend up the deck, toward the helm, marveling at the engravings in the wood and superior craftsmanship of the vessel. He found bugs and maggots in the hold, but he saw no birds picking at a fallen captain at his post or any trace of human remains on the commander's deck. Where were the people? He briefly wondered if those who lugged the corpses died in the comforts of their cots below deck.

The sound of a door creaking shut might have gone unnoticed had the pair been less vigilant or more in awe of their surroundings. Both men raced down the steps leading below deck, and Nisiris deflected the blade swung at them, and with the next swing, he disarmed his assailant, knocking his saber away, keeping its tip at his opponent's throat. The man might have fought more, were his face not puffed and sickly. There were three like him, with crossbows, but Nisiris saw the shaking arms that held them, and the fevered sweat, which made their hair greasy. He searched for signs of plague and saw only disease which took advantage of wounds untended. He flared his nostrils and kept a firm grip on his hilt.

"You're not soldiers," the man who attacked him stated. He appeared to be a decorated soldier rather than a sailor, though Nisiris could only assume, based on how he'd seen them dressed from a distance. "You will come no further."

"We spotted the ship and called up not ten minutes ago. Your sails are damaged, but we were about to inspect the helm and rudder," Vared said.

"And our swords, I see," accused the officer. "I should gut you now, thief."

Nisiris could kill the man swiftly enough. They thought him a scavenger, not the son of someone who could have taught him to use a weapon. They were fevered and weak, arrogant mainlanders through and through. "You've not the strength to manage the ship, do you? Why did your ship flee the battle?" he asked. "Are you traitors or cowards?"

The leader snorted, and a man raised his bow. Nisiris moved instinctively, drawing blood from the leader and slicing through the crossbow of the man to his left. Vared likewise drew blood when his friend attacked. Nisiris knew the men Vared attacked were dead, while he'd left the petty sailor wounded.

Vared made to finish off the leader. Nisiris grabbed the survivor's arm. "Tell me what cargo you have here worth killing two men who might have saved your worthless lives."

The sailor was his age—a young man, but no youth. "I am a simple sailor," he said after a pause. "I merely follow orders. Are we far from land or the hand of the Tenageen Imperium? Even if you are pirates, if you have a ship you can maneuver, you will be greatly rewarded."

Vared clunked the back of the sailor's head with his hilt, sending the man to the floor. "I'll go see to what they were protecting then."

Nisiris nodded and checked the bodies to ensure they were deceased. He quickly examined the officer's sword, immediately preferring his plundered model, but took his knife and was about to take the man's gauntlets when Vared called.

"Nisiris, I think we have something here worth more than a ship."

Nisiris followed Vared down the narrow passage and through an embellished door. They came upon a group of clerks shaking in a finely-crafted room behind a long war table. It was larger than his mother's home, decorated with carved birds and beasts and painted gold and green. Maps of the world, particularly the southern sea, covered the back wall, in addition to more books than Nisiris had never seen. He'd heard of the splendor of the Imperial City, but he didn't think he would ever see it himself.

One stood out from the others by age and dress. Though his clothes marked him an officer, his face revealed he was a youth. He wore too long a sword at his side and had rings on his fingers and jewels on his gauntlets, but he had not escaped the sickness, as his face was gaunt and pale.

"How did you get past our guard?" he asked.

"You were right," Nisiris said to Vared.

"Do not step further!" shouted the boy. "I am Prince Rasere of Tenagee, and I demand—"

At best, Nisiris thought the youth might have been the son of a warlord. Both men instinctively moved and seized the prince and dragged him back toward the door. Vared let go, only to slap at the peacocks, who made to protect their young lord. The boy had less strength than a bent fisherwoman.

Once the prince's hands were bound, Nisiris and Vared barred the door to the room behind them.

"We should set the ship on fire," Vared said.

"No. We'll need those clerks to talk," Nisiris said. "We'll get a prince's ransom for him."

"You will suffer for this!" the young prince shouted.

Vared hoisted the youth over his shoulder. "To the scow, then?"

Nisiris grinned and nodded, but upon climbing to the deck, saw their small fisher boat speeding away in the distance to the north. He and Vared turned their heads instinctively and watched the lone warship bearing down from the opposite direction.

"Nisiris," Vared asked. "What do we do?"

"Warlord Penthor's ship," the youth said, hope in his voice.

"Knock him out," Nisiris said. "They'll be upon us soon. We'll pretend like we were here to offer aid. They'll think us foolish fisherman, nothing more."

"They've no doubt spotted our fishing vessel," Vared said, panic rising in his voice.

"They'll not waste time pursuing it," Nisiris reasoned. "Unless they sink it on instinct."

"You stupid pirates," Prince Rasere snapped. "I'll see you feed the birds at the hanging cages in Port Iol!"

"Boy, if we have no alternative but death, you'll meet the abyss before us," Vared snarled. It was probably the smartest thing he'd ever said. The boy's face paled as the large man made his way to the railing.

"Wait!" the prince cried. "I'll make you a deal. Untie me and help Warlord Penthor's men aboard. I will reward you. What is your pleasure? If it is wealth, my family has jewels. If it is women, I have an uncle who collects only the most beautiful—"

"Steel," Nisiris said.

"What?" the prince asked.

"My grandfather served the chief of this island, but when he was slain, my line was sword-bearer no more," he said. "I would be able to wear steel."

"My uncle is your king as well," the boy claimed.

"Vared and I have no problem with your king, only his law, which says we cannot carry real weapons," Nisiris lied. "If I am your man, I see no objection to being allowed to bear a sword."

"Is that all?" the youth asked. "You have it."

"What promise do we have?" Vared asked.

"You have my word as a Tenageen gentleman, that you shall be given blades before the dawn. We have more weapons than arms fit to wield them."

Vared glanced at Nisiris, who bit his lip and nodded. They slit the boy's binds and put him on his feet. "How do we go about signaling them?" Vared asked.

"Release my aides. They will tell you where to find the right flags to signal the other ship."

Vared went below deck. Nisiris wished they hadn't been so careless, but his friend was smart enough to dispose of the bodies of the men they'd slain before releasing the clerks. There were other survivors onboard, but they were all sick, too weak to get up. Nisiris fancied himself a traitor, while the prince gave him orders and Nisiris did as he was told. He ran up the proper flag and caught ropes thrown from Warlord Penthor's ship then tied them snug.

"There is much death on this ship," he cautioned, as the first sailors boarded. "Prince Rasere is sickly. Be cautious with him."

After the grunts took control of the vessel, the Imperial sailors were followed by decorated officers with their seabirds and plumed helmets. They took one look at the prince and shouted for aid. Men dressed in brightly-colored satins and with swords decorated with gems boarded, and the prince was lifted onto a litter and taken to the other ship. Nisiris became invisible as orders were given to search and begin repairs on the ship.

"They seem to have taken the dead to the hold over there." He pointed with his chin. "My friend Vared is with the others below deck.

Most of them are sick."

"Who are you?" one of the officers asked.

"Nisiris, son of Hadeen," Nisiris said, bowing at his waist as his father taught him. "I hail from Tredonia."

"You're a fisherman?" asked a decorated officer. Nisiris wondered how he kept from sweltering under all his layers. The macaw on his shoulder ruffled his feathers. "I assume your friends were aboard that small fisher-boat we saw escape in the past half-hour."

"Our friends are superstitious," Nisiris said. "They thought this was a ghost ship. They likely believed you were coming to claim their souls."

"Why did you board?" the officer asked.

"We saw the boat on the horizon and curiosity got the best of us," Nisiris answered. "We called up and received no answer, so we boarded and searched the vessel."

"Indeed," said the officer before turning his attention to his men. "Take these two men to our brig and see their swords are inspected."

Nisiris resisted the urge to fight, instead following the soldiers across the planks to the smaller vessel. It was a much plainer ship than the damaged one they had stumbled across, but it did not stink of maggots and the sails seemed to be in good repair.

"Any other ideas?" Vared asked once they were led below deck and shown the small cells which were to house them. At least they were left alone.

"We have the word of a prince," Nisiris said. "They would have killed us outright."

Vared snorted and walked to the lone porthole. "I was wrong. The storm will be upon us before nightfall."

Nisiris followed his friend's gaze to the darkening sky. He told himself the storm would make the prince sick, and hopefully he would die. The officers would know nothing and release them to fish and plot once more. They were served no dinner but roused before the rains began. The reddening sun hung deep in the horizon, almost hidden completely by bulbous black clouds, which threatened strong winds over thunderclaps.

Prince Rasere saw them on the deck, seated on a cushioned wicker chair. He still seemed sickly, though he wore a new, however slightly oversized raiment and his hair had been combed.

"Kneel before the prince," a soldier said.

Nisiris and Vared did so.

"I did not expect to see traitors so easily bend knee," the prince said.

Nisiris stood, scowling. "We had a deal."

"I am honor-bound to keep my word. You gentlemen may have your steel." The prince motioned. Archers kept Vared and Nisiris from rushing forward once they were given old sabers. "There is a tradition of the Imperial family. We have a sacrificial duel to honor the dead, though in the cities they are happy with mere cuts and bruises, even in the grand arenas. Hopefully, one of your deaths will appease the fallen sailors and let them find rest. The survivor will be taken to the mainland and trained as a warrior for the arena games, where you will have your steel and find glory, and may one day win your freedom. My wager is on the large one."

Nisiris snorted. Vared was bigger and stronger, but he was also clumsy. "I'll not kill my friend," Nisiris said.

"Then you will both be tied to the front of two ships until you're brought to the mainland, fed and watered so you'll not die. Once you're properly broken, you will be sold to work, either the mines, or the fields," the prince said. "I care not which. It's your decision."

No choice at all. He felt the winds snatch water from the ocean, spraying the nobility and the captives alike in a salted mist. Torches flickered in the rising wind. "Vared, I do not think we can fight those here," he said finally.

"No," Vared said. "I would prefer a warrior's death."

Nisiris bowed his head and unsheathed his blade quietly. He waited for Vared to draw. "Let's not prolong it. Know if you kill me, I'll keep your place in the hall next to me."

Vared drew his weapon, but Nisiris saw no edge in his eyes. Nisiris realized he had no desire to live as a slave, either. He caught the prince's gaze. "I will remember your honorable words. Know mine: If not by my hand, may my line undo yours, sparing neither your descendants, nor your uncle's crown."

"If he talks again, castrate them both," the prince said.

The choppy waters made the princeling grip rope for support, but movement on an uneasy deck was second nature to Nisiris and Vared. Nisiris struck at his friend. Vared acted on the defensive, but he didn't defend once. As the rains started, Nisiris threw his sword at the nearest soldier, ran toward the darkness, then jumped over the railing and into the sea.

He swam down as long as he could and hoped drowning would be half as glamorous as the death which awaited Vared in the victor's circuit. When Nisiris finally dared to stop plunging down into the dark water, he knew not up from down as he struggled through the raging waters. He breathed air suddenly.

The darkness of the storm was all that kept him safe from their lanterns and archers. He thought he heard Vared's screams over the shouts of the sailors and rolling thunder as the waves battered against his face, forcing him down. The storm was cover, but it also kept him from seeing the stars, so he could not navigate back to Tredonia. He swam blindly in the cold water, until at last he caught a piece of driftwood, which did nothing besides help him stay afloat in the thrashing salt waters.

~ * ~

Nisiris woke on a sandy shore, when a seagull pecked at his face. He scared it away by stirring to cover his eyes and cursed himself, for if nothing else, he could have drunk the seagull's blood until he found safe water. His ears rang, and his tongue felt too large for his mouth. He finally saw what saved his life. It was a piece of broken mast from Prince Rasere's ship.

He'd landed on a beach of some sort. Salt crusted his eyelids, and sand was everywhere it shouldn't have been. Lush trees swayed in the distance. He looked to the sky.

He didn't recognize the pale sands of this beach. He knew he couldn't have wound up back on Tredonia.

His body ached from salted blisters, and his clothes were torn. Thirst drove him to his feet. There were a few other segments of timber washed up on the shore, but there was no sign of a river or a creek he could follow inland. His ability to navigate was poor, so he followed the shore. If his throat didn't ache, he would think he landed in paradise. Gulls passed overhead, and just as he was tempted to seek out shade and wait out the heat he saw stark white pillars in the distance. He quickened his pace. As he neared the marble pergola, Nisiris crouched low and searched for people, moving in the bush and moving slowly so as to not upset the foliage. He spied manicured gardens and intricate wooden archways entwined with strange red flowers on a vine, until he realized they gated a pool and a grand white villa—several strange, yet not unpleasing buildings marked the island, but they were few.

He checked for signs of guards or servants, but thirst made him rash. He crept to the pool and tasted it, finding it clean and fresh. Thirsty, he abandoned sense and lapped greedily, unaware of his surroundings until he heard a woman scream. Nisiris glanced up to hear men shout, but he didn't know where they were until a pair appeared behind some of the ornamental shrubbery, knocking their bows at him.

The men wore rather pathetic armor. White satin covered their chests and elaborate, rather than functional, gauntlets graced bronzed arms, which held their fancy swords and bows. Nisiris put his hands up and tried to apologize, and three more fellows dressed in the same strange draping fabric appeared from another garden path. A man went to strike him.

Nisiris reacted, grabbed his hand, and twisted it back. He let go before the order was given to shoot him. "I meant no harm, I only wanted a drink!"

His arms were seized, and he was dragged away from the marble pool. Nisiris was thrown to the grass and someone demanded, "Who are you?" At least they spoke the same tongue.

"Nisiris of Tredonia, son of Hadeen," he muttered. "I was shipwrecked. I didn't mean to scare anyone. I was merely thirsty." He rose to his elbows, and someone booted his back. He spat out a mouthful of sand.

"We'll ask what we want to know. He doesn't look like a scout."

"Ask him what vessel he crewed for, and if there are any more of his kind lurking about."

"He doesn't look like a sailor. More like a fisherman."

Nisiris chanced staring up at the men surrounding him. He saw no women among the guards, but he could hear more people behind him, including female voices. He turned his head to see several young women watching, but someone kicked him between his shoulder blades and told him to remain still. Nisiris forced his rage down. He wasn't fresh enough to fight a pair of them, let alone five armed men.

"March him several miles from here and tie him to a tree," said the leader. "If there are any other survivors, they'll likely go to his aid. If not…"

Arms grabbed his and forced him up. Nisiris struggled when he saw ropes and chains, choosing a quick death than to linger and starve. He reached for a belted dagger and slashed wildly. The gauntlets saved the man, but they instinctively released him. Backing off, someone gave the order to shoot.

"No," a woman said, "Outlander, drop your weapon, and I'll call off my guards."

The men did not change their stances, though the archer lowered his sight. "My lady—" began the most decorated of the men.

"Did I not make myself clear?"

Nisiris released the dagger and kicked it toward the owner, before turning to look at the woman. She appeared of age with him, her deep chestnut hair styled intricately in a chignon with heavy-hooded sea-blue eyes on a round face as well as a strong, prominent nose. Her clothing was rich looking, yet foreign to his eyes. Not Imperial.

"I do not think he meant us harm. I do, however, find it odd he was able to come so near us." She cast her gaze at the leader of the guardsmen.

"My lady." He bowed lower. "My men did not see any ships, and they were quick to respond to this trespasser."

"All of you? I wonder who guards the rest of my house. My enemies need but a breath's notice to strike you all down," the woman said. "Nisiris, son of Hadeen of Tredonia?" She cocked her head. "Captain, have him fed and given proper clothes, so I might receive him inside my villa. If he requires a bath," she paused, smiling at Nisiris, "have him do it in the ocean."

~ * ~

While he found the clothing of good quality, Nisiris thought it rather impractical and felt more like a pet then a guest one he donned the long tunic and trousers. They didn't trust him enough to shave himself, so an elder woman trimmed and styled his hair.

"Food?" he asked, once he was deemed decent to enter the lady's house.

The woman didn't acknowledge his question. Instead, she gestured for Nisiris to follow her inside the manse, however through the servant's entrance and nowhere near the marble pool. He wondered why the woman would show him kindness. He snickered, recalling stories of sailors, who claimed sirens lured ships toward rocks and ancient tales of island witches turned hapless sailors into food. Allowing his imagination to wander, he supposed he'd make a great tusked boar to Vared's ox. Nisiris tried not to think of Vared too much. He'd seek out his friend once he found his way off the island. The thought of being some sea-witch's pleasure slave was preferable to tales of one-eyed ogres, and the like.

Nisiris wasn't sure where he was taken but the building seemed open and clean. He heard unfamiliar music and they entered a large room featuring white curtains overlooking the sea. The chestnut-haired woman listened to her maidservants play their pan flutes, mandolins, and bongos as they sat on mats and pillows. There was a low, central table laden with rich cheeses and exotic foods, as well as more simple fare of fish and common fruits Nisiris recognized.

"Ah, a vast improvement," the sea-eyed woman said over the music. "Come and sit with me."

The woman and her company supped and paid him little attention. Water was plentiful, served in crystal goblets though several women appeared to be drinking garnet-colored wine. To his surprise, several who were obviously servants were dressed almost as well as their mistress. Nisiris's mouth watered, but he hesitated, even after he saw one of the young maidservants help herself to a plump orange.

"You may relax," his hostess said. "For this meal, consider yourself my guest."

"Thank you," he said. "I would know the name of my hostess."

"Elza," she said. "I am one of the rulers of this island."

"Lady Elza, what island is this?" Nisiris asked, sitting where she gestured.

"Mazala," she said. "We are situated far south of Tredonia. How long were you shipwrecked?"

He hesitated and caught some of the eyes of the girls who were playing instruments when they began to giggle and whisper to one another. Elza clapped her hands, and the chime of her bracelets silenced the music.

"You may go elsewhere," she said and waited for them to leave the room.

To his surprise, he was left alone with Elza. She wore a simple knife at her side. There were guards outside the room, but he needed only an instant. How could she not fear him, a stranger?

"As you were saying?"

He was suddenly compelled to be truthful. "I jumped ship," he stammered. "I was going to be sold as a slave, and I thought I could swim back to my island during a storm. I'd rather be dead than chained. The waves carried me further out to sea. I grabbed a piece of broken mast and woke up on your shore."

"I see."

"To whom is Mazala sworn?" Nisiris asked. "I've never heard of this island."

"You speak of the Empires?" she asked. "Neither. Mazala is free of both Hontue and Tenageen influence. The security you saw is to keep pirates at bay. You would not believe how far raiding parties set out."

"I would," he said, finishing his apple and reaching for a sprig of grapes. "We've had raiding parties from the Glass Mountains attack villages on our shores, as far as old Kesir could tell."

"Tredonia is under the protection of the Tenageen Empire," Elza said.

"Protection? If you're within their stone walls, you're protected enough, I suppose," Nisiris said. "They don't even allow us islanders real weapons to defend ourselves. We sharpen rocks for spears and use shells for arrowheads. There have been fewer raids in the past few years, but perhaps the pirates know the Empire has beaten them to the plunder."

"I saw the way you fought," she said. "Impressive for a common fisherman."

"My grandfather was an esteemed swordsman. He was slain when my father was a youth. My father taught me everything he knew."

"Your father must worry about you now."

"My father was taken into the Imperial army when I was still a boy," he said. "The son of one of my island's greatest warriors, probably to row a galley plank. He was either captured or killed. If he's alive, he's long forgotten his birthplace."

Elza frowned. "Your mother?"

"She has buried two husbands and three children," Nisiris said. "No doubt she will make an offering at the temple and light a candle, hoping to guide my soul back from the sea. She is a good woman, but she has more to concern herself than one of her many sons."

"What about your woman, and your sons?"

"I have none."

"Why not?" she asked. "Is it because you are poor?"

"No. It is because..." he stammered. "...I am a rebel. I would give my life restoring glory to my island. I would not see a woman be made a widow and my sons killed because of my actions."

Elza smiled. "No wonder you chose to jump ship than live a life of servitude."

She stood, and Nisiris stood with her. He followed her to the open balcony. The sands were white, the view of the white-capped waves, once too familiar seemed majestic from where they leaned against the marble parapet. He wondered how far away he was from Tredonia and if Vared lived. He looked to Elza, the sheer fabric of her shawl playing in the breeze, but he could not read her expression.

She watched the rolling waves of the sea. "Tell me, Nisiris, are you good with a sword?"

Good? Good in what sense? He was fast, and that was often *good enough.* He had no innate grace or skill, that required better instruction than old memories, and playing swords with other boys, besting those who had no real talent. "I've no way to tell," he admitted. "My father trained me with the best replicas we had. I could beat boys both older and bigger than me while I was still a boy. How is it your island remains safe from the Empires?"

"Hontue wars within itself, and Tenagee has claimed a few islands. It's hardly an empire, though they've been pressuring the small kingdoms surrounding them to submit. Puppet kings are plentiful these days. We are small and unnoticed for the time being," she said. "However, I fear we cannot remain unseen forever. I wonder," she wrapped her arms around her torso, bowing her head, "how much longer can we go unnoticed?"

"I know nothing of the mainland, but it is said the Honturian Empire once held almost the entirety of the known world in its hand. In time, it crumbled and fell, and now the one who sits on the throne balances warlord against warlord."

"Indeed," she said. "There are so few things that stand the test of time."

"The sea," Nisiris replied. "It is said that when the lands fall, the sea swallows them up. The sea birthed the land and will take it back once more."

She laughed. He bit his lip and bowed his head, feeling foolish. He couldn't match wit and words with his peers, much less this woman. "My lady, as much as I enjoy your company, I would ask why I'm here. You have treated me kindly, when most would have had me killed, enslaved, or imprisoned. Why would you call a foundling man a guest?"

"In short, you interest me, rebel."

"Why?"

"You carry yourself like a warrior," she said simply. "As opposed to my guard who carry on as dullards. I'll be blunt: I've no interest in making you my prisoner, but neither will I help you back to Tredonia. You'll see few ships pass by," she said. "Of course, you may swim, or take your driftwood boat. I'll not like it much if you begin to decimate my island to fix it."

"Aren't you worried I'll cause trouble?" She didn't answer him. "Is there a town nearby?"

"No," she said. "You're more than welcome to explore the island. It's not large, though it's several miles across at most. Everyone lives here, with me and my master."

"Your master?"

"It is a term of endearment from teacher to student. He is away right now. Vorun will return when it suits him, but it might be years. You may have steel here if you will join our guard."

"Will they accept me?"

"They will if I tell them to."

~ * ~

Her word wasn't good enough. Nisiris spent the next few days being beaten and insulted by men with half his talent. He tried to find camaraderie and found out much later the commanding officers were not well-loved by their subordinates. The best he could hope for was the master to bring in another to their number to be the new target as they took to boring island patrols and protecting the manor grounds, though he was seldom allowed to go into the jungles or the cliffs he found the woman to be truthful—Mazala had no villages or other people living across its small expanse. As guardsmen, their duties were many and varied. In addition to guarding what seemed like paradise, they also worked to maintain the building and helped prepare dinner.

"What does Lady Elza have to fear?" Nisiris asked the one guardsman younger than he, as they peeled potatoes one afternoon. "Why would she need help and protection in this place, if no ships venture near?"

"Pirates, or ships of the Empire, it makes no difference," the youth said. "Were you truly shipwrecked?"

Nisiris wondered if Elza spoke of him to the others. It would build no brotherhood to be caught in a lie. "I jumped overboard preferring to take my chances with the sea than the word of a nobleman," he said. "I was to be sold as a slave. The storm gave me cover but carried me further out to sea. I survived because I clung to a piece of broken mast."

"I've always been a slave," the youth said.

"Do you not like your lot here?" Nisiris asked.

"It is better than most," the youth admitted. "I wonder about the world beyond this island. I was born on the mainland and brought here when I was very young. It is silly to even think of leaving. I have heard that there are lands where men are free, to the far north, but across frozen landscapes. We would be run down by men and hounds, let alone the monsters of the deep. There are no ships here on the island, and we seldom see any on the horizon. Even if we were to craft a vessel in the forest, I would not think any land we were to come to would welcome us."

"The island has no vineyards, and the compound has only a small herb and vegetable garden," Nisiris said, frowning. He'd seen more flowers than fruit in his few patrols. "How do they get supplies?"

"Lady Elza is a witch," the youth said. "I'm just happy to see the food appearing in crates."

A pair of their fellow guardsmen entered the kitchen and made their way to Nisiris and the youth. "Has the new louse any skill with the peeler?" asked the first.

"Better than with a sword," said the second. "Pity he wasn't born a woman. He'd have a future."

The first picked up a peeled potato. He was one of the largest among the men. "This one's a mite smaller than his bruises." He tossed it at Nisiris, who let it bounce off his shoulder.

The second walked to the flagons of wine. "You're more than like to help them."

The larger man smiled at Nisiris and the other guard. He had missing teeth and the face of a boxer with curled ears. He knocked the bowl of water where Nisiris rinsed the potatoes after they were cut, splashing water over his tunic and pants.

Nisiris fought the urge to ram his potato peeler into the man's throat. Brawling outside of practiced fighting would have him put under the whip, or worse. Who knew what badly wounding or killing one of them would gain him?

"What stays your hand? Scared of upsetting the lady and what she does when she turns into a regular sea serpent?" The larger man laughed. "Come on, Idero. Let's leave them to their work."

Nisiris thought he saw remnants of wine stains near the flagons.

"You can tell they've nothing better to do," the young guard muttered.

Nisiris furrowed his brow before putting down the potato and peeler.

"Where are you going?" the youth asked.

He was tempted to speak to his superior, but he bumped into one of the giggling ladies who called him out for being so earnest in his steps. "Unless your lady has a spell to remedy poison, you're best not to slow me down," he replied curtly.

The woman grabbed his arm and took him into unfamiliar halls and was told to wait on a bench when she entered an adjoining room. He was surprised to see Lady Elza with one of her male servants, though obviously not a bodyguard for he only had a matching dagger to the lady at his hip.

"Tell her what you told me," the woman said.

"I didn't tell you anything," Nisiris said lowly. He caught the young man's gaze, but kept his eyes locked on Elza's. "I think... I don't know him well... Idero? I think someone tampered with the wine. Throw it out, all of it."

She scowled. The young man spoke up. "A rather expensive endeavor. What proof do you have?"

Nisiris's tunic had almost dried, and he hadn't stained hands at the moment to suggest he was even in the kitchens, but Elza crossed her arms. "Thank you for your suspicions, Nisiris. We will deal with it. Are you getting on all right with the other men?"

He wished he was more tactful with words. "You were right about your island being quite small. I haven't had a chance to explore the surrounding cliffs and jungle yet."

"That's not what I asked."

"I'm not sure being a rank and file guardsman suits my nature, Lady Elza. I still know if any harm befalls you, we'll all be held suspect."

"Is that the only reason you're here?" she asked. He didn't reply quick enough. "Wait here. I think I'll have you as my guest again this evening. Some nicer clothes this time, perhaps." She turned to go back into the room.

"Please my lady—don't dress me like one of your peacocks," he said. She paused, laughed, and continued.

Nisiris thought she forgot about him by the time someone came with a small bundle of clothing. He'd started to grow out a beard, like the other older guards, but his was trimmed into a goatee that, he later admitted suited him, but at the time he felt once again like a small lap dog. Elza appeared to look him over briefly, and this time had him escort her into the familiar banquet room.

The lady drank visibly from a clear goblet for all to see during their feast.

He really didn't like that he was seated at her left side and given a teal cloak none of the other guardsmen were given. His lady wore a form-fitting gown of gold and brown with a teal sash, and jewelry of jade and gold, and seemed more interested in the seemingly new selections of songs on the mandolin than his concerns.

"You're not eating," she said as he moved the fish and scallops around his plate. "They'll notice."

"I've not eaten by your side since I joined your guard," he told her quietly.

"Stop staring at them and eat something." She made a show of enjoying the red grapes, tossing them into the air and catching them with her mouth, giggling like her maidens, when she missed.

"What if I'm wrong?" he asked. "I feel like a fool for suggesting it without proof, but…"

"But if you are right," she said, "we must not let them believe you are here for any other reason." She put a hand on his shoulder.

He closed his eyes as she kissed him. She smelled of lavender and some exotic spice he couldn't place. He did not realize his hands were on her ribcage and starting to explore until she put hers on top of his.

"Later," she said, her soft painted hands relieving his strong ones. "Now eat something. You're going to need your strength." She popped a grape into his mouth, before turning her attention from him.

He dared not catch eyes with the other guardsmen. There was no going back to the main ranks now. Nisiris decided to drown his sorrows on the fattiest piece of pork he'd ever seen, when Elza downed her goblet and asked for another, only to drop the goblet when the serving girl neared.

"My lady, are you all right?" the serving girl asked, as other servants picked up the crystal shards.

Nisiris watched Elza grow pale. She rose on unsteady feet, and two of her maidservants rose to assist her. "I feel light-headed..."

She fell backward suddenly, into the arms of the maidservant Nisiris had spoken to in the hallway. He reached for Elza. The woman's face was white, and she appeared to be sleeping. He heard the guardsmen behind him shout, "Lady Elza has been poisoned!"

"Everyone remain calm. Inspect the lady's wine!" a more authoritative voice ordered.

"He was by her side the entire meal!" snapped the larger man, who'd been with Idero in the kitchen earlier.

Elza's servants rushed to her side and took her from the room. He heard screams from the hallway and wondered, briefly, if she was the only one who drank the poisoned wine, though he later wondered if he had any on his lips. *How did he know what bottle to poison? Others have been drinking...*

While his thoughts raced, Nisiris's arms were seized. "You are sure?" the captain asked Idero.

"I saw him in the kitchen with Tulleroy," Idero said. "He's been on kitchen duty today."

"Where's the antidote?" the captain asked Nisiris. "Tell us, now!"

"Shipwrecked, indeed! He was sent to assassinate her," Idero said, pointing "If she dies, the real master will find out, and we will all be executed. Slit his throat!"

"I was peeling potatoes," Nisiris said, eyeing his accuser. "We've all eaten them. You were the one near the wine while he distracted me," he said, gesturing at the larger man with missing teeth. "You've not had a cup all night. Care to tell us why?"

Gas pellets exploded at the far side of the room, and servants and men at arms gasped for air. His accuser drew sword, turned and knocked the nearest guard out of his way. "Let's go!"

The larger man nodded, and both men fled the dining hall. The captain ordered Nisiris released and archers to slay the fleeing pair then he trailed after his fellow guardsman. Nisiris smelled blood in the corridors, no doubt guardsmen on duty during the dinner hour relaxing, for theirs was a quiet shift. They likely had no idea what was going on, save for the ruckus down the halls.

The archers were poor shots. The men made it to the beach.

"If they make it to the jungle, we'll lose them in the night," said one of the men. "How did they get so far ahead of us?"

"They've been in our ranks for years," said another guard as they huffed and ran.

Nisiris sprinted ahead. With the exception of the youngest, the other guards, while generally large and strong, were fat and slow from inactivity. Nisiris gained upon the pair, the slender man being faster while Tulleroy tired. Before the larger man turned to face Nisiris, the pair were blinded by an intense shock of light beyond the men, coming from the surf, which had pulled back for a moment. The waves parted and two humanoids, taking the appearance of being wrought of blue fire, until the flame melted to reveal their human forms. Nisiris recognized the one has being from Elza's wake from before. One put his hands out to the men, the other pointed to the sea, but both Idero and Tulleroy drew swords. The mage pointing to the sea did not heed the warnings of the first.

"*Nagamba!*" one of the guards behind Nisiris cursed, halting.

He did not know why they halted, but he knew the curse—the man feared death who uttered that word—it was only used when ghosts were thought to be involved. Nisiris had no time for superstition, but neither was he sure of what to make of the lady's students as they hovered above the now strangely still waters surrounding them, though the waves began anew.

The large man faced Nisiris while the slender man went after the two men above the waters. There was a strange, almost humming sensation Nisiris couldn't place coming from the man.

One of her students fell wounded to the waves, while the other flew out of range. *He can dance in the air?* The smaller man focused his attention on the flyer, though he wasted no time at lunging and stabbing the bloodied man who clutched at his wounds, seemingly surprised at the sight of his own blood.

"You saw far too much," the large man muttered before striking toward Nisiris.

He was a much heavier man, but unlike the others his girth was over muscles ripe with power and he seemed to enjoy swordplay. When their blades met, he pushed Nisiris back. He pivoted at the second strike, making the man fall forward, using his weight against him. Nisiris almost struck him from behind, but the other assailant turned his attentions to Nisiris and caught his neck with his whip, choking him.

"Finish him!" Idero ordered.

The large man turned to skewer Nisiris, but the mage rained down fire in small, liquid clumps no wider than a man's thumb, but enough to make Tulleroy squeal in pain and flee. Though it squeezed his windpipe, Nisiris cut through the braided coil and gasped for air as the man's fire brushed against his flesh and rolled away from the intense heat. Thankfully his fine clothing had taken most of the damage. The backs of his arms were bare, his skin blistered. While his head still spun, he sensed more bright light behind him.

He was caught up in a strange sensation, and he experienced a strange sense of ease, when every fiber of his being told him otherwise. It was like being lulled. He almost dropped his weapon, his mind told him to grip it tighter as he fell to his knees.

The sensation narrowed and moved beyond him. He realized he'd gotten caught in something not intended for him.

"Tend to Nisiris," Elza said simply as one of her maidservants knelt by his side. "Can you not even take them alive?" she demanded of her flying student and put out her bangled hand and made strange motions through the air. The larger man clawed at his throat and writhed, as if being strangled with an invisible rope.

"Be careful, my lady," the mage hovering above them shouted. "He's armed with—"

A long knife, Nisiris realized. His senses still somewhat dulled, almost pacified, he leapt up to protect Elza from the assassin's strike. He met the knife with his sword and struck the man's arm, not severing it, but badly cutting it, revealing the two bones near the elbow.

He went to strike again and cleave the man's head in two, but Elza said, "Stop, Nisiris. I need to know who sent them."

He would have disobeyed the order, but his arms froze. Nisiris stood by her, ready to leap into action, but obedient. His comrades had finally decided to become men and chained the large man, their numbers rendering his might useless. Idero lay sprawled in the sand, clutching his wound as Elza and her servants surrounded him. Nisiris hardly expected her to look back at him.

"Nisiris, I am safe," Elza said. "You are wounded."

"I will heal," he said. His vision tunneled and his ears rang, and an unfamiliar pain emerged from behind his eyes. One of Elza's students helped him sit down. He felt dumbly peaceful, like it was all right for him to sleep, but the sensation died when Idero grunted and turned his knife inward. His arms shook, and Nisiris could only see the whites of his eyes.

"I don't think so," Elza said, removing the knife from Idero's hand. His body continued to shake as his knife came close, but barely grazed his skin. "You're not going to pass beyond a realm where I can't touch you. Tell me," she said, running her fingers through the man's hair, as if a mother were soothing her child, "who sent you, witchslayer? It will go easier for your comrade if you cooperate. I will find out. You will talk. Eventually. You all do."

"We were after your master," Idero croaked. "Vorun. We knew he'd rush back here if he received word you were dead. We thought we could blame the Tredonian..."

"You've been among my staff for several years. How many times have I passed by when you could have struck?" she asked, smiling. "You were patient, if you had gone against my enemy, I would say well-played." She turned her back on Idero and walked to Nisiris. "And now, what to do...?"

~ * ~

Nisiris wasn't sure how he fell asleep. He seldom remembered his dreams. His grandmother told him she used to have visions in her sleep, and warnings. She would tell her grandfather tactical advantages, and even professed to know when the island was doomed to bend knee. Many old women claimed to have such visions, and Nisiris had no time for visions or gods, who could not give him steel.

He dreamed of the sea through her eyes, which gave way to ships aflame, banners burning. The thought of Rasere's death comforted him. Visions of Vared bloodied, fighting for his life among a crowd of well-bred spectators, victories met with jeers and the roar of the mob made bile rise in the back of his throat.

Nisiris woke, not in the guard quarters, but in what he could only describe as a woman's room, given the strange art adorning the walls and too-soft sheets. His arms were stiffly bandaged, and he had one of Elza's students offered him water almost immediately.

"Where is Elza?" he asked, sitting up. He was topless, but unsure if he was naked beneath the sheet. "Is she safe?"

"She will be happy to know you are awake," said the young woman, guiding the cup to Nisiris's lips. "She has instructed me not to leave your side, but I can have her told you are awake. Would you like more rest? I have herbs, which will ease your pain."

"Nani," Elza said. "Do not pester him." She leaned against the doorway.

Nisiris straightened and, recalling the kiss from earlier, cared less about the sheets, but she walked over and tried to force his shoulder down. He let her think she could but paused halfways down.

"Nani, leave us," she said, before catching Nisiris's gaze. "In the future, you will not be so careless. My servants can heal bad injuries but there will be scars."

"Are your other guardsmen afraid of scars?"

She gave him a thin smile. "Nani, so help me..."

The girl scurried out.

"You called them witchslayers," he said once Nani left them.

"Are you a witch?"

Elza sat on Nisiris's bed. "*Witch* is one of their words for us," she said. "Some call us wizards, sorcerers, I prefer the term *mage*. Idero was a witchslayer—Tulleroy his ally."

"You can fly?"

"We call it levitation."

"You came from the sea," he said. He sputtered, "You...you took poison willingly!"

"I imbibed a drug which would appear as poison before dinner, instructing my students what would likely happen. If nothing had happened, one of my trusted men would have revived me and let rumor carry. I was worried the treachery had rooted itself quite deep, and there were others who would have helped them. One spooked, and then the other ran to his aid. We caught them in their panic, though I am not entirely convinced they acted alone. Would you like some wine? It is not drugged or poisoned. As for coming from the sea, it is something I make my students practice. We need to be able to move quickly over great distances. Water and mirrors tend to work well. You will see my students perform it often."

"One of your students was slain, wasn't he?"

She frowned but nodded. "Whoever sent them did an impeccable job. They were even given weapons to make our magic weaker."

"Witchcraft and sorcery?" Nisiris asked.

Elza smiled, running her fingers through his hair. "I can teach you a few tricks, if you like, though, it may cost you." she said. She kissed his forehead, but Nisiris seized her shoulders. Grinning like a cat, she let him pull her toward him. Nisiris tried not to flinch when she touched his dressings. "I told you that you'd need your strength. Rest now."

"Don't put me to sleep again."

"I am going to see my master in the morning," she said. "I'd have my knight accompany me."

"Knight?" he asked.

She smiled and stood up. "You said being a guard didn't suit you. I don't suppose you'll object to being my...bodyguard?"

He watched her leave before he sank back into the bed. "Is that what they call it on this island?" he asked the ceiling.

Out Now!

What's next on your reading list?

Champagne Book Group promises to bring to readers fiction at its finest.

Discover your next
fine read!
http://www.champagnebooks.com/

We are delighted to invite you to receive exclusive rewards. Join our Facebook group for VIP savings, bonus content, early access to new ideas we've cooked up, learn about special events for our readers, and sneak peeks at our fabulous titles.

Join now.
https://www.facebook.com/groups/ChampagneBookClub/

Made in United States
North Haven, CT
01 June 2022

19739903R00146